Chapter One

The Mouse Hunt

"I *am* a real cat. I am a *real* cat."

Smokey shakes her head as she stands outside Autumn Amelia's bedroom door listening to the daily self-pep-talk and knowing Autumn only half believes herself.

"Autumn!" Smokey calls. "I've got an important meeting this morning. Miss Fluffington wants to talk to me about a new account, so I need to leave early. Are you making breakfast, or should I grab something on the way?"

"Coming," Autumn calls.

A skittering noise comes from behind the door, followed by Autumn's frustrated cry of "Oh, this stupid floof!" Smokey pictures her fluffy sister slipping on the tufts of fur between her paw pads.

"You really should do something about that," says Smokey as she heads for the stairs.

Smokerina, or Smokey as she is called, is Autumn Amelia's older sister. They share the cottage in Wild Whisker Ridge that they've inherited from their parents. Autumn presides over the kitchen, rarely allowing Smokey to cook, for which Smokey is grateful.

"Granola and berries in cream since you're in a hurry, okay?" asks Autumn.

"Perfect."

Smokey smooths her gray skirt over her Russian Blue fur.

Autumn, a calico Maine Coon with black markings around her eyes that look as though she lost a fight with a mascara brush and thick double-layered fur in a crazy-quilt pattern of gray, white, and burnt orange, can never seem to look as pulled together.

"Ms. Fluffington says this account is the biggest Fluffington ArCATecture has ever had," Smokey says while setting the table.

"What's it for?"

"I don't know. That's one of the things she'll tell me today. I hope she's going to give me the lead on it. Whatever it is."

Autumn carries a pitcher of cream from the refrigerator. On her way to the table, her paws slip, the pitcher flies into the air, and Autumn Amelia lands on her rump in the middle of the floor. Smokey, grabbing for the pitcher the second it leaves Autumn's paws, catches it in mid-flight.

"Nice save, Smokey!" Autumn says, still on the floor.

"I'm always on guard when you're carrying food."

"It's the darned floof," says Autumn. "I can't get a grip on anything."

The floofless Smokey gives a mild snort as she sets the pitcher on the table.

"You needn't snort, Smokey."

"Snorting is vulgar. I never do it."

"You did and you know it," says Autumn, wiping the puddle of cream up from the floor. "Someday I'm going to glue floof to your paws while you're sleeping and see how you like it. We'll see who's snorting then."

Smokey can't repress a laugh. Autumn Amelia turns away, but not before Smokey notes that Autumn's jaws are clenched in an attempt to staunch her own laughter.

After breakfast Smokey dashes upstairs for one last check of her clothes and makeup. Once certain every fur is perfectly in place, she descends the stairs to find Autumn crouched low on the living room floor peering under the hutch, muscles tense, whiskers twitching.

Not this again. Smokey enters the living room, making sure her claws click on the floor so that Autumn is aware of her presence.

"What are you doing?" Smokey asks, though she knows all too well.

"Shhh! You'll spook him."

"Who?"

"The mouse. Who do you think?"

"Autumn, there is no mouse."

"Yes, there is. I heard him. He's under the hutch."

"Autumn Amelia you've been imagining a mouse in this cottage forever. I'm telling you there is no mouse."

"How do you know?" Autumn's tail thumps.

Smokey was considered a great huntress in her youth, in the years before Autumn Amelia's birth. Autumn has never caught a mouse. Smokey knows Autumn has no idea why cats catch mice and wonders what her gentle, peace-loving sister would do if she did catch one.

"I can see it," says Autumn, her head half under the hutch. "I think it's a mouse. Please be a mouse. Oh, please be a mouse."

Pitiful. Smokey shakes her head.

"I can't take it anymore. I'm going to get it. Come here mousy!" calls Autumn, charging the hutch, her right front paw sliding underneath, head up, the bulk of her body slamming into the bottom of the hutch making the glass doors above rattle. Autumn's outstretched arm flails in vain. She rolls onto her back, feet in the air, her other forepaw gripping the front of the hutch. Terrified that she might flip the heavy piece of furniture onto herself, Smokey yells, "Autumn stop! You can't do it that way!"

Autumn freezes. The impulse to laugh at the spectacle of Autumn Amelia wrestling with the living room furniture overtakes Smokey and for a moment she says nothing. Once she trusts herself to speak calmly, she says, "If you want to catch a mouse you must be subtle, use stealth, and intelligence. Now come away from the hutch and let's see if there's really a mouse under there."

Slowly, Autumn extracts her arm while wiggling back into an upright position.

"Watch," Smokey commands, crouching low until she's eye level with the bottom of the hutch. Slowly, she creeps forward, body tense, every inch of her on high alert. Smokey knows there's no mouse under the hutch, she would have sniffed it out, but old instincts take over, memories of the hunt kick in. She can't restrain whisker twitches, chittering jaws, and the rush of adrenaline.

Behind her she hears Autumn's whispered pleadings, "Please be a mouse. Please be a mouse. Oh, please let there be a mouse."

Just as Smokey comes even with the space between the floor and the bottom of the hutch, she feels a paw tap gently on her back. "Remember what you promised, Smokey."

Smokey sighs as the adrenaline rush fades.

"Don't worry, Autumn. If there's ever a mouse in this cottage, it's yours." Then extending a paw under the hutch, she grabs a clump of fur with her claws and draws it out.

"Is this what you saw?"

Autumn looks at a fluffy clump of her own fur. It's forever dropping off only to be found in tufts and balls all over the cottage.

"Well...maybe. I guess so."

"I have to get to work," says Smokey, straightening up.

Autumn heaves a heavy sigh. "I'll go clean the kitchen."

Chapter Two

Work

Smokey has worked for Fluffington ArCATecture for several years, starting as a junior architect and working her way up to senior. She dreams of one day owning her own architecture firm, though the thought of starting from scratch and working her way up to something as successful as Fluffington's is a daunting prospect. Still, it's a dream that creeps into her thoughts too often to ignore. She imagines herself striding the halls of the Faunaburg Office Tower, the site of Fluffington ArCATecture, with the sophisticated air of Abigail Fluffington. She'll have to begin small, probably a few rooms in a strip mall. But she could do it. She's young, talented, confidant.

Smokey knocks on Abigail's office door, hoping that whatever project her boss wants to see her about is another stepping-stone on her way.

"*Entré*" calls Ms. Fluffington. "Ah, Smokerina. Do have a seat."

Smokey sits opposite Abigail, only the vast expanse of a mahogany desk between her and the elegant cream-colored Persian.

"We have landed a huge account." Never one for small talk, Abigail gets right to the matter at paw. "It was Rufus Tailwagger's idea. He was so excited when he told me about it. You know how that dog is. Once he gets an idea into his head, he's like a... well like a dog with a bone, I suppose."

Smokey knows all about Rufus Tailwagger. He's one of the best PR dogs in the business; a huge Siberian Husky with piercing blue eyes and a long, bushy tail that's always wagging. The more excited he becomes, the more his tail wags. Once while explaining an idea for one of his dog parks to the Fluffington staff, his tail became so animated that he accidentally swatted Paulie Pomeranian clear across the room. Paulie was fine and Rufus was horribly embarrassed, but it did serve as a warning to give a wide berth to that dog's tail.

"What's his idea?" Smokey asks, trying hard to feign interest in yet another variation on a dog park.

"As you may know, Rufus has some close feline friends. On his last visit to them they started talking about the plethora of dog parks in Faunaburg while there's nothing at all for cats."

Smokey's ears twitch. "Is he suggesting a cat park?"

"I suppose you could call it that, though it would be quite different from a dog park, cats having other needs. Rufus wasn't exactly sure what should be in it, not being a cat himself, though his friends did make a few suggestions. A catnip garden, some weatherproof kitty condos, etcetera, etcetera." Abigail waves her paw like a queen dismissing a servant.

"Do we have a space for it?" Smokey asks.

"Yes, the lot behind those old high rises. You know, off Rodent Way."

"Rodent Way? Did he think that was a good place for a cat park?"

"It has very nice features. It's large. There are lots of tall trees for climbing and claw sharpening. The soil has good drainage so there's no pooling of water anywhere that will get our feet wet or create mud puddles after a rain." Abigail's lips curl ever so slightly. "That's precisely the reason the dogs have never wanted it. They do so like to roll in mud, though heaven knows why."

"Did Rufus have any other ideas besides catnip and condos?" Smokey asks, deciding not to push the idea of looking for a different location yet.

"That's where you come in." Abigail leans across the desk as if about to impart a state secret. "You may be surprised to learn this, Smokerina, as I'm sure it doesn't show, but I am well into my seventh life."

Smokey does not have to feign her shock, not that she isn't aware of Abigail's advancing age, but that the Grand Dame Fluffington is actually admitting to it.

"I know it's hard to believe." Abigail wraps her feather duster tail around herself so that the tip rests on the edge of the desk and strokes it lovingly with a freshly licked paw.

"I'm going to be forthright with you, Smokerina. This is the largest account we've ever received. Rufus mentioned it to Miguel Gato. He loved the idea so much he purchased that land parcel from the city."

Smokey's jaw drops. Miguel Gato, owner and CEO of Gato Enterprises, a multi-national firm he inherited from his father who inherited it from his father before him, is the single wealthiest cat in Faunaburg.

"We're talking millions, Smokerina. He wants to go all out. It will be the first cat park in Faunaburg. For all I know, it may be the first in the world. It must be both tasteful and spectacular."

Smokey swallows hard. "That's a tall order."

"Indeed, it is, but you're my best architect. I want you on this project. Delegate everything else you're working on now to the rest of the staff. Include some of the best juniors to bring them up a notch or two. Dedicate all your time and effort to this project."

Stunned, Smokey stares at Abigail.

"Well? Do you accept the project?" The tip of Abigail's tail thumps the desktop.

"Yes, of course! I never dreamed of such an opportunity."

Abigail's tail stops thumping as she smooths the tip with her paw.

"Surprised? Your work is brilliant." Abigail leans in close again. "If this is a success, I'll make you my partner. If and when I do retire, Fluffington's will be all yours."

Smokey draws in a sharp breath. Excitement, anxiety, confusion, and joy all combine in one inexplicable emotion.

"Oh, Miss Fluffington, this is amazing!" I can't even...I don't know what to say!"

"Take a moment to collect yourself, my dear. You must succeed at this project first."

Smokey nods. "Of course. I won't let you down, Ms. Fluffington!"

"It's taken me decades of hard work to build this firm. I want to be sure that after I'm gone it's in the paws of a cat capable of carrying on what I've started. Now, let's go tell the rest of the staff." Abigail rises from her chair. "About the new account and you taking the lead on it, that is. The rest is between us. You understand, Smokerina?"

"I do."

"Good. I'll call Rufus and Miguel to tell them you've agreed to take on the project. Rufus will want to meet with you. Stay out of the way of his tail. I'll have the surveyor's maps, city ordinances, permits, etcetera, etcetera on your desk by lunchtime. Congratulations, Smokerina. I am available anytime for consultation. I'll expect frequent updates and detailed reports."

Smokey fights the urge to jump to the top of the window frame and leap from one to the next. Instead, she follows her boss out of the office and stands proudly beside her as Abigail calls together the entire staff of Fluffington's. Smokey barely registers the applause and congratulatory head bonks.

Once the staff returns to work, Smokey makes a beeline for the basement. There she races up and down the hallways, doing zoomies in and out of the janitors' quarters, sending squirrels and chipmunks diving into mop buckets for cover. She runs until she's exhausted and can safely return to her office with some semblance of composure.

* * *

I'll start with the birthday cake, thinks Autumn Amelia. She sets out all her baking implements, ready to begin.

Autumn produces her creations for a local bakery, Furry Confections. When she began with Furry's she worked on the premises. Soon Tabby Furry, the bakery owner, noticed two things. First, Autumn was the best baker Tabby had ever encountered. Phenomenal was the word Tabby used. Not only could she make bakery staples to perfection she also concocted new recipes so delicious that customers began asking for special orders made specifically by Autumn Amelia. Sales increased to the point where Tabby had to hire two bakers to handle the everyday items so Autumn could focus on her special creations.

The other thing Tabby noticed was that food was disappearing. A customer might stop in to pick up a batch of cookies. Plenty had been baked, some had sold, but there should have been some left. Yet they had all vanished. This happened with several items. One day Tabby strolled through the back of the main kitchen, an area set aside for Autumn, and found her deep in thought, writing out ideas, while absentmindedly eating one salmon scone after another. The container for those scones was supposed to be under the glass in the shop's counter.

Tabby confronted Autumn, who apologized, explaining that eating while she worked gave her inspiration for new desserts. "I need different tastes in my mouth. It inspires me."

"But do you have to eat so much?" Tabby asked.

"I only ate one," said Autumn.

"Really?"

Autumn followed Tabby's outstretched paw pointing towards the bin and gasped.

"That bin was full, Autumn."

Both cats stared. There were only two scones and some crumbs.

"Oh my!" said Autumn. "I must have been too lost in thought. I'm terribly sorry. But look what I've made," she said, grabbing a nearby loaf pan. The aroma of warm cinnamon wafted under their noses. Autumn cut a slice of the pound cake she had just covered in salmon mousse frosting and handed it to Tabby.

Of course, the salmon mousse cinnamon pound cake began flying out of the shop as fast as Autumn could bake it.

Autumn promised to be more careful about her inspirational snacking. She had every intention of making good on her promise. For her part, Tabby tried hard to overlook Autumn's indiscretions. It was obvious that she was a baking genius and honestly didn't realize how much she was eating during her lapses into a trance-like state while new recipes presented themselves in her head.

Autumn, however, was simply incapable of keeping her promise. One afternoon as she was spreading a delicate ocean white fish frosting over a cookie with the circumference of a small cake, Autumn overheard Tabby talking on the phone in her office.

"I just don't know what to do," she heard Tabby complain. "She's the best baker I've ever known, and I come from a long line of bakers. She's turned Furry Confections into one of the most popular spots in Wild Whisker Ridge. Customers are coming from surrounding towns just to try out something made by

Autumn Amelia. Without her we'd just be a run-of-the-mill bakery. On the other paw, she's eating all my regular inventory and my other bakers are frustrated when they can't find ingredients and the customers get peeved when we've run out of bakery staples early in the day. Why just today a cat came in for a box of tuna chip cookies and there were none to be had. The cookie jar was missing, and I had nothing to offer. That jar was on the counter and full to the brim the last time I checked. I'm in a terrible quandary."

Well, that's just ridiculous, Autumn thought. *She must know I brought the cookie jar back here for inspiration, but I only ate a couple, and she could have come and boxed some up for her customer.* Autumn sighed. *I suppose I can do it myself and put them out front.*

She grabbed some empty boxes from the shelf and set them next to the jar, then put her paw in to draw out some cookies. Deeper and deeper went her paw until all she could feel was the ceramic bottom and a few crumbs. Autumn drew out her paw and stuck in her head.

"Oh dear," she said to the inside of the cookie jar. "I've done it again."

Pulling her head out, she picked it up and carried it to Tabby's office. She knocked and when Tabby called, "Come in," she set the jar on her boss's desk. "I'm afraid we have a problem," she said.

Tabby peered into the empty jar then looked at Autumn. "Yes, Autumn, I'm afraid we do."

With tears glistening in her eyes, Autumn removed her baker's apron with the words FURRY CONFECTIONS emblazoned across the front and held it out to Tabby.

"Autumn, what are you doing? You're not quitting, are you?"

"What else can I do? I'm causing an awful problem for you, but I can't stop eating everything. It seems to be the only way I can think up new recipes." Autumn began to cry so hard she could no longer talk.

Tabby stood and threw her arms around Autumn. "No, you can't go. No one can bake like you. Let's sit down and think about this."

"I can't think of a way to solve this problem," said Autumn, taking a seat across from Tabby's desk.

"I can't afford to lose you, Autumn. On the other paw, I can't afford to lose half my inventory, either."

They sat quietly for a while, Tabby thinking hard about a solution. Suddenly, Tabby said, "I've got it! How would you feel about working from home? You could do your baking there and eat all the treats you want. I'll even supply a few to help you with your inspiration. When we get special requests, I'll send you a list. When you finish, you can bring everything over or I can send a courier, so you won't have to waste time driving back and forth. That way you'll still be working for Furry's but you won't be tempted to eat everything in the shop."

"That would be wonderful!" said Autumn, sorry to be exiled from the bakery, but delighted that Tabby had found a way to keep her on staff.

"And I'm going to give you the title of Specialty Baker," said Tabby. "And a raise to go with it."

"Really?" asked Autumn, feeling a little better about herself.

"Your special confections are what bring in the customers and keep them coming back."

On the way home that day, Autumn wondered how to explain to it all to Smokey. As she neared the cottage, Autumn thought, *I think I'll start with, "guess what, Smokey. I got a promotion and a raise today!"*

* * *

It has been two years since Autumn began baking for Furry's from home. Today's first order is a cake for a kitten's birthday party. Autumn chooses a cake mold in the shape of a party dress. After adding her favorite secret ingredient — powdered moths — she makes the dough and pours it into the mold. While the cake bakes, Autumn mulls over flavors and designs for the frosting while absentmindedly munching from a jar of candied dragonfly wings. By the time the cake is finished baking she has decided on a light ocean whitefish butter cream with tuna flavored polka dots. The buzzing of the timer pulls her from her reverie, and she looks at the candied wing in her paw. *Wouldn't these make adorable bows for the party dress?* she thinks, popping the wing into her mouth.

Once the cake is cool enough, she whips up the frostings. Autumn deftly spreads the whitefish butter cream across the dress-shaped cake making frills down the front and ruffles along the hemline. She squeezes the tuna polka dots here and there all over the cake, careful to keep them all close to the same size.

And now for the finishing touch. Autumn goes back to the table and grabs the glass jar that, just this morning had been full of candied dragonfly wings, only to find it completely empty.

"Oh no!" she exclaims. "I've done it again!" She looks at the dress cake and thinks how perfect it would be with a row of dragonfly wings down the center and a few more at the waist. "They would have looked like perfect little ribbons," she says, stamping her paw.

Candied dragonfly wings are Autumn's own creation. She's made a wide array of insects an integral part of her baking, but dragonflies are her favorite. She carefully cooks them with sugar and leaves them to dry and cool for hours until they become hard like sugar candy. It's a long, complex process, but the result, glistening wings in brilliant colors that burst with sweetness when crunched, can't be beat for either taste or beauty.

Why did I have them out here? She wonders. *I didn't even know I was going to use them until I started thinking about the frosting.*

Autumn looks over her list of orders again and then at all the ingredients set out for the day's work. "Aha!" she exclaims. "The toasted crickets are missing. I simply grabbed the wrong jar. Well, that explains it, but now what am I going to do about the dragonfly wings?"

She heads for the pantry to retrieve the toasted crickets and looks around for a substitute. *Hmmm...mocha covered ants, roasted grasshoppers, catnip drenched praying mantises – not for a kitten's cake.* "Drat! I don't see a thing that will work. Oh, I could just bite myself!"

Just as she's about to give up, something in the corner, way in the back on the very top shelf catches her eye. *Is that what I think it is?* she wonders. Autumn proceeds to the back of the pantry, climbs the shelves, tipping over boxes and bags along the way. Finally, she reaches the top. Yes! An extra jar of candied dragonfly wings sits glistening in front of her.

Jubilant, Autumn grabs the jar and begins her descent, jumping from shelf to shelf when she suddenly slips on her floof. When her feet go out from under her she misses the shelf on which she was supposed to land. Tightening her hold on the jar only makes it slide through the floof on her front paws, sending it rocketing into the air. All four paws flail wildly trying to get a purchase on anything. The skittering of her paws from shelf to shelf, then to the boxes below breaks her fall allowing her to land safely on all fours. *But where has the jar of dragonfly wings gone?* She doesn't recall the sound of glass breaking. Autumn wanders through the pantry and finally finds the jar lying on its side on a five-pound bag of moth flour.

Opening the jar, she sees that only a few wings have been damaged.

Autumn arranges the intact wings on the cake while eating the broken ones, then stands back to take in the full effect.

The kitten's party dress with polka dots, ruffles, and frills is set off to perfection by the sparkling bows of red, blue, green, and purple. Autumn claps her paws wishing she could be there to see the delight on the faces of the kittens when they get their first glimpse of it. Quickly, before anything can happen, she grabs a cake box, slides it in and ties it up with string. Then she calls Furry's.

"The cake for the kitten's birthday party is ready," she tells Tabby. "Please send a courier to pick it up. What? No, there are no nuts or acorns. It's okay to send the squirrels. Thanks, Tabby. I'll bring the rest of today's orders over later. I want to get this cake on its way. I know the Mama cat will be in soon to pick it up and I have lots more baking to do."

Autumn peers into the pantry, sees the mess she's made and shuts the door, not looking forward to cleaning up at the end of the day. *Oops! I just need one thing*, she thinks and, going back into the pantry, she empties the contents of a small jar into her apron pocket.

Autumn is about halfway through the next item on the list when the doorbell rings. She wipes her paws on a towel and, taking the boxed-up cake, carefully carries it out of the kitchen and through the living room where she opens the front door.

The Squirrel brothers stand before her, each of them wearing a hollowed out walnut shell for a helmet. Their tandem bicycles with the cart attached to the back is behind them in the semi-circular driveway.

"Here it is," says Autumn, handing the box to the squirrels. "Be careful with it. Don't go too fast. I want this to get to Furry's all in one piece."

"What is it?" asks Simon Squirrel.

"It's a cake for a kitten's birthday party."

"Any acorns in it?" asks Simon's brother, Sam.

"No. No acorns."

"What about walnuts?" asks Simon.

"No walnuts, either."

"Peanuts?"

"Almonds?"

"Sesame seeds?"

"Sunflower seeds?"

The Squirrel brothers take turns naming off their favorite foods so fast Autumn's head begins to swim.

"No. No. No. There is nothing in that cake that a squirrel would want."

The squirrels finish securing the box in the back of their cart, then run off.

"Get back here right this minute!" Autumn calls as the brothers chase each other around the trunk of a nearby tree. They run back to stand side-by-side in front of her.

"That's better. Now give me your full attention." She looks at them sternly, paws on her hips.

"That is a very special cake. The kitten whose birthday it's for is a tripod. Do you know what that means?"

The squirrels nod. "Means she's only got three legs instead of four," says Simon.

"That's right. You boys have a special mission to get that special cake back to the bakery in perfect condition so that the Mama cat can pick it up on time for her very special kitten's very special day. Do you fully understand the importance of your mission, men?"

The squirrels sit up tall and puff out their chests. "We do!" they declare.

"Good. I know you'll do just fine. Now, hold out your paws."

The Squirrel brothers cup their paws and hold them out in front of them. Autumn reaches into her apron pocket and deposits a mix of nuts and seeds into each of the brother's paws which they immediately stuff into their mouths."

"Fank ew, Mish Autumn," they say.

"You're welcome. Now get going."

Autumn watches Simon and Sam hop onto their bikes and pedal off.

"Remember what I said, boys. Be careful!" she calls.

"I'm glad that's done and out of my paws," Autumn mutters to herself as she heads back to the kitchen.

Autumn Amelia is just boxing up the last batch of cookies when her cell phone rings.

"Hi Smokey. What's up?"

"Autumn, I have the most amazing news! I don't want to tell you over the phone. Just pull out a bottle of catnip champagne and put it on ice for when I get home."

"This must be big news. C'mon, tell me," Autumn pleads.

"Not until I get home."

"Fine. Do you want me to make something special for dinner?"

There's silence for a moment then Smokey says, "Let's go out for dinner."

Autumn drops into the kitchen chair with a thud. "Really?" she asks. "Are you sure? With me?"

Smokey giggles. "Yes, with you. And Jasmine. I'm going to call her right now and see if she can join us. You get that nip-pagne on ice, okay? Gotta go. See you tonight, Autumn."

Autumn sits at the table in stunned silence wondering what on earth could have happened that would make Smokey want to go to a restaurant with her. Come to think of it, what restaurant could they even go to? Most of the restaurants in Wild Whisker Ridge are off limits to Autumn. She has a terrible habit of snatching food off passing plates as they are being carried to other diners. She doesn't mean to do it, doesn't even notice the waiters carrying big trays of dinner plates. It's as if the food is just floating by. The sight and smell overcome her and without realizing it, her paw reaches out for whatever catches her attention.

In a small, close-knit community like Wild Whisker Ridge, Autumn Amelia is too well-known and loved to be officially banned from any of the local restaurants, but she knows they're afraid to see her coming especially since the last time she was at The Feeding Bowl. Upon exiting the ladies' litter room she'd sniffed the aroma of tuna and crab casserole fresh from the oven and followed her nose to the kitchen instead of going back to her booth. The owner had to get Smokey to drag Autumn out of the kitchen. As Smokey led her away, Autumn called over her shoulder to the astonished chef, "Needs more cream and a little bit of nip and parsley sprinkled over the top to make it p-u-u-ur-fect!"

Since then Smokey has seriously curtailed Autumn's trips to restaurants. Autumn was, however, gratified to hear that The Feeding Bowl had taken her suggestion and the tuna and crab casserole had become their bestselling dish. Word throughout Wild Whisker Ridge's restaurants is that Autumn Amelia could become a world-renowned chef if she could only keep from eating the entire contents of the kitchen.

All the way to Furry Confections and back Autumn ponders what could have made Smokey relent. Upon returning, she whisks the cottage into shape, cleans up the mess she made in the pantry and takes a bath. About an hour before Smokey is due home, Autumn pulls a bottle of Fluffy Tails Catnip Champagne from the cabinet and sets it in an ice bucket to chill.

Chapter Three

The Restaurant

The thought of going to a restaurant begins to outshine Autumn's curiosity about Smokey's news. She paces the cottage floor thinking of all her favorite dishes, one food after another dancing through her mind like an edible chorus line. When Smokey arrives home, Autumn is sitting on the living room floor, staring into space, so engrossed in her food fantasies that she nearly jumps out of her fur when Smokey taps her on the shoulder.

"Excited about going out to eat, Autumn?" Smokey asks, giggling.

Autumn nods vigorously.

Smokey sighs and shakes her head. "Please wipe your mouth, Autumn. You're drooling. Dog's drool. Cats don't."

Autumn wipes her mouth and follows Smokey into the kitchen, murmuring to herself, "I *am* a cat. I *am* a cat."

In the doorway, Smokey stops, turns around, holds Autumn's face between her paws and says, "Yes, Autumn Amelia, you most certainly *are* a cat." Then she turns back towards the kitchen. "Let's break open that nip-pagne!"

"Don't keep me in suspense any longer." says Autumn watching Smokey grab two champagne flutes from the cabinet. "What's the big news?"

Taking the bottle from the ice bucket, Smokey announces, "This morning, Abigail Fluffington made me the sole lead on the biggest account Fluffington ArCATecture has ever had."

"Smokey! That's terrific!"

"There's more. She said that if I do a good job on this project, she's going to make me her partner and, when she retires, I will get to take ownership of Fluffingtons!" With that Smokey pops the cork on the bottle.

Autumn claps and jumps up and down, her paws skittering all over the kitchen floor while Smokey laughs and pours the nip-pagne. She lets Autumn finish her wild dance before handing her a flute and clinking glasses.

"We've got to change," says Smokey. "I've made reservations at Top Cat. Jasmine's going to meet us there."

Autumn stands in the kitchen doorway, watching Smokey hurry up the stairs.

"Aren't you coming?" Smokey calls.

"I don't know, Smokey. Top Cat's a pretty fancy restaurant. I've been there once. Remember? Are you sure you want me to go? Maybe you and Jasmine should go alone."

Smokey descends the stairs and walks back to Autumn Amelia.

"Autumn, this is the most exciting thing that's ever happened in my entire life. I want to celebrate it with my sister and my best friend."

"But I'll embarrass you. You know I can't help myself. You should have seen what I did with the candied dragonfly wings this morning."

Smokey laughs, a little snort escaping. She covers her mouth with her paw.

"I don't want to ruin your special night," Autumn explains.

"The only way you can ruin it is if you don't come. Don't worry. Jasmine and I think we've got a way to keep everything under control. Now come upstairs and let's get ready."

* * *

When they pull into the parking lot at Top Cat, Jasmine is waiting for them. Another Russian Blue, Jasmine and Smokey look enough alike to be identical twins. In fact, they are often mistaken one for the other. Watching them frolic excitedly in front of Top Cat's fancy, carved door, Autumn thinks the two could easily be supermodels, envisioning them gracing the covers of Catmopolitan or Glamour Puss.

Smokey and Jasmine stride into Top Cat like they own the place. *And here I am, big old furball waddling along behind*, thinks Autumn. She doesn't have long to feel sorry for herself. Upon entering the lobby all her senses become heightened to the extreme. She hears the rattle of dishes and sees plates of food being carried in one of the dining rooms just beyond the lobby. But it's the smells that really carry her away. The mixed aromas of roasting meats, simmering sauces, stewing seafood, and baking desserts nearly have her in a swoon.

"Smokerina! Jasmine! Darlings, what a pleasure to see you!" Jacques, the maître d', a tuxedoed French poodle, steps from behind his desk to kiss the air next to each cat's cheeks. "It has been a while. So good to have you with us, darlings."

"We're celebrating tonight, Jacques. "I've made reservations for three," says Smokey.

Jacques looks at his seating chart. "Ah, *oui*. The corner table in the back by the window." Jacques looks up from his chart and, for the first time, notices Autumn Amelia standing behind the two Blues. "Oh, yes...Oh, my. Well. I see you've brought your sister with you. Good evening, Miss Autumn. A...um...pleasure to have you dining with us."

25

Autumn barely hears Jacques. Her nose is too busy sorting out the various aromas. She has the uncanny ability to separate individual scents even when a multitude are mixed together. *Swordfish, hollandaise sauce, lemon méringue, coq au vin, bananas foster, beef bourguignon, fresh cream, tomatoes...*

"Autumn. Autumn Amelia." Suddenly Autumn is aware that Smokey is tugging on her fur.

"What?"

"We're going to our table now."

"Oh. Okay. Sorry, I was just smelling all the ingredients."

"In what, pray tell?" asks Jacques.

"Everything, of course."

"Of course," Jacques sighs and rolls his eyes. "Well, if you ladies will follow me, I'll show you to your table."

Before turning towards the dining room, Jacques leans close to Smokey's ear. He speaks in a low voice, but Autumn overhears. "Do you think there's a chance we can make it to your table without our patrons' dinners disappearing as your dear sister walks past them?"

Smokey glances at Jasmine and winks. "We've got that covered."

"Autumn, would you be a dear and carry my purse for me?" Smokey holds her clutch out to Autumn.

"Mine, to if you wouldn't mind," says Jasmine, handing hers to Autumn as well.

"Lead on, Jacques," says Smokey.

They form a line, Jacques in front, then Smokey, then Autumn, paws full of purses, and finally Jasmine bringing up the rear, gently nudging Autumn with a "hang onto those purses, Sweetie," every time Autumn's head turns in the direction of a passing tray. They make it to the table without incident and Smokey ushers Autumn into the seat closest to the window.

She and Jasmine have her boxed in where she can't reach passing trays of food.

"See, Jacques. No problem," says Smokey, triumphantly.

"The night is still young, Mademoiselle Smokerina. Your waiter will be here momentarily." Jacques bows and departs with a flourish.

"He can be a bit of a snob, can't he?" Smokey says to Jasmine.

"A bit," she replies. "But for a French poodle, he's not that bad. Now for heaven's sake, Smokey, tell me your news before I burst from curiosity."

* * *

"That dinner was delicious!" Smokey tosses her purse on the table by the front door and heads into the kitchen for a glass of ice water. "Did you have a good time, Autumn?"

"Tell you later. I need the litter box."

Smokey knew Autumn had needed to go before leaving Top Cat, but had begged her to wait until they got home. It was bad enough that all the waiters were taking circuitous routes to their assigned tables to avoid passing Autumn. When their waiter had asked Autumn what she'd like to order and she'd said, 'one of everything' Smokey had to ask him to give her a few more minutes. Finally, Smokey and Jasmine convinced Autumn to narrow her choice to one meal with the promise that she could have a few bites of theirs. They'd used the pocketbook trick again on the way out. They'd had a fabulous dinner, great conversation, and lots of laughter, so when Autumn announced just before leaving that she needed to use the restroom, Smokey had a moment of terror and panicked.

"Autumn, couldn't you wait until we get home?"

"I really have to go, Smokey."

27

"Please, just try. We'll be home in fifteen minutes." Smokey knew she was being unfair, but she couldn't stand to have this perfect night ruined at the end.

Autumn sighed. "Fine, but hurry."

I must be sure to praise Autumn for showing great restraint tonight, Smokey thinks.

Smokey pulls her cell phone from her purse to check her schedule for tomorrow and, noticing that she missed a call, taps the screen with one claw to play the message.

Hello, Miss Smokey. This is your cousin, Greyson. I just wanted to give you and Autumn the news that I've officially retired and now that I've got some free time on my paws I'm wondering if I could pay a visit to my two favorite cousins. I'll try calling again tomorrow.

Autumn comes out of the bathroom and joins Smokey in the kitchen.

"Well, that's a relief! And to answer your earlier question, yes, I had a very good time. Though I have to say I did feel a bit silly carrying around three pocketbooks."

"Yes, but it kept your paws off food that wasn't yours, didn't it?"

"I suppose."

"Well, I think you did a marvelous job. Not a soul in Top Cat can say you weren't the perfect customer. I think you're getting better, Autumn."

Autumn laughs. "If you think that, you should have been here this morning. I ate an entire jar of candied dragonfly wings then made a disaster of the pantry looking for more. Now I'm all out and you know how long it takes to make them."

"Maybe you'll get some help."

"What do you mean?"

"Listen." Smokey plays the voice mail message.

"Greyson's coming to visit!" Autumn exclaims. "How long has it been since we've seen him?"

"A couple of years, I think."

"Autumn glances at the clock. "It's not too late. Let's call him back now."

Smokey taps the call back icon. Greyson picks up on the second ring.

"Greyson, hi, this is Smokey. We got your message. Autumn's right here so I'll put you on speaker phone."

"Hi Greyson!" says Autumn.

"Well, hello there, Miss Autumn. How are you?"

"I'm great. How are you?"

"Fine and dandy."

"When did you retire?" asks Smokey.

"A few months ago. At first, I was keeping busy fixing things up around the house and yard, but before long I found myself just rattling around without much to do and I thought, 'why not go see my cousins up north?' That is, if you've got time and room for a guest."

"Of course, we do," cries Autumn. "Smokey just got a super exciting new project at work that could lead to a huge promotion and now you've just retired so we've got lots to celebrate!"

"Hmm…" muses Greyson. "A big project that could lead to a promotion. Sounds like you're going to be busy Miss Smokey. I don't want to be an imposition. I could come another time when it's more convenient."

"Don't be silly," says Smokey. "This project will take a while to complete, and life will just have to go on around it. It might even help to bounce ideas off you. Besides, Autumn works from home and she could use a little help. How good are you with dragonflies?"

"Dragonflies?" Greyson chuckles. "What do you do with dragonflies?"

"I candy them and use them for baking decorations. I used the last of them today to make bows on a kitten's birthday cake, so I need to make more."

"Can't say as I've ever done that, but I'm willing to try my paw at it. When is a good time for me to come?"

"Anytime," says Smokey.

"Come now!" says Autumn.

"Hold on, little ladies. Let me check my calendar. How about the week after next? I'm pretty sure I can get a flight that Friday. Would that work?"

"Looks good for us," says Smokey.

"All right then. I'll talk to you once everything's been confirmed. See you soon."

"It's getting late," says Autumn as Smokey puts away her phone. "Let's do Evening Chant before I fall asleep."

Smokey and Autumn head for the back yard. Gazing up at the stars and moon, they join paws and link tails as in unison they chant:

"Oh Great Creator of all the exists, we thank you for the day that was and the night that is.

We thank you for our fur and whisker, tails, and claws.

We thank you for how you have made us with amazing balance, lightning speed, great agility, able to see at night, and all the things that make us cats.

We thank you for the sun that warms our fur, the wind that blows our whiskers, the grass that tickles our toes and settles our stomachs, for trees to climb and flowers to sniff.

Oh, Great Creator, watch over us throughout the night and guide us through tomorrow."

When their chant ends, each cat bows her head, offering her own silent pray. Back in the house, they bid each other goodnight.

Chapter Four

Rodent Way

Smokey can feel them watching her. Yet every time she catches a glimpse of beady eyes or twitching noses they disappear. She tries to keep her mind on her conversation with Rufus Tailwagger. *Pay attention*, she tells herself. *This is important.*

Smokey and Rufus have spoken on the phone a few times and met in her office once, but this is the first time they've been onsite together. Smokey needs to get a good look at the plot of land, walk the perimeter, visualize what might go where. She'd never had a problem with any of her other projects. Ever since Fluffington's had expanded into landscape design, Smokey had distinguished herself as the best in the firm. All the dog parks she'd designed had been a snap. She can stand in a seemingly empty spot and see, touch, and smell everything she envisions. It is something akin to the trance that comes over Autumn Amelia as she concocts new recipes. All Smokey need do afterwards is put it on paper drawn to scale and slowly watch it come to life. Once the builders and landscapers finish, it is always just as her vision predicted.

Today something is different. She isn't slipping into her usual designing daydream, and it has nothing to do with Tailwagger's presence. She feels on high alert as if she is the prey for something lurking in the tall grass edging the land parcel.

"What do you think? Great potential, right?" asks Rufus Tailwagger. "Loads you could do with it." A little breeze breaks the dead still of the hot summer day. Smokey realizes that it's Rufus's tail betraying his growing excitement and moves out of the way.

"It is large so there's plenty of room. I like the way the trees are spaced. I've been thinking a lot about trees lately. They're so integral to the landscape design and, for cats especially, trees are an important feature."

"Trees? Oh, yes, that's right. You cats like to climb trees. You've got some tall ones here. Tall. Thick. Great stuff. But what about the descending issue? You don't think that will be a problem?"

"Descending issue?"

"Yes. You know. Cats run willy-nilly up a tree and can't come back down. A problem. Quite a problem."

Smokey steps up to a massive oak. "I'll take care of that in my plans," she says, looking him in the eye. "Besides, trees aren't just for climbing. They're also for claw sharpening. See?" She stretches up, sinking her claws deep into the bark.

"Yup. Yup. I see. I see." Rufus takes a step back as Smokey deftly kneads the tree trunk leaving ragged scratch marks before disengaging her claws.

They continue to walk together. Some ideas start to form in Smokey's mind. She's on the verge of slipping into her design trance when something moves in the grass beside her. Her eyes dart to the right where she spies a long, thin tail disappearing into a hole in the ground.

"So, what have you got? Any ideas frolicking in your head yet?"

Smokey returns her attention to Rufus.

"A few. I like your friends' idea of a catnip garden. It could go practically anywhere on this parcel, so I'll watch for a spot that gets good sunlight. I'm thinking of running some sky bridges on varying levels from tree to tree. That way cats can move from one tree to another without having to get down first. And we can put in ramps from the ground to the bridges for the elderly and physically challenged kitties. Ramps would also address the...ahem...descending issue."

"Yup. Yup. Good. All good. I like it. I like it a lot." A breeze starts up again and Smokey quickly scampers ahead of Rufus, keeping herself safely away from his tail.

"Rufus, how much of this grassy area is included in the parcel?" Smokey asks, pointing to the lush, overgrown fields surrounding the sandy soil and short grass interior.

"Oh, all of it. All of it. The parcel goes right out to the streets on all four sides."

"It's a huge space. We could clear some of the tall grass to make a playing field. I know Faunaburg already has a brusselball field—"

"Yup. Beautiful job you did on that," Rufus interrupts. "Love playing there myself."

"Thank you. But as I was saying that field is on the other side of the city and caters to a rather sophisticated crowd what with the adjacent spa and all. I don't think it would create competition or ill-will to put one here as well."

"Nope. Nope. Not at all. Good idea. I like it."

Smokey looks over the expanse of wide-open space. "Those are the thoughts that come immediately to mind, but there's still so much room. I'm going to have to let my imagination run wild and see what else I come up with. Of course, I'll talk to my cat friends for their input." An idea suddenly occurs to Smokey. "My friend Jasmine is a freelance web designer. I'll ask her to set up an online survey for ideas from all the cats in Faunaburg and the surrounding area. It will be a real cat community space if they can all have input about what will be here. It will help to ensure that we're creating something the cats really want and will use." Smokey feels excitement rising, nascent ideas beginning to form. Yet in the back of her mind, she knows something isn't right.

"Good, Smokerina! Great stuff indeed!"

Smokey is glad she's placed herself in front of Rufus as his tail is now waging at alarming speed and cutting a swath in the tall grass behind him.

The onsite meeting comes to an end as Smokey and Rufus return to their cars. As she reaches for the door handle, Smokey once again feels the intensity of eyes on her. The fur stands upon her back.

"There is one thing that's bothering me about this parcel," she says in a hushed voice.

"What's that?"

Smokey gestures towards the high rises just beyond the field of tall grass. "It's awfully close to Rodent Way."

"What of it?"

"An awful lot of rodents have lived in this area for generations. They think of this whole section as theirs. They may not take kindly to any changes, most especially not to a cat park."

"Smokerina, you're forgetting that this parcel was sold by the city to Miguel Gato. It's in private ownership now. The rodents have no say in what's done with it."

"I haven't forgotten. It's just that having lots of cats take over a big section so close to where they've always lived might make them feel...you know...threatened."

"Are you worried about what a bunch of rodents think?" Rufus laughs. "Doesn't seem very cat-like."

Smokey stiffens. "I've evolved."

"If you don't want this project, Smokerina, I can speak to Abigail Fluffington and have her reassign it, though frankly, it would be a great loss. I was delighted when I heard she'd assigned it to you. But if your heart isn't in it..."

Smokey feels a knot form in the pit of her stomach. "Oh, but it is! I assure you I'm overjoyed at having this project. I'm just concerned. What if the rodents protest?"

"They haven't a paw to stand on. The parcel stops short of Rodent Way. We won't be encroaching on their territory, so there really is nothing they can say about it."

"Legally, that's true. But I noticed a lot of them in the fields as we were walking. I felt them watching us. I felt their hostility and fear. They aren't going to like it. I don't want there to be any trouble. It will make for bad PR."

"You needn't worry. Putting a positive media spin on it is my responsibility. Hopefully, we can head off any ill-will or protesting, or whatever these critters might have in mind before it ever begins. You just do what you're best at and come up with some great designs. Let's meet again soon to talk about your progress."

As Smokey drives back to the office her thoughts alternate between ideas for the park and concern about how the rodents might react. *I don't just want to put a good spin on it*, she thinks. *That will only last so long, and the rodents certainly won't buy into it. What on earth are we going to do?*

Chapter Five

Greyson Arrives

"He's here! Smokey, he's here!" Autumn bounces up and down as Greyson's rental car pulls into the driveway.

Smokey hurries to join her at the door as a handsome cat in a sports jacket and hat steps out.

"Welcome, Greyson!" they call, throwing their arms around him.

"This is a grand welcome. You ladies are looking lovely, I must say."

"We're so happy to see you!"

"How was your trip?"

"Are you hungry?"

Smokey and Autumn fire questions at him while nearly swallowing him up in paws, tails, and fur.

"Ladies! Let me get my suitcase and then I'll answer all your questions."

The sisters back away, still bouncing with excitement.

"Let me show you to your room," says Smokey. As they enter the cottage, she directs him to the guest room just off the living room. "It's right this way and the bathroom is next to it. That will be yours for as long as you are here."

"I just made lemonade," says Autumn. "Would you like some?"

"I'd love a glass," Greyson calls over his shoulder.

Once Greyson is settled, they all make themselves comfortable in the living room.

"That lemonade hits the spot," says Greyson. I was parched!"

"How do you like being retired?" asks Smokey.

"It's okay, I guess, but it's really a semi-retirement. Too much of my heart is in that job to leave it altogether."

"It must be very rewarding helping animals who've been through natural disasters," says Autumn. "I can see why it would be difficult to leave."

"And you worked so hard going from field work all the way up to Chief Executive Officer," Smokey adds.

"My decision to retire was not easy. However, I am getting on in years and I was beginning to find that I just couldn't keep up the way I once did. There are others, younger, with more energy, better ideas, and far more tech savvy. I could see they are the future of PAWS UNITED, so I groomed the ones I felt were best suited to take over, eased them in and myself out. I'll still keep my paw in, though. As long as there's breath in my body and animals in peril, I'll do what I can. Meanwhile, it's good to enjoy life a bit."

"We're glad you thought of visiting us," says Autumn.

"You two were at the top of my list. It's been far too long since we've seen each other. Now, Smokey, I want to hear all about this big project you're working on."

Before Smokey begins explaining, Autumn excuses herself to start dinner. "We're having grilled halibut with peach and pepper salsa. I hope you like it," she tells him.

"Sounds fabulous."

Smokey and Greyson continue their conversation while Autumn works in the kitchen, blithely humming a favorite tune. When she returns to announce that dinner is ready, she is caught up short by what she thinks is a scurrying sound in the wall behind her.

"Shhhhhh!" she commands.

Startled, Smokey and Greyson stop talking and stare at Autumn Amelia who is perfectly still, eyes bulging, every strand of fur standing on end.

"What's wrong?" asks Smokey.

"Didn't you hear it?" Autumn whispers.

Over the past week Autumn's fruitless nocturnal mouse hunts have recurred every night.

"The mouse," Autumn whispers, her voice suddenly husky and rough.

"There's a mouse?" Greyson asks.

"No," says Smokey.

"Yes!" says Autumn. "And he's in the wall. He'll come out tonight, I'll bet you anything."

Greyson stands. "I am at your service, m' ladies. If a mouse appears, I assure you I will take care of it so you can both sleep soundly and not give it another thou—"

Suddenly, Greyson is on the floor, flat on his back, Autumn Amelia standing atop him, her face inches from his.

"Don't you dare!" she cries. "If there's a mouse in this cottage, IT'S MINE!"

Smokey jumps to her feet. "Autumn Amelia, that's rude! You let Greyson up this instant!"

"Only when he promises. Promise, Greyson. Promise right now. If there's a mouse in this cottage, promise you won't touch it."

Smokey sighs. "Greyson, you'd better promise, or you'll never get off the floor. I'll explain later."

"Umm...okay. Autumn, I solemnly swear not to so much as lay a paw on any mouse I see during my entire stay here."

Autumn stares into his eyes for a moment, then steps off his chest, one paw at a time. Smokey assists Greyson to his feet and dusts off his fur. "I'm very sorry," she whispers in his ear.

"Quite all right. No harm done," he assures her.

Sidling up next to Autumn, Smokey asks, "Did you come to tell us that dinner is ready?"

"Oh. Yes. That was it. Dinner is ready."

"Good," says Smokey. She turns to Greyson, smiles, holds out a paw and says, "shall we?" while simultaneously giving Autumn a sharp swat with her tail.

The three cats enjoy a delicious dinner followed by fresh whipped cream topped with raspberries served in glass goblets.

"Do you cook like this every night, Miss Autumn?" Greyson asks.

"Most nights. I love to cook."

"And eat," says Smokey.

"I must say this is the best dinner I've had in quite some time. May I help you with the dishes?"

"Oh, no. I'll do them," says Autumn.

"Truly, I don't mind lending a paw."

"No, Greyson. You're our guest. And you haven't had the best welcome. I'm awfully sorry for knocking you down. It's just that...well I..." tears form in Autumn's eyes. "I can't really explain it, but I need to catch that mouse myself and when you said you were going to do it, I got scared that you would and then I'd never catch a mouse and I'm not a real cat and..." Autumn chokes on her words, unable to continue. "Excuse me, please," she stammers, rushing from the room. Halfway up the stairs, she calls down, "Leave the dishes. I'll do them later."

Greyson looks at Smokey, puzzled. "Dare I ask what that was all about?"

Smokey sighs. "It's a long story. I'll tell you later when I'm sure we'll have some time alone. I don't want her to hear us talking about it."

"Is she alright?"

"She's fine. It's just this obsession she's got about not being sure she's a real cat because she's never caught a mouse."

"It sounds to me like there's more to that story."

Smokey nods. "But now's not a good time."

"I see. Well, you can tell me whenever. Or not. It's not my business. Meanwhile, should we clean up these dishes?"

"That would not be a good idea. Autumn will want to do it herself. Why don't I make us some catnip iced tea?"

"Sounds terrific."

Smokey makes three tall glasses of iced tea. "Let's take ours outside," she says. Then she calls upstairs, "Autumn, Greyson and I are going outdoors. I've made iced tea. I left one for you on the counter."

As they stroll through the yard, sniffing flowers and letting the evening summer breeze ruffle their fur, they can hear the clack of dishes and know that Autumn has returned to the kitchen.

"One thing's for sure," Greyson confides to Smokey. "My stay here will certainly be interesting."

Chapter Six

Autumn's Secret

It's one o'clock in the morning. Autumn is wide awake. She's certain the mouse is running around the living room but doesn't dare check. Before going to bed, Smokey made her promise that no matter what she thought she heard she would not get up in the middle of the night to chase a mouse, or as Smokey had insultingly called it, an *imaginary* mouse. It wouldn't do to have Greyson's sleep disturbed by Autumn slamming into furniture just outside his door. Autumn considered her earlier behavior and reluctantly agreed to a moratorium on all nocturnal mouse hunts for the duration of Greyson's visit. She will honor her promise, but the sound of tiny scurrying feet coming from the living room is driving her crazy. She can't believe Smokey doesn't hear it. Autumn tries to sleep, but the more she attempts to put it out of her mind, the louder the scurrying grows.

It's no use, Autumn thinks. *I'm obviously not going to sleep*. She throws back the sheet, crawls out of bed, and heads for her closet.

There isn't much on the closet floor other than a few small boxes. Autumn keeps it that way on purpose. She wants a very private space for when she needs to do her secret thing that nobody, not even Smokey, knows about.

Autumn moves the few boxes until she comes to the smallest one and brings it to the center of the closet floor. Opening the box, she carefully unwraps a small, glass pirate ship from several layers of tissue paper, replaces the lid and sets the ship on the top of the box, settling down next to it.

When she and Smokey were kittens, Mama Cat had taken them on a trip to the seashore. They'd just finished lunch and were strolling along the wharf when Autumn spied the glass ship in a gift shop window.

"Mama, look!" She exclaimed, pointing to the ship. "Isn't it beautiful?" Spellbound by its smooth glass and gleaming colors, she begged, "May I have it? Please?"

Mama Cat sighed. "I'm sorry, Autumn. If I buy something for you, I'll have to buy something for Smokey, too, or it wouldn't be fair. I simply don't have enough money."

"Oh. Okay." Autumn tried hard to speak without a catch in her voice. Though still a kitten, she knew Mama Cat struggled to give them what she could. Even this daytrip to the seashore was a rare luxury. She didn't want to make Mama Cat feel bad.

"Goodbye, ship." She waved as they walked away.

The rest of the day had been spent frolicking on the beach, chasing bugs, collecting shells, and building sandcastles. But the ship continued to tug at Autumn's imagination. She looked out at the sea and thought of herself on a real pirate ship, sailing off to exotic places as the Pirate Queen of the High Seas.

"Hey!" she yelled when Smokey dumped a bucket of sea water over her head. "What'd you do that for?"

"I was calling you and you wouldn't answer. It was the only way I could get your attention."

Sure it was, thought Autumn.

They had to walk back down the wharf when it was time to leave. When they passed the gift shop again, Autumn couldn't help stopping to look at the ship, her little pink nose pressed against the window.

She felt a soft pat on her back. "Autumn, baby, we have to go now."

"Can I stay just a little longer, Mama? I want to look at it for one more minute."

"Autumn, Smokey and I were almost to the next block when we realized you weren't with us. It gave me a scare. Now come along."

Autumn pulled herself away from the window, but this time couldn't hold back a sniffle. They continued down the wharf when Mama Cat surprised them by stopping, opening her pocketbook, and counting her money.

"What are you doing, Mama?" Smokey asked.

"Making a decision."

"What decision?"

"Well, that depends. Can you two girls be very grown up?"

"I *am* very grown up," Smokey asserted. Autumn rolled her eyes, which fortunately, Mama Cat did not see.

"Yes, Mama," said Autumn.

"Then I'll tell you what I'm going to do. I'm going to buy that ship, but only on one condition."

"What, Mama? What?" Autumn jumped up and down and spun in circles.

"Autumn Amelia, stop!" Mama Cat commanded. "You have to give me your full attention."

Autumn stood very still, using every ounce of restraint her kitten body possessed.

"I will buy that ship if, and *only if*, you girls promise to share it."

"I promise," Autumn readily agreed.

"Smokey?" Mama Cat asked.

Smokey gave Autumn a look of disdain. "Sure. Whatever."

"Okay, then. Let's go back and get it before the shop closes."

"Yippee!" Autumn yelled, racing back to the shop.

"Autumn Amelia, wait for us! Do not go into that shop until we get there."

Taking no chances on Mama Cat changing her mind, Autumn stopped short before the door, hopping from one paw to the other as she waited.

The clerk wrapped the ship carefully in several layers of tissue paper, then placed it in the box. Autumn carried the box all the way home, never taking the ship out for fear of anything happening to it. She couldn't wait to get home so she could set it on the little table in her room right between her favorite toys — the two little balls with jingle bells inside them.

Once they got home and Mama Cat went to the kitchen to make supper, Smokey snatched the box from Autumn's paws.

"Hey!" Autumn exclaimed.

"Hey, yourself. Mama said we have to share it. That was the agreement, the only way you got to have it in the first place."

"Smokey, you don't even care about it!"

"Doesn't matter. You have to share it with me. Mama said so."

"Fine. How do we do that?"

"Simple. I'm the oldest so I get it first. It's going to sit on my bureau until I say you can have it."

"That's not fair!" Autumn wailed.

"What's going on in there?" Mama Cat called from the kitchen. "You two had better not be fighting over that ship or I'll have to take it away from you."

"See," Smokey sneered. "You have to share."

"Sharing doesn't mean *you* decide everything or that *you* get to keep it forever!"

Autumn ran to the kitchen to tell Mama Cat her troubles. When they returned, Smokey was no longer in the living room. They found her in her bedroom, the ship sitting on her bureau.

"Smokey, you weren't even interested in that ship, and you know it," Mama Cat stated. "I do want you girls to share it, but you have to be fair about it. You will each take turns having the ship in your room for a reasonable amount of time."

"Fine," said Smokey. "One week."

"Okay," Mama Cat agreed. "But one week from today it goes to Autumn's room. I'm going to mark it on the calendar, so no one forgets which day."

"Why does she get to have it first?" Autumn complained.

"Because I'm the oldest," said Smokey and she stuck her tongue out at Autumn.

"Mama!"

"Let's go, Autumn. You can put the mark on the calendar."

Autumn dissolved into tears as Mama Cat carried her downstairs. When they got to the kitchen, Mama Cat sat Autumn on her lap, nuzzled her with her nose, and said, "Listen, baby, Smokey doesn't care one whisker about that ship. You let her have it for a week. After that she'll have to give it to you for your turn. Chances are she'll forget all about it before you week is even up."

"What if she doesn't?" Autumn had gulped out, still crying, but starting to calm down.

"Then you'll have to give it back to her for her week. You've made an agreement and you both have to stick to it. But, if she loses interest and doesn't want it back, she doesn't have to take it." Mama Cat kissed Autumn's nose and held her close. "Don't worry, Autumn. She's not going to stay interested for very long and the less fuss you make the better. If she thinks it's not bothering you, it won't matter to her anymore."

"Why, Mama? Why does Smokey want to make me sad?"

"Oh, darling, I wish I had a good answer for that. It's just a normal thing for kits to do. It's part of growing up. When you're both grown cats, it won't be this way anymore. But right now you and Smokey have to go through your growing pains."

Mama Cat had been right. The week of waiting seemed the longest in Autumn's young life, but when it finally ended and the pirate ship came to rest on the table in her room, it never left. Autumn had offered it back to Smokey when her own first week ended, but Smokey was on to bigger and better things by then. She told Autumn, "Never mind. I don't need a stupid pirate ship. You keep it." Autumn had been so happy she didn't even care that Smokey had called it stupid.

As a kitten, Autumn spent many an hour gazing at the ship, letting it take her to imaginary places. It was most helpful during times when Smokey was being especially mean to her. Then she could forget her hurt feelings and go off in her mind to the deck of her own pirate ship where she ruled supreme.

One day, shortly after Mama Cat had passed away and Smokey and Autumn were sharing the cottage they'd inherited, Smokey knocked on Autumn's bedroom door. When she didn't answer, Smokey let herself in.

"You okay, Autumn?" she'd asked. "You didn't answer when I knocked."

Autumn had been sitting by the table with the ship, lost in a reverie.

"Hmmm...what? Oh, I'm fine. I was just thinking."

"About what?"

"Nothing really." Smokey did not know about Autumn's pirate fantasies, and she was not about to reveal them.

"Are you sure. I knocked three times. You never answered."

"I'm sure. What do you want?"

"Are you going to make supper. It's getting late. Oh, you still have that?" Smokey asked, just noticing the pirate ship.

Autumn suddenly felt possessive. "Yes, I do. What's wrong with that?"

"Nothing. Are you sure you're okay, Autumn?" Smokey gave her a strange look.

"I'm fine. I'll make supper now."

Later that night, Autumn had decided to put the pirate ship away for safekeeping. She wasn't worried that Smokey would take it or make fun of her for still having it. They were long past those days. She'd simply felt embarrassed that Smokey had caught her daydreaming over the ship. Those daydreams helped her through some of the most difficult times in her life. She'd feel more secure if they could be kept completely private. So, she'd found the box that she'd brought it home in, wrapped the ship carefully in the tissue paper, replaced the lid and put it on the floor in the back of her closet. It was a place where she could get to it easily and where she could go to be alone with it whenever she needed to.

Tonight, with a for-sure mouse (at least she thinks it's for-sure) running around in the living room and she unable to catch it because of Smokey's tyranny, she needs the pirate ship. She turns on the tiny nightlight in the closet and closes the door. The ship gleams in the soft glow of the nightlight. A tear rolls down her face with the first thought that always comes to her when she sees the pirate ship. *Mama Cat, I miss you so much.* Then, slowly, as she stares at the ship, she lets it work its magic and before she knows it, she is standing on the deck, the Pirate Queen of the High Seas, chasing down a band of marauding mice. Smokey and Greyson are subordinates, and she fires orders at them as they race with the wind, gaining on the mouse ship.

Chapter Seven

Niptucket Island

"Hurry up, Autumn! We're ready to go," Smokey calls up the stairs. A large cooler sits on the living room floor. Smokey paces while Greyson relaxes in an easy chair reading the morning paper.

"I'm coming," Autumn calls back.

"So's winter," Smokey mutters.

Smokey, up extra early in a hurry to get started, has made breakfast. Still half asleep, Autumn staggers downstairs yawning and nearly tripping over her own tail.

"Let's go!" Smokey says, once breakfast is cleaned up.

They pile into the car and head off for the ferry that will take them to Niptucket Island.

"Is there anything you specifically want to do while we're on Niptucket?" Autumn asks Greyson.

"That lighthouse Smokey told me about this morning sounds interesting."

"You must mean the one at Moss Head. That's Smokey's favorite. What else are we going to do? A whale watch? A boat tour?"

"Sure," says Smokey. "And we'll have a picnic on the beach at lunchtime. There are some nice little shops on Niptucket, too."

"Sounds wonderful," says Greyson.

As they settle into their seats on the ferry's deck, the morning sun gleams off the water while a light breeze ruffles their fur. A family of Yorkshire terriers sit right in front of them, the three little pups yipping as they squirm and wiggle, jumping over each other vying for their parents' attention.

"They are so adorable!" Autumn exclaims, the puppies' antics fully reviving her.

"Really?" asks Smokey looking annoyed.

"Well, I think they are." Autumn leans forward. "Hey, pups," she calls. "Is this your first trip on a ferry?"

"Yip! Yip! It is!"

"You're going to love it. Just wait 'til we get going. The ocean is so big you won't believe it!"

"Yip! Yip! We can't wait!"

The ferry begins to move. Autumn giggles as she watches the pup's heads turning, looking this way and that. They see seagulls and yip at them. They see fish jump out of the water and yip at them. They see passengers walk by and yip at them. Their parents try to keep them still, but their enthusiasm overtakes them. They jump up and down, tumbling about the deck. A wave tosses the boat just enough to send one pup sliding backwards under his seat headed straight for Autumn Amelia. She scoops him up in her arms, gives him a kiss on top of his head and hands him over the seat to his mother. It strikes her so funny she can't stop laughing. Smokey rolls her eyes while Greyson chuckles to himself.

Once on Niptucket Island, Smokey suggests heading straight for Moss Head Lighthouse.

Greyson whistles when he sees the imposing structure. "This is impressive," he says.

The sign at the entrance explains that the lighthouse was built in 1870 and stands over two hundred and twenty-five feet high. "I can't wait to see what it's like inside."

"Aren't there lots of lighthouses in Palm Ray?" Autumn asks.

"Yes, but somehow I've never paid much attention to them."

"Let's go in," says Smokey. "The inside is my favorite."

Upon entering the lighthouse, they find themselves in a small mudroom leading to the kitchen. There is an old-fashioned stove, a sink with a pump handle, a little wooden table and two chairs. Just beyond the kitchen is a small sitting room. Windows in both rooms look out over the water.

"Do you want to go upstairs?" Autumn calls from the sitting room.

The three of them ascend the circular staircase to the second floor. From the top stair they step directly into a bedroom.

"Look," says Smokey. "If you go up another flight you come out into the second bedroom. All the rooms are stacked atop each other.

Greyson strolls about the master bedroom. "This must have been where the lighthouse keeper and his wife slept. I assume the room upstairs was for their children.

"That's right," says Smokey. "Those are their pictures." She points to a set of framed sepia-toned photos on the bureau showing a family of Irish setters. The keeper wore a coat with five regulation triple gilt buttons on the side.

"We can go up to the tower, but we'll have to climb a lot of stairs to get there," she says.

"Lead the way, Miss Smokey!"

Opening a door in the master bedroom, they step onto the sky walk. At the other end is a stairway enclosed in stone. The chilly air is damp and musty. Smokey, in the lead, stops short.

"Look up," she directs.

The spiral of stairs continues.

"Gorgeous, isn't it?" she says. "It makes me think of a nautilus shell."

"It does, Smokey, but I wouldn't have thought of that. I'll bet as an architect you appreciate those types of things more than the rest of us. What about putting something like this in the cat park?"

"Great idea!"

As they continue up the stairs, Smokey's mind races with thoughts of how she can incorporate her favorite aspects of the lighthouse into the cat park. When they finally reach the top, they are standing next to the giant lantern.

"Wow! Look at the size of this!" Greyson exclaims. "I'd love to know how it works."

"There are panels that explain everything," says Autumn, pointing out the boards along the walls.

Greyson goes from each panel back to the lantern trying to piece together how the inner workings operate. The sisters admire the lantern for a moment then step onto the balcony. They breathe in the salt air and watch the seabirds fly above and below them.

"I'm getting hungry," says Autumn.

"Me, too. We'll find a nice spot on the beach for our picnic when we're done here."

Greyson soon joins them. "What a spectacular view," he says.

Smokey agrees, then asks, "Are you hungry, Greyson?"

"I could go for some lunch. Let's head out."

About halfway down the spiral staircase, Autumn says, "You know what I think the lighthouse builders should have done?"

"What?" asks Smokey.

"They should have put in a chute so instead of walking down all these stairs the lighthouse keeper could just slide down. It would have been faster and a lot more fun."

Greyson laughs. "You're right, Autumn. Another thought for your cat park, Smokey."

"But don't have it made of plastic," says Autumn. "Sliding down a plastic chute would make my fur all staticky."

Smokey bursts out laughing.

"What's so funny?"

"I was just thinking of you with your fur full of static. By the time you got to the end you would have changed from a cat to a porcupine!"

Greyson tries to stifle a laugh.

"Yeah, that's hilarious," says Autumn.

Smokey drives them to her favorite beach. They remove the wicker picnic basket from the cooler and carry it to a semi-secluded place on the sand. Smokey unfolds a large blanket while Autumn unpacks the basket. After a cold lunch of chicken drumsticks, egg and tuna salads, and lemonade, they relax in the sunshine letting their food digest.

"Are you going for a swim, Autumn?" Smokey asks after Greyson returns from taking the picnic basket back to the car.

"A swim?" Greyson asks. "Really? You actually go in the water, Miss Autumn?"

"Don't forget, she got Mama Cat's Maine Coon genes. Water doesn't penetrate her fur as quickly as it does ours, so she doesn't mind getting wet."

"Actually, I like it," says Autumn. "Unless you want to go somewhere else right away, I'd enjoy a quick dip."

"I'm in no hurry," says Greyson, "and, honestly, I'd like to see a cat swim. That's a new one on me."

"I'm going to the changing room to put on my bathing suit. Be right back."

Smokey and Greyson sit on the blanket looking out over the water. Lots of dogs splash about in the ocean, but no cats. A minute later, Autumn runs past them, kicking up sand as she goes, then dives straight into the sea. Greyson sits up straight, hardly believing his eyes.

"Can she really swim?"

"She's a good swimmer," Smokey assures him.

Other beach-goers stare in Autumn's direction. Several dogs splashing nearby stop to watch. Autumn swims out a little way, then turns so that she's parallel to the shore. She swims a strong, steady line.

"Wow!" bark some of the dogs.

After her swim, Autumn returns shaking the excess water from her fur.

"Autumn, stop! You're getting us all wet!" Smokey and Greyson roll out of the way.

"Sorry," Autumn says, dropping down on the blanket. "I need to lie in the sun while my fur dries."

"Fine, but keep on your own side," Smokey commands.

Once Autumn is dry and changed back to street clothes, they roll up the blanket and return to the car. "I think if we hurry, we can make the last whale watch of the day," says Smokey as they head off to buy tickets for the tour.

On the ferry trip back to the mainland, Greyson can't stop talking about the whale watch. "I still can't believe I saw two humpback whales up close. When that second one rose out of the water, he was right next to us, and I swear his eye was as big as I am."

"It's an awesome sight," Smokey agrees. "But I'm still amazed you haven't done much beach stuff considering all the years you've lived in Palm Ray."

"You know, Smokey, I've been thinking about that all day. I've been so busy working all these years that I've never stopped to look at what was right in front of me. I loved my job, but now that I'm retired, I need to do more than just relax. It's time to become aware, to notice what I was missing."

Once in the car, heading for home, Smokey realizes it's nearly supper time. She suggests they stop for take out on the way back.

"I would love to take you ladies out to dinner," Greyson offers.

"Um...to a restaurant?" asks Smokey.

"Of course." Greyson laughs.

Think of something, quick! She thinks. Taking Autumn to a restaurant with her and Jasmine was one thing. They both knew about Autumn's problem and managed to control it. Greyson knows nothing about it. "That's really thoughtful, but you don't have to."

"I insist. You've taken me to such wonderful places all day."

Smokey glances at Autumn in the rear-view mirror. Her head is resting on her paw against the car window, her eyes closed.

"Actually, Greyson," she whispers. "Autumn is almost asleep. I think she's too tired to go out to dinner. There's a really good sandwich shop that we have to pass on the way home. Why don't I just stop there."

"Okay," Greyson agrees. "If Autumn is too tired, she won't enjoy it. But before I leave you two must promise to let me take you out to eat one evening. You pick the restaurant, but make sure it's a nice one. Only the best for my cousins!"

"Okay," says Smokey. At least she is off the hook for tonight.

Once home they eat the sandwiches, clean out the picnic basket, then sit in the living room to talk. Autumn can barely keep her eyes open. "I'm sorry," she says, "but I can't stay awake any longer. I think the sea air tired me out. If you don't mind, I'm going to bed."

"Sleep well," says Greyson. "I think I'll turn in, too."

As Smokey makes her way up the stairs, thoughts of the day return bringing a barrage of ideas for the cat park. In her dream she sees Autumn sliding down a chute in a lighthouse with a whole family of mice on her lap, all of them yelling "whee!"

Chapter Eight

Dragonflies and Brusselballs

"Looks like I'm just in time to help," says Jasmine, exiting her car after pulling into the driveway behind Autumn Amelia.

"Autumn went shopping," says Smokey meeting her friend in the driveway.

Smokey has invited Jasmine over to meet Greyson. Once the introductions are over, Jasmine grabs one of the bags from Autumn's car and follows them into the cottage.

"Tell us what to do, Miss Autumn," says Greyson as they set the bags on the counters.

Autumn puts two bowls on the table then takes a huge jar of dragonflies from one of the grocery bags.

"Please separate them," she instructs. "Bodies in this bowl. Wings in that one. Smokey, please show Greyson how to do it without tearing the wings."

Autumn puts the groceries away while the other three set to work.

"Do you have a game today?" Smokey asks Jasmine.

"Yes. At three o'clock."

"What do you play?" asks Greyson.

"Brusselball."

"I've never heard of it."

"It's only played around here, but it's very popular," Jasmine explains. "There's a brusselball court in Faunaburg. Smokey designed it."

"Jasmine's on one of the official teams," says Smokey. "She's really good."

"Brusselball is a game made up by a local cat," Jasmine explains. "A bunch of us were having a big summer party over at Dexter's house."

"Dexter works in the same office building as me," Smokey interrupts.

"It was potluck," Jasmine continues. "All the guests were supposed to bring something to eat, and a cat named Arnold brought Brussels sprouts. Can you believe that? Brussels sprouts. Yuck!"

Greyson makes a face.

"They weren't cooked or anything," says Smokey. "We didn't know what to do with them."

"I figured out what to do with them," Autumn interjects.

"Yes, but not 'til later. Besides, that's another story," says Smokey.

"Anyway," Jasmine continues, "Some of us started batting them around. Arnold was like, 'hey, that's food, not a toy.' So, a few of us took a bite. Big mistake!"

Smokey makes a horrible face, sticking out her tongue and saying, "Bleck!"

Greyson laughs.

"Poor Arnold," says Jasmine. "He looked mortified even though he admitted he'd just grabbed them up at the grocery store on the way and didn't know what to do with them either. He said, 'I think you're supposed to cook them first.' Honestly, even cooked we couldn't imagine them being anything but disgusting."

Autumn snorts. "Because you don't know how to cook them properly."

"We'll get to that, Autumn," says Smokey.

Jasmine picks up the story again, "So one cat, I think it was Merlin, said, 'I know what we can do with them.' He started kicking them around. Then he said, 'Let's form teams and make up a game. We'll call it brusselball. So, we went out to Dexter's backyard and started playing, making up rules as we went along. That was the beginning of brusselball. Since then, real rules have been devised and there are several teams from all the towns around Faunaburg."

"That's right," says Smokey. "And Jasmine is one of the best players. If we get a chance before you leave, we'll take you to see the brusselball court I designed where most of the games are held. There are fields on the edges of the court where Brussels sprouts are grown to keep a steady supply since we go through a lot of balls in the course of a game."

"Are you on a team, too?" Greyson asks Smokey.

"No, but I play a lot. When the official teams aren't using the courts, anyone can play. There's a spa there, too, with changing rooms, a massage room, a workout room, and a health food court. It's very popular."

"If you designed it, I'm sure it's spectacular. So, what is the story about Miss Autumn and the brusselballs?" asks Greyson.

"Brussels sprouts," Autumn corrects him.

"Well," says Smokey. "The most important rule of the game is 'don't bite the ball'."

"Why? Is there a penalty for biting it?"

Smokey laughs. "Yes, but not anything that affects the game. If you bite it, you taste it. Yuck!"

"I see," Greyson laughs, too.

"But Autumn, being Autumn, caught the ball in her mouth during a game and naturally she bit into it. Instead of spitting it out in disgust like the rest of us, she stood there in the middle of the court, chewed it up and swallowed it. The entire game came to a halt while every player stared at her in disbelief."

Greyson turns to Autumn Amelia, now stirring something in a pot on the stove. "Did you actually like it, Miss Autumn?

"No. It was awful."

"Then why did you eat it?"

"I knew it was a vegetable and meant to be eaten so I decided to figure out what it needed."

Smokey can hardly contain her laughter. "It was hysterical. Autumn walked off the field just like that in the middle of the game, picked a few more Brussels sprouts from the field and we didn't see her again for over an hour."

"What were you doing, Miss Autumn?"

"Experimenting."

"She took over the kitchen in the food court and started cooking," says Jasmine.

"That's right," says Smokey. "By the time the game was finished, she had come out with a steaming plate of Brusselballs—"

"Brussels sprouts," Autumn corrects again.

"Pardon me," says Smokey. "Brussels sprouts. Anyway, she'd sautéed them in a butter and garlic sauce, and started serving them to everyone. Most were terrified to try them, but finally a few gave in."

"And?" asks Greyson.

"Yes, Smokey...and?" Autumn turns towards them, paws on her hips, one foot tapping.

"And they were delicious. She had to go pick more and make enough for all the players.

Autumn turns back to the stove, but not before Smokey glimpses the look of triumph on her face.

"Of course, Autumn has been all but banished from the brusselball court ever since," she declares.

"Whatever for?" asks Greyson.

"Because whenever she goes, she spends all her time harvesting brusselballs...excuse me...Brussels sprouts and the players started worrying she wouldn't leave enough in the fields."

Greyson laughs.

"Are those wings finished yet?" asks Autumn.

"All done, Miss Autumn. Here you go." Greyson hands her the bowls. "What can we help with next?"

"I have to start the drying process and finish everything for the sugaring. It's complicated work.

Thank you for the offer, but from this point on I'll need to do it myself."

"That, I think, is Autumn's way of telling us to get out of her kitchen," Smokey explains.

"I have to go, anyway," says Jasmine. "I've got to get to the court to warm up before game time."

"It was very nice meeting you, Miss Jasmine," says Greyson. "I hope I'll get to watch you play sometime."

"Nice meeting you, too, Greyson."

"Would you like to go for a walk," asks Smokey after seeing Jasmine out.

"Sounds like a fine idea. Lead the way. Miss Autumn, we'll leave you to work your magic," Greyson says, giving her a peck on the cheek.

Smokey and Greyson stroll across the meadow and onto a path in the woods.

"Smokey, you still haven't told me why I was attacked for offering to catch a mouse when I first got here. I can't help but be curious as all get out. Autumn seems so sweet and compassionate. Why is she so obsessively intent on catching a mouse? Does she have a vendetta against them?"

Smokey laughs. "No, nothing like that. Honestly, if she ever does catch a mouse, I've no idea what she'll do with it, but I'd lay bets she'll kiss it on top if its head and let it go."

"So, what's that all about then?"

Smokey sighs. "I'm afraid it's my fault," she says, her tone turning serious.

"How so?"

They come to a log lying across their path. "It's a long story, Greyson. Why don't we sit down?"

Chapter Nine

Smokey's Explanation

(A Sad, But Necessary Chapter)

"Do you remember my Mama Cat, Greyson?" Smokey asks as they hop onto the log.

"I sure do. My family moved south shortly after you were born. I was already nearly grown by then, so I have lots of memories of Aunt Lucy. I especially remember how kind and gentle she was."

"As you know, I came from her first litter. There were four of us. Life was very hard. We didn't have this cottage. We didn't have any place to live. Mostly we roamed the woods and bedded down in the bushes. Papa Cat couldn't find a job. We scavenged for food, mostly mice, moles, bugs, whatever we could catch."

"Our family did the same. That's why we left," says Greyson. "Mama and Papa thought there might be more opportunities somewhere else. It was a hard way to grow up."

"Yes, but I didn't realize it at first because I didn't know anything different."

"What happened to your litter mates, Smokey? I know something happened, but my parents would never tell me."

Smokey looks down, absentmindedly picking at a piece of wood sticking up from the log. "Hawks," she whispers. "They swooped into the bushes one day and made a grab for us. It happened so fast. The others were sleeping, but I was awake, so I guess I had a slight advantage. I ran. I'm the only one who made it."

"I'm so sorry." Greyson puts his arm around Smokey's shoulder, giving her a squeeze.

"It was the first time Mama Cat left us alone. She thought we were old enough to leave while she helped Papa hunt. When she got back, we were all gone. I heard her calling and came back to the bush. I had to tell her what happened. She thought it was her fault for leaving us. After that she kept me close all the time. She took me everywhere with her and never left me for a minute."

Smokey cries, unable to continue. Greyson tightens his arm around her shoulder and strokes her head. "It must have been awful."

Smokey swallows. "It was just the three of us then. Mama and Papa were more determined than ever to keep me safe. They taught me everything about how to survive. I learned what to hunt and what wanted to hunt me and how to hide from them. I hated winter. It was harder to hunt. Some days would go by with no food at all. I was cold and hungry. I quickly realized it was hunt or starve so I made it my mission to find out where mice go in the winter. Mama and Papa told me I was a real survivor. There was so little in my life that felt good or comfortable that praise from them became everything to me. I became an expert mouser."

"They must have been proud of you."

"I think so. They said they were. But I always saw something in their eyes, especially Mama Cat's, that I didn't comprehend whenever I brought back a mouse. She always said, 'good job, Smokey,' but there was something I can't explain. A sadness that I picked up on but didn't understand."

"She probably wished there could be another way for you...a better life."

Smokey nods. "I know that now."

"But things turned around for your family. You have that lovely cottage now and you're well educated with a good job. Everything worked out in the end."

Smokey nods. "Worked picked up again and Papa got a job. Actually, he got three of them. Then he bought the cottage, and we moved in. When I started school, Mama Cat got a job during my school hours so Papa could drop one of his. It was nice at first. We had a safe, warm place to live and not long after we moved into the cottage, Mama and Papa stopped hunting and started shopping at the grocery store. Mama sang while she cooked. She was so happy. We were finally eating food we didn't have to hunt for ourselves and eat raw."

"It must have been a big change for you. Did you like the food?"

"Did I ever!" Smokey looks up, gazing at the treetops. She smiles, but tears shine in her eyes. "Things changed so much. Eventually, Papa got a really good job so he could quit the others. He put a lot of money away. He was very frugal and said we couldn't touch it except for emergencies. I think the experience of being homeless made an indelible impression on him."

"I'm sure it did," Greyson agrees. "It had the same effect on my parents."

"Then there was the day that Mama and Papa told me more kittens were coming." Smokey laughs. "I didn't understand. 'Coming from where? Who's moving in with us?' I asked. That's when they had umm...*the talk* with me."

Greyson chuckles. "How did you feel about that? More kittens, I mean. Not 'the talk.'"

"I felt conflicted. Sometimes I was excited and couldn't wait. Other times I wished they wouldn't come at all. I wanted to keep Mama and Papa all to myself."

"So, normal then?"

Smokey smiles at him. "I suppose."

"I take it that was the litter Miss Autumn was born into?"

"Yes, but it wasn't a litter. Autumn turned out to be the only kitten. I guess it happens sometimes."

"What did you think of her?"

"I thought she looked weird and gross at first, but when she got a little bigger, she was kind of cute. Mama and Papa gushed over her, even when she was still ugly. That really irritated me."

Greyson laughs. "Again, sounds totally normal to me."

Smokey stares at the leaves on the ground.

"What are you thinking about, Smokey?"

"I was very jealous of her. When we'd first moved into the cottage and things improved, Mama Cat still made me the center of her life. Then Autumn Amelia showed up and they started making such a fuss over her. I felt as though they'd forgotten me. On top of that it wasn't long before we lost Papa Cat."

"What happened?"

"He worked late one night in the winter and when he left his office only the night janitor was still there. Later he told Mama Cat that he'd heard coyotes howling in the distance and warned Papa, but Papa told him he'd heard them too and thought they were far enough away for him to get safely to his car. He was wrong."

Smokey puts her head in her paws and cries. Greyson turns her to him and wraps his arms around her. "I'm so sorry, Smokey."

"Papa always reminded us never to let our guard down, to stay alert and keep our skills sharp just in case. How could he make such a terrible mistake?"

"Even the smartest cats can miscalculate sometimes. No one is perfect."

"Mama Cat and I were devastated. Autumn was still a baby. She hardly knew what was going on, so she didn't need much comforting. Mama hugged me all the time and let me sleep in her bed for a while. Even though I was horribly upset over losing Papa at least I felt I had some of Mama's attention back." Smokey's words come out in a rush with gulps and catches in her voice.

"Then Autumn Amelia got sick. Mama took her attention away from me and gave it all to her."

"She was a good Mama Cat, Smokey. She had to take care of her sick kitten. I'm sure she didn't neglect you completely and she probably couldn't stand the thought of another loss." Greyson speaks the words gently into Smokey's ear as he continues to stroke the fur on her head and back.

"I know that now, but then I was hurt and confused. I didn't understand anything."

"Of course not. How could you? You were just a kit, yourself."

Smokey cries on Greyson's shoulder for a long while then pulls away, wiping her eyes.

"Autumn got better, and life went on, but part of me was always angry with Autumn or jealous of her, I guess is more accurate."

"Why?"

"She was born into the cottage and good food. She'd never had to hunt a day in her life. She didn't know what it was like to go hungry or spend an entire winter outdoors in the cold and she didn't have a clue about the terror of knowing that she could be the prey. She didn't know what it was like to lose someone you love."

"She lost her Papa."

"Yes, but she was so young, she didn't really understand. You can ask her. She'll tell you she barely remembers him. You can't miss what you never knew."

"True, but it's still not easy to grow up without a Papa Cat. But you're right. You had an awful lot to overcome that she never had to deal with. So how does Autumn's desire to catch a mouse play into this?"

"That's the part that's my fault," says Smokey. "From the time she was old enough to understand I used to tease her because she'd never caught a mouse. I did it simply because I knew it upset her. I told her that real cats catch mice, and I was the best mouser ever and that she couldn't be a real cat if she never caught a mouse. Once I even caught one and brought it to her just to tease her with it. It was still alive. Mama Cat saw and made me let it go. Later she took me aside and told me that we only caught mice and other animals when we were homeless and had no choice and she wished I'd never had to do it. She said she was glad that Autumn had never had to catch her own supper and hoped she never would. I understand now what she meant, but then I thought she was saying that I wasn't as good as Autumn. It really hurt.

"So, I continued to tease Autumn and I finally had her convinced and I mean *totally* convinced that she wasn't a real cat, and no one knew what she really was. She cried and cried. Mama Cat was very angry with me. She spent countless hours trying to convince Autumn that she was a real cat and insisted that I tell Autumn I'd only been teasing her and that of course she was a real cat, which I did, albeit half-heartedly, but the damage was done. When she got older, Autumn finally claimed to believe that she was a real cat, but the idea that she might not be is still in the back of her mind. I think the only way she can truly convince herself that she's a real cat is if she catches a mouse."

"I see." Greyson strokes his chin. "If catching a mouse would do the trick, have you ever thought of getting one and putting it in the cottage without her knowing about it so she can catch it?"

"I've thought of it but decided against it."

"Why?"

"Two reasons. The first is that for her to believe it, it has to be real. If she has any suspicion at all that I set it up it won't work, and she might get angry with me."

"And the other reason?"

"I'm afraid."

"Of what?"

"She was never taught to hunt. That's why I kind of hope a mouse never does show up in the cottage. What if she can't catch it? It will devastate her. Then she'll be certain she's not a real cat. Heaven knows how she'll react."

"Good point."

"Any suggestions?"

"Yes. First of all, stop blaming yourself. You were a young kit, who had been through a very rough early life before things got better. Then, when you were still young, you lost your Papa Cat in a tragedy. You had the normal reaction of a young kit when a new kitten enters the family, but you had to deal with grief and loss at the same time. Give yourself a break!"

Smokey smiles through her tears. "Thank you, Greyson. This is the first time I've ever told anyone. It feels good to let it out and be supported."

"Good. Now, what to do about Miss Autumn? Are you sure catching a mouse is the only way to resolve her identity crisis?"

"I can't think of any other."

"If you're not willing to risk setting it up for her, the only thing you can do is leave it to fate."

Smokey sighs. "I guess. I so wish I hadn't done this to her."

"Now, Smokey, what did I just tell you?"

"I know, but I can't help feeling responsible and it's not just the mouse thing."

"There's more?"

Smokey nods. "Mama Cat was sick for a while before she died, and she knew it was coming. Autumn and I were grown up by then, but still living in the cottage with her. One day, Mama Cat was feeling particularly ill and called me to her bedside. She told me that she regretted not teaching Autumn any survival skills. She taught her how to cook and sew, how to keep house and make repairs, keep a budget, and all the things necessary for running a household. But she never taught her to hunt. She did tell her to be careful of coyotes, but she didn't go into much detail. I think it was hard for her. She was so happy to have at least one kit who didn't need to be taught about all the rough things in life that she sheltered her from them."

"Considering everything you all had been through, that's understandable."

"I guess, but by the end of her life she worried about it. I mean you must have noticed that Autumn is, well...different."

"Delightfully so!"

"No, Greyson. You don't understand. If life circumstances should change, she'd never know how to take care of herself. I would never want to go back to living the way I did when I was young, but if I had to I could do it and survive. Autumn wouldn't have a chance. That's what Mama Cat was worried about. She felt she'd failed her in that respect. So, she asked me to watch over and protect her. That's what I've been trying to do ever since. In a way, I'm trying to atone for what I did, but beyond that, I love Autumn. I've long since outgrown my childhood jealousies and I see what a truly good soul she is. But I also see other things."

"What other things?"

"She has certain...I don't know what to call them. Idiosyncrasies, maybe."

"Like what?"

"Like what she does when she cooks. She eats at the same time and doesn't know she's doing it. She takes food off of other's plates and eats it but doesn't realize what she's doing. That's why she can't go to restaurants anymore. More than once she's wandered into their kitchens and taken over the cooking without planning to. She just finds herself in the kitchen without even knowing how she got there. Don't you find that odd?"

"I'll admit that's a bit out of the ordinary, but on the other paw, she's an amazingly gifted chef. I'll bet she's improved the food on more than one occasion."

Smokey laughs. "True. But she also eats half their inventory while she's at it. That doesn't always go over well."

"Is that all?"

"No. It's hard to explain, but sometimes she doesn't seem quite, you know, normal."

"Define normal."

"She's just different. It's not anything bad. She'd never harm a soul. She just doesn't have any sense that not every creature is thoroughly good. I mean, if she ran into a coyote, she'd probably invite him home to dinner. That's why I feel the need to protect her. She just can't completely take care of herself."

"I don't think you're giving Autumn enough credit. She may have perfectly good survival skills that are just different from the type you learned. You might want to try letting go a little and letting her be who she is because from what I can see who she is, is pretty darn wonderful."

Smokey wants to believe Greyson. "Do you think I'm being controlling?"

"I wouldn't say controlling, but maybe a little too sheltering."

"I don't know, Greyson. If anything ever happened to her, I'd never forgive myself. I promised Mama Cat I'd take care of her."

"You've kept that promise. But what would happen if you fell in love and wanted to get married? Would you insist that Autumn live with you and your new husband? How do you think that would go over?"

"I've never even thought of marriage. I'm too focused on my career."

"Possibly. Or could it be that you've never let yourself think of it because of what it would mean to Autumn?"

"Maybe," Smokey concedes.

"Here's another thought, Smokey. What if Autumn falls in love and wants to get married?"

A snort mixed with a laugh escapes Smokey. "I can't picture Autumn married."

"Why not? She's a lovely cat with an endearing personality. I have a feeling she'd make a marvelous Mama Cat. Why couldn't it happen?"

"That's all true, but she's so innocent. Sometimes I think of her as still a kitten."

"You may think of her that way, but a man cat might see her very differently. And if that happens, then what?"

"I don't know. I guess I'll have to be sure he's right for her and that he'll take care of her and—"

"Um...Smokey," Greyson cuts her off. "Aren't those Autumn's decisions to make?"

"I don't expect you to understand, Greyson, because I can't explain it properly," Smokey blurts out. "You haven't lived with her. You don't realize how much help she needs navigating through life."

"I think she does just fine. Maybe you're too close to forest to see the trees. Try letting go, Smokey. You don't have to do it all at once and I'm not suggesting you abandon her. She'll always be your sister and you'll always love and care about her. But you have to let her find her own way. I think she can do it."

Smokey sighs. "I'll think about it. I'm not sure how to reconcile my promise to Mama Cat with letting go of protecting Autumn, but maybe you're right. Maybe I do need to find a better balance."

Chapter Ten

The Invitation

"You certainly have some interesting tins, Miss Autumn." Greyson sits at the kitchen table looking over Autumn's array of cake tins. Smokey has returned to work and Greyson is spending the morning helping Autumn Amelia with her baking.

"Whenever I see an interesting tin, I always pick it up. That party dress mold was a real find."

"I'll bet."

"I'd better clean up and get everything over to Furry's. I can't believe how quickly we finished. I'm never done before lunch. It must be because I had a great helper."

"My pleasure." Greyson's cell phone rings. "Excuse me."

Autumn gathers up her dishes and baking implements.

"That sounds wonderful," she hears Greyson say. "Autumn finished early so we can drop everything off at the bakery and head over. See you soon."

"Who was that?" asks Autumn.

"Smokey. She mentioned to her boss that I was visiting, and her boss suggested we all go out to lunch together. We're to meet at Smokey's office after we deliver to the bakery. We can take my rental."

Greyson starts loading the baked goods onto the large carrying trays.

"That can't be right," says Autumn.

"Am I putting them in the wrong order?"

"No, Greyson. That's not what I mean. Smokey couldn't possibly have meant for us both to go. Just load the trays into my car. I'll take everything to Furry's and you can head straight to Faunaburg."

"Of course, you're invited, Autumn. You heard me tell Smokey we'd both be there, didn't you?"

"I don't go to restaurants. I can't. I have a...um...problem." Autumn fidgets with her apron, twisting it in her paws.

"I know. Smokey told me."

"She did?" Autumn feels heat rise in her face.

"She had to since I kept insisting on taking the two of you out to a nice restaurant while I'm here."

"You can't do that! I mean, you can take Smokey, but not me. If she told you, then you must understand why."

"I think there are ways to work around the problem. Don't you?"

"I did go with Smokey and Jasmine to Top Cat to celebrate Smokey's new project."

"And how did that go?"

"Fine, I guess."

"See."

"But that was just Smokey and Jasmine. This is Smokey's boss, Abigail Fluffington. Smokey wouldn't want to risk being embarrassed in front of her. I don't want to risk it either."

"If you don't go, I won't either."

"You have to go."

"Then I guess you do, too."

Autumn looks into Greyson's eyes. "Are you certain I was invited? What exactly did Smokey say?"

Greyson clears his throat. Pretending to hold a cell phone to his ear, he says in a silly falsetto, "Hi, Greyson. I was telling everyone here at work that you are visiting from Palm Ray. When my boss, Ms. Fluffington, heard she told me to call and invite you to lunch. Can you come?"

"Aha!" says Autumn. "See. She didn't say a word about me, did she?"

Greyson returns to his normal voice. "And I said, 'That sounds wonderful. Autumn finished early so we can drop everything off at the bakery and head over.' And Smokey said," Greyson returns to the falsetto, 'meet us at my office. It's Fluffington ArCATecture in the Faunaburg Office Tower. The address is—"

"Greyson, stop that!" His falsetto makes Autumn laugh so hard her knees buckle.

"So, I told her *we'd* meet them at her office. Never once did she say you couldn't or shouldn't come."

Autumn wipes away tears from her laughing fit. "Still, she didn't exactly invite me and I'm not one to invite myself."

Resuming his falsetto, Greyson says, "Except into restaurant kitchens!"

"Greyson!" Autumn doubles over with laughter.

"Miss Autumn Amelia, the best way to overcome a problem is to face it head on. So, let's get going."

"I can't go dressed like this," says Autumn, recovering from her laugh attack. "Ms. Fluffington is sure to take us somewhere nice for lunch. Shorts and a tee-shirt won't do."

"You're right. I'll get these trays into the car and put on some slacks and a dress shirt. You run upstairs and change. I'll meet you in a minute."

"You're really asking for trouble, you know," Autumn calls over her shoulder as she heads up to her bedroom.

"Good!" He calls back. "I love an adventure."

* * *

Smokey sits at her desk staring at her phone. "What just happened?" she asks herself.

This morning while milling around the lobby, getting coffee and pastries, she'd told her colleagues about her cousin visiting from Palm Ray. Shortly afterwards, Abigail Fluffington had knocked on her door.

"Your cousin sounds very interesting. I'd like to meet him. Invite him to lunch. My treat."

It was as quick as that. When she'd called, Smokey hadn't mentioned Autumn. Greyson had taken it for granted that she was invited, too.

Now what am I going to do? She wondered. *I can't call back and uninvite her.* Smokey taps her claws on her desk. *Maybe Autumn won't come. She'll find a way to squirm out of it.*

Smokey goes to her drafting table. She draws a line or two then thinks, *what if she does come? Ms. Fluffington isn't expecting her. I'd better warn her.*

"Come!" Abigail's voice commands from behind her closed door.

"Ms. Fluffington?" Smokey pops her head inside.

"Yes?"

"I called my cousin."

"He's coming?"

"Yes."

"Wonderful!"

"There might be a slight problem."

"Do come in, Smokerina." Abigail motions her to a chair.

"Well, you know my sister, Autumn Amelia, works from home?"

"I believe you've mentioned it. She's a baker, correct?"

"That's right."

A spark of recognition dawns in Abigail's eyes. "I do remember! She's the one who made those positively scrumptious cupcakes you brought to the office Winter party last year." Abigail licks her lips at the memory. "The ocean whitefish frosting was to die for!"

"That's her," Smokey acknowledges.

"What about her, dear?"

"Well, Greyson is home with her and when I called, he seemed to think I meant for the both of them to come to lunch. I didn't say anything about Autumn, but he must have assumed it because when I hung up, I realized he'd said, 'we'll see you soon.' I'm awfully sorry, Ms. Fluffington."

"Is that all? Think nothing of it. I'd love to meet your sister. I can tell her myself how much I enjoyed her cupcakes. I'm sure having your sister along for lunch will be delightful."

Smokey smiles wanly, thinking, *you may be in for a big surprise*, before returning to her office.

* * *

Just before noon the building's receptionist buzzes Smokey to say that Greyson and Autumn Amelia have arrived.

Drat! She thinks. *Why couldn't Autumn have found a way out of it?*

Smokey goes to the hallway.

"Hey, Smokey, this is a pretty fancy office building," says Greyson stepping off the elevator with Autumn Amelia on his arm.

"Glad you like it. Fluffington's is down the hall."

They follow her down the long hallway to the double doors with the words Fluffington ArCATecture etched across the frosted glass. As she opens the door, Smokey turns to give Autumn a questioning look.

"I tried," Autumn whispers, but it's all she can say before they enter Fluffington's lobby. Cats and dogs are coming and going from various offices.

"Smokerina, this must be your cousin." Elton, a dalmatian, stops on his way to the lunchroom to greet them.

"Yes. And my sister, Autumn Amelia."

74

"Nice to meet you both," Elton says, shaking paws. "Are you the one who made the cupcakes for last year's Winter party?" he asks, turning to Autumn Amelia.

"Yes, that was me."

"They were out-of-this-world fantastic! I hope you're going to make them again this year."

Abigail Fluffington's door flies open, and the elegant Persian enters the lobby in a flourish of cascading fur, her plumed tail sweeping along behind her.

"Ah, there you are," she says, heading towards them.

Elton excuses himself and heads for the lunchroom.

"Ms. Fluffington, I'd like you to meet my cousin, Greyson."

"A pleasure," she says, lifting a perfectly manicured paw.

"The pleasure is mine, Madam." Greyson bows and kisses the air above her paw.

She glances sideways at Smokey. "Your cousin is a charmer, Smokerina." Then to Greyson she says, "I am so glad you could join us. I do apologize for the short notice. I found out only this morning that you were visiting and, as I'm booked solid tomorrow and leaving on a business trip on Wednesday, today was the only day I had available. Thank you for being so accommodating."

"I'm honored by the invitation. It's not every day I get to dine with three lovely ladies."

Abigail laughs softly, dipping her head coquettishly, then turns to Autumn. "You must be Smokerina's sister, Autumn Amelia." Abigail holds out her paw. "So very nice to meet the cat who can bake like a perfect angel."

Autumn shakes Abigail's paw. "It's nice to meet you, too. "I'm glad you liked my cupcakes."

"Liked them? I've never had cupcakes that tasted so heavenly in my life. Here it is half a year later and I'm still swooning at the thought of them."

"Thank you." Autumn looks at Smokey, not sure what to make of Abigail.

Smokey just smiles and says, "Shall we go?"

"In a moment, Smokerina. I'm afraid I have a phone call I absolutely must return before we can leave. I promise it will only take a minute and then we'll be on our way. I thought we'd go to The Scratching Post. It's my favorite lunch spot. Meanwhile, why don't you show Greyson and Autumn Amelia around."

"So, this is where your genius is unleashed," says Greyson as they step into Smokey's office.

They look at the desk, worktables with double computer monitors, drafting tables, rows of wide filing cabinets holding blueprints, and an assortment of drafting tools, and stacked cubbies with all sorts of odds and ends.

"Is this your current project?" asks Greyson, pointing to the large sheet of paper on the drafting table.

"Yes, that's the cat park. What do you think?"

"I like the sky walks in the trees," says Greyson. "And the ramps for the elderly and disabled kitties. That's a nice touch. What's this?" He points to a partially finished figure in the center.

"A tower. I was inspired by the lighthouse on Niptucket Island so I'm toying with the idea of adding something similar to the park. It wouldn't be a functional lighthouse, more a lookout tower, but it could have function rooms, maybe a big fire pit where the lamp would in a lighthouse with seating and tables out on the balcony."

"Very creative. Miss Autumn, come tell Smokey where to put the chute." He turns to look for Autumn who's been wandering around the office looking at everything, only to find she is no longer there. "Where's Autumn?"

Smokey turns around. "Oh, no. How could she have slipped away so quickly?"

Trying not to panic, Smokey walks to the reception desk in Fluffington's lobby. "Claudia, did you see my sister, the fluffy calico who came in with Greyson?"

"She went that way." Claudia points.

"The lunchroom," says Smokey.

Greyson laughs. "Why am I not surprised."

Smokey knits her brow. "Let's go get her."

They find Autumn Amelia sitting among Smokey's colleagues.

"An herbed goat cheese would be the perfect complement to those veggies," Autumn instructs one dog. "And I'd add more basil to that pasta salad," she tells another.

"Autumn, take a taste of this beef stew, would you, please? A large Doberman requests. "My wife made it last night. It's good, but I've always felt it was missing something."

Autumn scoops a spoonful into her mouth. "Needs wine. A dry white wine. And a little green pepper. Then it will be perfect."

"She's certainly in her element," Greyson notes.

Just then Abigail emerges from her office headed in the opposite direction.

"Ms. Fluffington, we're in here," Smokey calls.

Abigail walks to the lunchroom door, taking in the scene.

"The chef is holding court. Delightful!"

Smokey notes with relief that Abigail's tone is genuine.

"I hate to break this up," says Abigail, "but we must be on our way."

"Of course, Ms. Fluffington." Smokey strides to Autumn and whispers in her ear.

"I'm sorry everyone. I have to leave," Autumn announces.

Abigail talks as they cross the lobby toward the frosted glass doors. "I do apologize for taking longer than expected. The second I hung up from the call I had to return, the phone rang, and the caller ID said it was Miguel Gato. One takes a call from Miguel Gato, now doesn't one." It was not a question.

"Miguel Gato is a local businesscat," Smokey explains to Greyson. "He purchased the land for the cat park."

They enter the elevator.

"A local businesscat does not begin to describe Miguel Gato," Abigail says as the elevator begins its long descent to the lobby. "He's the wealthiest cat in Faunaburg and practically anywhere else for that matter."

"A multi-millionaire," says Smokey.

"Billionaire," Abigail corrects. "If rumors are to be believed. And in this case, I have no trouble believing them."

"I see," says Greyson, a bemused smile playing around his whiskered mouth.

Worry nags at Smokey. "Everything's okay with plans for the cat park, isn't it?" she asks.

"Oh, yes. He just wanted a progress report."

"Good. That makes me feel better," says Smokey letting out a sigh. "Now we can all enjoy our lunch at the Scratching Post." She gives Autumn a stern look.

The elevator doors open. With Abigail in the lead, they emerge, headed for the building's main doors.

"Where is my head today?" says Abigail. "I completely forgot to tell you. I told Miguel that I was taking you out to lunch and he insisted we meet him at his private club. Forget the Post. We're going to Miguel's." She glances back at the others. "In his private dining room, of course." Abigail throws open the main doors, stepping triumphantly into the bright sunlight.

Smokey, who has been walking between Greyson and Autumn Amelia, stops short, grabs a paw of each in her own and says, "Oh my blessed whiskers! I think I'm going to faint."

Chapter Eleven

Miguel's

"Miguel, darling, so good to see you." Abigail greets the sleek black cat as she struts down the hallway of Miguel's private club, her gossamer shawl billowing behind her.

"Abigail, my dear, you're looking radiant, as always." The two cats meet in the middle of the hall exchanging kisses in the air.

Abigail introduces Smokey and Autumn Amelia. Then she turns to Greyson, taking his arm in both paws, tugging him a bit closer. "And this is Greyson. Our visitor from Palm Ray who I told you about on the phone."

Abigail lets go of Greyson's arm long enough for him to exchange a hearty pawshake with Miguel. "Very pleased to meet you, Señor Gato."

"Please, call me Miguel. All of you. Shall we?" Miguel makes a sweeping gesture towards the doors at the far end of the hallway.

Entering through the double doors, they find themselves in a luxuriously appointed room. There is one round table in the middle with a rich chocolate brown cloth draping it to the floor. On the table are five place settings, each with a layer of plates and bowls topped with a bundle of silverware wrapped in burgundy cloth napkins and gold ribbon. Each setting has a water tumbler and a wine glass.

"Ladies, please..." Miguel holds out a chair for Abigail. Greyson does the same for Smokey and Autumn.

Reproductions of famous paintings hang on walls painted in deep, rich ocher. Recessed niches hold intriguing, exotic curios. Built out from the far wall is a fully stocked bar with a door on either side. The door to the left of the bar opens and a greyhound wearing an immaculate white shirt and black vest takes up his place behind the bar.

Miguel turns in his chair. "This is Maxwell, my private bartender. Maxwell, a gin catini, please. And what can he get for you?" Miguel asks his guests.

"I'll have a catmopolitan, if you please," says Abigail.

"Smokerina?" asks Miguel.

"Perhaps a sparkling water," she says, glancing in Abigail's direction.

"If you're worried about drinking on work time, don't," Abigail states. "Normally, that would be off limits, but today is special so order whatever you please."

"Smokey relaxes. "I'll have a mojito with nip."

"And for you, Autumn Amelia?" asks Miguel.

"I'll have a ginger ale, if you don't mind."

"You may have whatever you like," says Miguel.

"Greyson?"

"A Tomcat Collins sounds good. I haven't had one in quite some time."

Abigail leans towards Miguel. "I assume Gustav is whipping up something scrumptious?"

"Would he do otherwise?"

Abigail throws her head back and laughs. "Never!"

Turning to the others she says, "Gustav is Miguel's private chef. He has cooked for royalty in four countries and is considered one of the best chefs in the world."

"Or, if you ask him," interjects Miguel, "*the* best chef in the world."

"Really?" Autumn Amelia's asks. "I would like to meet him."

"You might not know what you're asking," says Miguel with a chuckle and a wink at Abigail. "Gustav can be a bit temperamental."

"That's an understatement," says Abigail, flipping the tip of her shawl at Miguel. "Seriously, though, Miguel, our Autumn Amelia here is quite the little chef herself."

"Is that so?" he asks, looking at Autumn with new interest.

"Oh, indeed. Last year for the office Winter party she made the most scrumptious cupcakes. Here it is July and we're all still raving about them."

"Perhaps sometime you would bake some for me?" he inquires.

"I'd be happy to. But I don't just bake. I cook all sorts of things. Cooking is my favorite thing in the whole world."

"I see. Well, I do hope Gustav's dishes meet with your approval."

Maxwell arrives with the tray of drinks, sets each one at their places, then returns to the bar.

"It's true Señor...I mean Miguel," says Smokey. "Autumn is an amazing chef. Not on the level of Gustav, of course, but she has a gift for cooking. I don't know anyone who hasn't been impressed by her talent."

"I'll vouch for that," Greyson adds. "In the short time I've been here, I must have gained ten pounds and it's all due to Autumn Amelia."

"She's even improved on some recipes in local restaurants," Smokey tells him.

"Really?" asks Miguel. "Here in Faunaburg?"

"Well, no," Smokey admits. "In Wild Whisker Ridge, where we live."

"Autumn, dear," says Abigail. "I didn't know you cook as well as bake. You are a cat of many talents."

"Where did you study?" asks Miguel.

"Study?" Autumn asks.

"Yes. What culinary institute did you attend?"

Autumn laughs. "The one in my Mama's kitchen. She taught me all the basics and I just went from there."

"How charming!" says Abigail.

Miguel dabs his mouth with a napkin, attempting to hide a wry smile.

"It is amazing that without professional training Autumn Amelia is one of the best chefs I've ever encountered, and I have traveled the world in my line of work," says Greyson. His eyes meet Miguel's with a look that politely, but silently dares him to utter anything remotely condescending.

The door on the other side of the bar opens and the tuxedoed waiter, a Rhodesian Ridgeback enters with the first course. He places small glass bowls filled with berries and wedges of melon in whimsical shapes and topped with fresh whipped cream before each of them. They dig into their fancy fruit cups with gusto.

A few minutes later the same door opens again. The waiter removes the empty fruit cups, replacing them with steaming bowls of wild mushroom soup topped with grated cheese.

"This smells heavenly," Autumn croons.

"Have you had this before?" asks Miguel.

"Never." Autumn swallows a spoonful. "It's wonderful!" she exclaims.

"Gustav isn't one to give away his recipes, but with something like a soup, well, perhaps he could be persuaded," Miguel concedes.

"No need," says Autumn. "I know what's in it."

"I thought you said you've never had it before."

"That doesn't matter. Now that I've tasted it, I know what's in it and how it was cooked."

"How is that possible?"

"I can just tell. I do it all the time. All I have to do is taste something, well sometimes just smell something, and I know everything that's in it."

"Truly?" asks Miguel. "Tell me what you think is in this soup."

Autumn takes two more spoonfuls. "To feed the five of us, I would say two tablespoons of olive oil, one chopped onion, a pound of porcini and white button mushrooms, one and a quarter cup of milk, three and three fourths cup of hot vegetable bullion, seven or eight slices of French stick bread..." Autumn takes another spoonful. "Eight. It's eight slices. Three tablespoons of melted butter, two minced garlic cloves, three cups of finely grated Gruyere cheese, salt, and pepper."

Smokey watches, amused as Miguel, Abigail, and Greyson stare at Autumn Amelia, eyes wide, mouths agape.

"Maxwell!" Miguel calls.

The Greyhound's head snaps up. "Señor?"

"Tell Gustav to write down the ingredient list for this soup immediately. If he balks tell him I said to do it no questions asked."

"Right away, Señor Gato."

Maxwell disappears through the side door. He reappears moments later with a slip of paper which he hands to Miguel.

"Well?" asks Abigail.

"Miss Autumn, would you mind repeating the ingredients?" he asks.

As she lists them, Miguel ticks off each one on the paper. When she finishes, he places the paper in the center of the table so the others can see it, too.

"Astonishing!" he exclaims, tapping the paper with his paw. "Word for word, she got it exactly right."

"Well done, Miss Autumn," says Greyson, sharing a triumphant smile with Smokey.

"I am very impressed," Abigail says, staring at Autumn.

"It's nothing," says Autumn finishing the last of her soup.

The waiter returns, removes the empty bowls and sets down plates of filet mignon in a bourbon sauce. Fettuccine Alfredo and steamed asparagus with hollandaise sauce accompany the meat as side dishes. Maxwell follows behind the waiter filling each cat's glass with the finest Cabernet Sauvignon.

Smokey savors the beef, the sauce the best she's ever tasted.

"I certainly can't say I haven't been well fed on this vacation," Greyson observes, taking a bite of the meat.

"Tell me, Greyson, what do you do in Palm Ray?" Miguel asks.

"Actually, I've just retired. I was the CEO of PAWS UNITED."

"They do wonderful work rescuing animals from natural disasters. My company has donated often to PAWS UNITED. It's one of my favorite charities," says Miguel.

"We thank you for your contributions."

"My pleasure. But you said earlier that you've traveled extensively. Was that work related?"

"Most of it. I worked in the field before rising through the ranks. Frankly, I preferred the field work. There's no greater satisfaction than bringing assistance to those in dire need."

"I'd like to hear more about your work. You must have some interesting stories."

"I do. One that is dear to my heart is the time we rescued over two hundred animals that were trapped between the sea and a massive volcano on the verge of eruption."

"Sounds positively harrowing," says Abigail. "Do tell us about it."

Smokey glances at Autumn Amelia. She's obviously not listening to Greyson's fur-raising tale.

"Aha!" Autumn cries.

All talk stops as the others turn to look at her.

"Is everything okay?" asks Miguel.

"Divine!" she assures him.

"Excellent." He smiles broadly.

"I just figured out what's missing from the bourbon sauce."

Miguel's smile fades. "Missing?"

Smokey's heart sinks.

Autumn nods, her mouth full.

"You find something wrong with the sauce?" Miguel asks, sounding simultaneously concerned and incredulous.

"Certainly not. It's the finest I've ever tasted."

Miguel lets out a long breath.

"But I know how to make it even better."

They all look at each other.

"Better than a world-renowned chef?" asks Abigail.

"Yes. Peppercorns. And it should be slightly creamier." She turns to Miguel. "Would you like me to show your chef how to do it?"

Tears form at the corners of Miguel's eyes as he attempts to suppress his laughter. He clears his throat. "I would be happy to show you the kitchen after we've finished eating, Miss Autumn. I'm not sure if Gustav is in the mood for a cooking lesson, but we shall see what he says, eh?"

Autumn's whole face beams as Greyson returns to his story.

When they finish eating, Miguel turns to Autumn Amelia. "Ready?" he asks.

Autumn jumps from her chair. Miguel extends his paw to escort her.

"Won't you all join us?" he asks the rest of them.

"This should be interesting," says Abigail, getting up.

Smokey looks at Greyson who just grins and shrugs.

"Aren't you coming?" asks Abigail, halfway across the room.

"In a moment," says Smokey.

She turns back to Greyson. "This can't be good," she says. "How can we stop it?" Her heart races as she licks off the sweat beads forming on her nose.

"I don't think we can. Miguel and Abigail seemed charmed by Autumn. Maybe there's nothing to worry about."

"Improve my burgundy sauce!" an unfamiliar voice booms from the kitchen. "It is lauded in France! I have had standing ovations in the finest restaurants in Italy. The prince cat of Monaco heralds it as the best sauce in all creation. Kings and queens request it!"

Smokey's whiskers stiffen. "Oh, no!"

"Let's go," says Greyson, helping Smokey from her chair.

No one notices as they enter the kitchen to find Abigail, Miguel and Autumn Amelia clustered around a ginger tabby whose paws wave wildly in the air.

"Your sauce is wonderful, Mr. Gustav," Autumn says, interrupting his litany of self-praise by putting one paw on his shoulder and the other against his cheek. "I didn't say it wasn't good, only that it could be even better. Can you imagine how impressed they'd all be if you went back and the sauce they all love so much is even better than they remember?"

Gustav, a large orange cat with marmalade stripes and swirls making bold patterns throughout his fur, backs away. He jumps up and down, his fisted paws pounding the air with each syllable as he proclaims, "IT CAN NOT BE IMPROVED!"

"Oh, sure it can," says Autumn, unfazed. "Here, I'll show you.

A large pot of the sauce simmers on the stove. Smokey stares, dumbfounded as Autumn pulls a jar of peppercorns from the spice rack, shaking some of the contents into the sauce.

"What are you doing?" screams Gustav. "You are ruining my sauce!"

"No, I'm not. Now you settle down. You can't learn anything when you're in such a tizzy."

"Settle?...Learn?...From you?...A tizzy!" Gustav is nearly frothing at the mouth. At the counter directly behind him, a Beagle sous chef is chopping carrots and celery with abandon. Her front paws rapidly slice through the vegetables while her back paws dance a jig. A grin that couldn't be pried off with a crowbar stretches across her face.

Miguel stands behind Autumn silently watching in quiet amusement. Abigail looks both worried and intrigued.

"Now what else?" Autumn muses aloud as she strolls the kitchen, looking over all the shelves, into cabinets, and opening the great refrigerator. "Oh yes, the cream. It needs just a dollop or two more. Here we go," she says, letting a small amount drop from the container into the simmering pot.

"Señor Gato, stop her!" yells Gustav. "Why did you bring this bumpkin who thinks she can cook better than the Great Gustav into my kitchen?"

"It amused me to do so and, if you'll remember, Gustav, this place is called Miguel's not Gustav's, so it is really my kitchen."

"I cannot believe this! I cannot work like this! It is unthinkable. It is unbearable. It is—"

"I've got it! Ginger!" Autumn announces.

"What?" screams Gustav. "Ginger in my burgundy sauce? That is it. That proves she is insane. Get her out of here!"

Miguel laughs. "She's already added to your sauce. Why not let her finish?"

"Why not indeed? Why not let her take over my whole kitchen? And by the way, Señor, you do not cook. Therefore, it may be your club, but it is indeed my kitchen."

Autumn holds a freshly peeled and grated pawful of ginger out to Gustav. "See Mr. Gustav? Just this much. I know it sounds odd to put ginger in this sauce but trust me. I'm sure of this."

"You are sure of nothing! You are a raving lunatic!"

"Tsk! Tsk! Tsk!" Autumn drops the ginger into the sauce and stirs. "Mama Cat would send you to your room for talking like that," she admonishes. "Really, there is always something to learn. You needn't make such a fuss about it. Now, you'll want to keep stirring throughout the simmering process," she tells him.

The sous chef finishes chopping, tosses the celery and carrots into a large pot then executes a few pirouettes ending in a leap as she heads down the long counter to gather the rest of her ingredients.

Behind Autumn, who is completely absorbed in stirring the simmering sauce, Gustav grabs Miguel by the shoulders. "Señor! I have never been so insulted, so abused, so maligned in my life! Either you must get this ragamuffin out of MY kitchen at once or I will leave. Forever!"

"It's done," Autumn announces. She turns and holds out a spoonful of sauce with one paw beneath it to catch any drips. "Try it now," she instructs Gustav.

"After you've ruined it, positively destroyed the best sauce in the world, you ask me to try it? You are—

Autumn sticks the spoon in his mouth before he can utter another word.

Gustav's expression shifts from fury, to surprise, to confusion, to elation. "...a genius! That's what you are! A genius!"

"A genius, Gustav?" asks Miguel. "Are you sure?"

"Taste it!" Gustav demands.

"My pleasure," says Miguel. He grabs a clean spoon and samples the sauce. Miguel's eyes roll back in his head in ecstasy. "Oh, my whiskers, this is fabulous!"

Gustav turns to the sous chef, "Sally! A filet mignon that's cooked. Immediately!"

Sally quickly plates the meat and hands it to Gustav. "Pour it over the meat," he says to Autumn who ladles just the right amount across the steak. Gustav grabs a knife and fork and takes a bite. "It is food for the angels!" he exclaims. "My dear Seńor Miguel, where did you find this priceless gem of a chef?"

Miguel, when he stops laughing, answers, "In my dining room. And you'll never guess where she studied the culinary arts, Gustav?"

"Where? I must know. Who created this brilliance? They are to be commended."

"You tell him, Miss Autumn."

"Mama Cat," she says. "And you're right, Mr. Gustav. Mama Cat was the best cook ever."

"Who is Mama Cat? This is a chef of whom I've never heard. Why is that?"

"Because you've never met my Mama, silly," says Autumn.

Gustav gapes at her. "You mean your mother? Your own mother?"

"Who else would Mama Cat be?"

"She was a master chef in a culinary school, then?"

"No. She cooked at home for Papa Cat, Smokey, and me. She taught me everything she knew about cooking, and she told me to follow my own instincts, which is what I've always done."

"Amazing, isn't she?" says Miguel. "Well, Miss Autumn, this concludes our tour of the kitchen. We should get back to our table now. I can see that dessert is about to be served." Miguel gestures towards the Siamese pastry chef who is setting five chocolate lava cakes on a tray for the waiter to take to their table.

"They look delicious!" says Autumn. "May I say hello?"

"Of course," says Miguel.

Autumn approaches the pastry chef. Smokey follows quickly, afraid Autumn will want to improve on the dessert.

"Hi, I'm Autumn Amelia. I'm a baker by profession. I work for Furry Confections in Wild Whisker Ridge."

"Hi. I'm Sukey. If you bake as well as you cook, I would love to take lessons from you."

"Well, I sure wish I had a kitchen like this to bake in," Autumn tells her. "I work out of my own kitchen in our cottage. I used to work in at Furry's but...um…well it just seemed better for me to work from home. Even Furry's isn't as big and nice as this, though."

"Working from home sounds relaxing."

"You can come to my house," says Autumn. "It's nothing like this, but I'll bet we'd have fun. Sometimes it's lonely baking by myself."

"I'd love to," says Sukey. She leans towards Autumn and whispers, "Sometimes it's not so much fun to work here." Sukey inclines her head towards Gustav.

Autumn giggles. "I'll bet," she says. "So come to my house and we can bake in peace."

"You're on!"

Just as the cats are about to exit the kitchen, Autumn turns back. "Mr. Gustav, you can come to my house for a cooking lesson, too, if you want."

The sous chef nearly faints from delight.

They return to their seats just as the lava cake is being served.

"What did you think of Chef Gustav, Autumn?" Abigail asks.

"He's a bit testy."

The entire table erupts in laughter. Even the waiter nearly drops the empty tray on his way back to the kitchen and Maxwell suddenly collapses to the floor behind the bar to hide his hearty chuckle.

"Smokerina, I've just had a brilliant idea for the cat park," says Miguel, once he gets himself under control. "You must design a restaurant with your sister as the master chef and baker. She can have a whole staff under her, but as long as she's in charge, it will undoubtedly be a smashing success."

Abigail clinks her claws against her glass and looks at the others. "Perhaps Gustav could be her sous chef."

"Abigail, you are such an instigator." says Miguel.

Smokey's not sure what to say. On the one paw, there's no denying that Miguel is right about Autumn's abilities. On the other paw, he knows nothing of Autumn's idiosyncrasies, and she certainly can't tell him.

"A restaurant is a great idea, Miguel," she says, unwilling to commit herself further.

"Very well, then. It's settled."

"This has been a most splendid luncheon," says Abigail as Miguel walks them to the main doors of the club.

"Thank you again for showing me the kitchen," says Autumn. "I've never seen anything like it. Would you please give this to Sukey?" Autumn hands him a paper with her phone number on it. "I really would like to bake with her."

They arrive back at Faunaburg Office Towers and say goodbye at the main doors. Before heading for Greyson's rental car, Autumn takes Smokey aside and whispers to her, "I was afraid to come today, but I'm so glad I did. Everything turned out far better than I could have ever dreamed." She gives Smokey a kiss on the cheek and trots off with Greyson.

Smokey stands at the door, wondering if Autumn Amelia hopes to run a restaurant at the cat park or if she simply means she had a good time at lunch.

"Are you coming, Smokerina?" asks Abigail, holding the elevator for her.

"Yes," she says, feeling dazed.

Could Autumn really do it? She wonders. She can handle the cooking and baking. Of that, there's no doubt, but what about everything else? *I'll have to think carefully about this*, Smokey decides.

Abigail smiles at her on the ride up in the elevator. "That was quite the lunch, wasn't it?"

"Indeed," Smokey agrees. *Indeed.*

Chapter Twelve

A Rainy Evening

"That was a lovely dinner, Greyson. Thank you." Smokey hangs her raincoat in the closet upon entering the cottage.

"It really was," Autumn agrees. "And I didn't steal anyone's food or end up in the kitchen. That's twice in a row." She puts her umbrella in the stand. "At least at Top Cat, anyway. You can't count Miguel's. He brought me into the kitchen."

"You'll be the talk of Top Cat for days to come, but for different reasons than usual," Smokey teases as she takes Greyson's umbrella and raincoat.

"I'm glad you ladies finally let me take you out to dinner before I leave. I was beginning to fear it wouldn't happen. I'm just sorry tonight's weather is so awful."

"Didn't make a bit of difference to the dinner," says Autumn. "Besides, we need the rain. It's good for my garden. I'll go make some tea." Smokey and Greyson follow her into the kitchen.

They take their places at the table. Autumn fills everyone's teacup.

"Sounds as though we made it back just in time. That storm will be upon us any minute. I feel it in my whiskers," says Greyson as thunder rumbles in the distance.

"I have news," says Smokey. She bounces a little in her chair as a sudden thought flash into her mind.

"What is it?" asks Greyson.

"Ms. Fluffington came into my office this afternoon. She asked how much longer you are staying. When I told her you're leaving the day after tomorrow she said she couldn't possibly let you go without having us all over to her apartment for an evening of wine and cheese. Her business trip was postponed so she'll be home."

"Really?" asks Autumn.

"Yes. I meant to tell you earlier, but the storm distracted me." She turns to Greyson, "I always get distracted by storms. When one is coming it gives me the zoomies. I was racing all over the basement at work just before I left for home. Anyway, she said it will just be the three of us and her sister, Dusty, who lives with her."

"Ms. Fluffington's sister lives with her too?" asks Autumn.

"Apparently. I didn't even know she had a sister until today. She's not usually one to mix her personal and professional life. To my knowledge, no one from the firm has ever been invited to her apartment. I was astonished she asked me."

"Well, look at you, Smokerina!" Greyson says. "You're really coming up in the world if you're getting such invitations. First lunch at Miguel Gato's private club and now wine and cheese with Madam Fluffington."

Smokey laughs. "Actually, Greyson, I don't think it's me. You're the one she seems interested in. She's been asking lots of questions about you ever since you two met. I think she's rather taken with you."

"That's flattering to be sure. She seems a force to be reckoned with."

"She did build Fluffington's from scratch all on her own and now it's the biggest architectural firm in Faunaburg. She's a brilliant businesscat."

"She's certainly astute at hiring great architects."

"Oh, go on," she says, playfully pushing his shoulder.

"It's true, Smokey," Greyson assures her. "One of the most important attributes of being a great businesscat is having an instinct for hiring. She struck gold when she hired you. I'll bet she'd be the first to say so."

"Thanks, Greyson." Smokey can't smother a huge grin.

"So, Ms. Fluffington has a sister? Is she a business cat too?" he asks.

"I honestly don't know anything about her." Smokey turns to Autumn. "She did say she especially thought you would like Dusty. She seems to think you have a lot in common."

"How so?" asks Autumn.

"She didn't elaborate."

"Another cat like Autumn Amelia? That's hard to imagine," says Greyson.

"I don't think there could ever be another cat like Autumn." Smokey laughs. "She's one of a kind."

"I believe that."

Smokey giggles. "Autumn, do you remember what you did to the humidifier?"

"Oh, Smokey! Don't bring that up," growls Autumn.

"Why not? It was hysterical."

"I've got to hear this story," says Greyson.

"Fine, but keep in mind it happened when I was only in kittengarten." Autumn pours herself another cup of tea. "And it wouldn't have happened at all if Smokey had been doing her job."

Greyson looks expectantly at Smokey.

"It was late October or early November, I forget which," Smokey begins. "Anyway, the air in the cottage was getting dry so Mama Cat bought a humidifier one day while we were both in school and put it in the living room. Later that afternoon, Mama Cat said she had to run an errand and told me to keep an eye on Autumn while she was gone. She knew she would need to go back to work once we were both in school full-time, so I think she was testing me to see if I was ready to kittensit, but, of course, I didn't know that at the time."

"Yes, and what did you do, Smokey?" asks Autumn.

"I sat here at the kitchen table doing my homework while Autumn played in the living room."

"Homework? Really?" asks Autumn, giving Smokey an *oh, please!* Look.

"Well, I was going to do my homework, but then the phone rang, and it was one of my friends and, well, I got busy talking. You know how it is when two girl cats get talking."

"I can imagine," says Greyson.

"In Smokey's case it means they yak non-stop about nothing," says Autumn.

"Well, I had to stop when I heard a crash and Autumn's little baby voice from the living room saying "Oh-oh." I ran in there to find her sitting in the middle of the floor with the humidifier in pieces, a flood of water all around her and strange little things that looked like gray cookie crumbs hanging from her whiskers."

"You took the humidifier apart?" Greysor asks Autumn.

"She did a wonderful job of watching me, didn't she? Autumn asks. "I've always been curious about how things work. That little machine with the water bubbling through a clear plastic container and the mist billowing out the other side intrigued me. I had to figure out what made it work. The only way I knew to do that was to take it apart and see what was going on inside."

"Of course, that would be just the moment Mama Cat picked to return," Smokey continues the story. "You should have seen the look on her face. All that mess and Autumn in the middle of it.

"Mama Cat rushed to Autumn and sent me for towels to clean up the water."

"And Smokey said, 'I was in the kitchen doing my homework, Mama," Autumn interrupts. "Yeah, right!"

Smokey clears her throat. "Well, anyway, when I came back with the towels, Mama Cat asked me what Autumn had been eating. I said I didn't know. So, Mama asked her. Autumn looked at her and said, 'Just the cookie, Mama.'

"What cookie?" asks Greyson.

"That's what Mama Cat asked," says Smokey. "Autumn said to her, 'The cookie in the machine.' I had no idea what she was talking about, but Mama Cat began rummaging through the humidifier parts strewn all over the floor until she found the remnants of the filter. 'Is this the cookie?' she asked her, holding up a third of a charcoal filter."

"You didn't?" asks Greyson, staring at Autumn.

"It looked like one of those wafer cookies to me," says Autumn. "Again, I remind you, I was only in kittengarten."

"Got it," says Greyson. "Go on, Smokey."

Mama Cat had the same look on her face as you do, Greyson," says Smokey. "'Autumn, that's not a cookie. It's the filter for the machine and you're not supposed to eat it', she said. Fortunately, it was only charcoal, so it didn't hurt her. Then Mama Cat told me to help Autumn put the machine back together. I didn't have a clue how to do it."

"I did," says Autumn. "I'd taken it apart, so I knew how it went together."

"It's true," Smokey admits. "She had it put back together in no time. Meanwhile, Mama Cat went into the kitchen saying she was going to call Jerry Rabbit at Rabbit's Hardware and see if he had any more filters. That's when Autumn called out to her, 'Mama, ask if he has any other flavors. Charcoal's not that good.'"

Greyson bursts out laughing.

"I was hoping for chocolate," says Autumn.

"Oh my!" says Greyson once he catches his breath. "That is a good story. How long was it before Aunt Lucy let you kittensit again after that, Smokey?"

"It was a while. That night began the talks about RESPONSIBILITY," Smokey explains. "From that point on, Mama Cat was always giving me scenarios about what to do in various situations and drilling me on the importance of being *responsible*." Smokey emphasizes the word just as she remembers Mama Cat saying it to her.

"By the next fall when Autumn started first grade and Mama Cat went back to work, I knew all the first aid basics, cooking safety, what to do in case of fire, stranger danger, and anything else Mama Cat could think of."

"You must have become a first class kittensitter by then," says Greyson.

"I do remember one time in school when we were given a list of vocabulary words. We had to choose one of the words and write an essay about its meaning. Wouldn't you know, one of the words was 'responsibility'. I wrote such a good essay that my teacher read it to the class and put three gold paw prints at the top of my paper. I don't remember what I wrote except that the last line was, 'Never let your little sister eat a humidifier filter.'

"When I showed it to Mama Cat, she was so proud she had me read it aloud to her and Autumn. Then she stood up and applauded.

"I remember that" Autumn interjects. "She took us out for ice cream after supper. I had strawberry."

"So, when Aunt Lucy went back to work the next year you must have been the best prepared kittensitter in Wild Whisker Ridge," says Greyson.

"You would think," says Smokey. "But no one can really be prepared for Autumn."

"What else happened?"

"Well, let's see. There was the time she got stuck in the freezer trying to get popsicles. To this day, I don't know how she got in there."

"She really got shut in the freezer?"

"She wasn't shut in. I'd opened the door to get out the meat Mama wanted thawed for dinner. When I turned back to shut the door, she was in it, way in the back, trying to take popsicles out of the box. It was too high for her to jump down, so I had to climb the step stool and pull her out. The two of us nearly fell off the stool."

"I got my popsicle, though," says Autumn.

"Oh yeah. She never let go of that. Then there was the time she ate a bee."

"You ate a bee?" Greyson looks askance at Autumn.

"It was summer," Smokey begins. "We were playing out in the backyard late in the afternoon. I went inside to set the table. I always did that so it would be ready when Mama Cat got home. The next thing I knew, Autumn came running into the house screaming. I couldn't figure out what was wrong because she was so hysterical. Then I noticed her mouth was swelling. She kept pointing to it and saying something which I finally figured out was 'bee' and I deduced the rest."

"What did you do?" asked Greyson.

"I grabbed a bunch of ice chips and made her keep them in her mouth, replacing them as they melted."

"She put me up on the table and petted and hugged me until I calmed down too," Autumn remembers. I was really scared. It hurt a lot and it felt so strange to have my mouth all swollen up like that. Smokey kept feeding me ice chips and telling me I would be okay."

"Truthfully, I wasn't sure what to do," Smokey admits. "I knew ice was good for swelling but beyond that I was baffled. I wasn't sure if she'd swallowed the bee. If she had, I thought she might be swelling up inside, too, and I sure didn't know what to do about that."

"So that's why you kept asking me, 'where's the bee?'" says Autumn. "I thought you wanted to yell at it for stinging me."

"I was debating whether to get a neighbor for help or call an ambulance when Mama Cat came home from work and took over. I was so relieved. She said I'd done the right thing with the ice chips and the swelling was going down so Autumn didn't have to go to the doctor."

"Whatever possessed you to eat a bee, Autumn? Greyson asks.

"It was a misunderstanding," Autumn admits. "That night Mama Cat and I had a talk. It turns out bees *make* honey; they are not *made* of honey."

Greyson slaps a paw over his face as they all break into gales of laughter.

Autumn's cell phone rings. The others stifle their laughter so she can talk.

"Hi. Yes, I remember. I'd love to. Yes, Monday's fine. I start early, but you can come whenever you want. Sure, ten is fine. Let me give you the address."

"Who was that?" Smokey asks when Autumn hangs up.

"Sukey, the pastry chef from Miguel's. She sounded excited. She was talking very fast. Of course, she's Siamese so maybe that's just how she talks. Anyway, she's coming over on Monday morning to bake with me."

"Two great bakers putting their heads together. I wish I wasn't going to be gone by then," says Greyson. "You'll have an amazing dessert on Monday night, Smokey."

Lightning flashes at the kitchen windows, followed immediately by a loud clap of thunder.

"That's getting close," says Smokey.

"The rain's really coming down. Listen," Greyson observes.

The downpour on the cottage roof sounds as though a million pebbles are being pelted from the sky.

The doorbell rings.

"Who on earth would be out in this weather?" Autumn asks, getting up to answer the door.

Smokey and Greyson listen from the kitchen as the front door opens and Autumn says, "Oh dear, Your Highness, please come in, quickly. You're soaked to the skin."

"Your Highness?" asks Greyson.

Smokey nods looking bemused. "That's Holly Berry. She lives a few streets away." Smokey's voice lowers to a near whisper. "She's a very old cat. A few years ago she got the notion into her head that she's an empress. She's such a sweet old lady that we all just play along. It wouldn't do any good not to. She refuses to believe otherwise."

"I hope she doesn't live alone."

"No, she lives with her grandniece, Chrissy. She takes very good care of her, but occasionally the Empress manages to wander off. Looks like tonight's one of those times. I'd better help Autumn."

"I'll come, too."

Just inside the door stands a gray and white cat, her drenched nightgown stuck to her equally drenched fur.

"I'll get towels," Autumn offers, hurrying up the stairs.

"Bring my bathrobe," Smokey calls after her.

Greyson hangs back a bit.

"Greyson, would you be a dear an prepare some more tea?" Smokey calls to him. "I think the Empress could use a cup."

Autumn returns with towels and Smokey's robe. "Let's get you all dried off. You're shivering, poor thing."

The two cats briskly rub the Empress' fur to dry the worst of it then throw the bathrobe around her shoulders and tie it in front. Smokey leads the Empress to the kitchen while Autumn wipes up the puddles on the floor.

Greyson whisks the whistling teakettle off the stove as they enter the kitchen and pours the steaming water into a teacup.

The Empress eyes Greyson then looks questioningly at Smokey and Autumn who has just entered the kitchen. "You have a gentleman caller?" she asks. "It's a bit late in the evening, you know."

Smokey puts an arm around the Empress' shoulder and nudges her towards Greyson. "Your Highness, please allow me to present to you our cousin, Greyson, who is visiting us from Palm Ray."

The Empress's face brightens. "A cousin. Oh, I see. Well, that does make a difference."

Smokey mouths the word *bow* to Greyson. Gallantly, Greyson makes a sweeping bow before the elderly cat. "It is indeed a great honor to meet you, Your Highness," he says. "I hope you don't mind. I've taken the liberty of preparing a cup of the finest catmint tea for Your Highness' pleasure."

The Empress smiles. "How delightful. Thank you."

Greyson holds out a chair, seating the Empress at the table. Smokey whispers to Autumn, "Go call Chrissy" then seats herself as Autumn grabs her cell phone and slips from the room.

"What brings you here, Your Highness?" Smokey asks.

"I was feeling cooped up in the palace and decided to take a stroll."

"Doesn't Princess Christina usually accompany you?"

"Indeed, yes, but I could not find her, so I decided to go on my own. It's my realm after all. I can go where I please."

"Of course."

"I'm terribly sorry you got caught in the downpour," says Greyson.

"Downpour? Is it raining, young man?"

Greyson glances at Smokey.

"It has started to sprinkle a bit," says Smokey. Greyson smothers a smile as the rain pelts the windows. "We thought perhaps that's why you stopped here. To get out of the rain."

"Oh, I hadn't noticed. I just saw your house and realized I hadn't visited in a while. Of course, I didn't know you were entertaining." She looks at Greyson. "Is this young man your suitor?"

"No, Your Highness. This is my cousin, Greyson."

She turns to Greyson. "Where are you from?"

"Palm Ray, Your Highness."

"Palm Ray?" The Empress appears deep in thought. "Is that part of my realm?"

"I don't think so, Your Highness. It's rather a long way from here."

"I see. Well, when you return do give your sovereigns greetings from me."

"I'd be honored to, Your Highness."

Autumn returns to the kitchen and whispers to Smokey, "Chrissy is on her way."

"Are you more comfortable now, Your Highness?" Autumn asks, joining her at the table.

"I've never felt better!" She leans towards Greyson to pat his paw. "I've never been sick a day in my life, you know. I've a marvelous constitution."

"I'm happy to hear it."

The Empress turns her head, looking up and then from side-to-side.

"Is something wrong?" asks Smokey.

"I hear a strange sound. Do you hear it?"

"Do you mean the rain?" asks Autumn.

"Is it raining?"

"It is. Raining like mad! But it's fine with me. It's good for my garden."

"You have a garden? What do you grow?"

"Vegetables, flowers, and herbs," says Autumn.

"Sounds lovely. I had a garden once, I think." The Empress closes her eyes for moment. "Yes. Yes, I did. I remember now. I grew roses, peonies, hollyhocks, foxtail, bachelor's buttons, black eyed Susans, and daisies."

"It sounds lovely," says Autumn. "You must have been happy when it rained. It made your flowers grow."

"Yes, but too much rain is not good either. Tell me, has it rained enough to suit your garden yet?"

"It's probably enough for now, though it doesn't sound as though it will stop anytime soon," Autumn answers.

"If you'd like it to stop now, I will make a decree for you."

"You don't have to do that, Your Highness. I'm sure it will be fine."

"No. No. I insist. To thank you for your hospitality. Bring me paper and a pen, please."

Greyson gives Smokey a questioning look. Smokey widens her eyes and shrugs.

"Right away, Your Highness," says Autumn. She goes to the kitchen drawer, returning with a pad of writing paper and a pen which she sets on the table.

The Empress picks up the pen and in perfect script she writes:

DECREE

I, Holly Berry, Empress of Wild Whisker Ridge and its environs, do hereby decree that enough rain has now fallen to water all gardens for the time being. Until further notice, all rain shall cease and desist.

She signs her name at the bottom and hands the paper to Autumn Amelia.

"Thank you, your highness. That is most kind of you."

"Think nothing of it, dear." She winks at Autumn. "We gardeners must stick together."

The doorbell rings again. This time it's Chrissy, a gray and white tiger cat, carrying a raincoat and umbrella.

"There you are, Auntie," she says to the Empress. "I've been worried sick. I was looking all over for you."

"My dear, you needn't have worried. I simply went for a walk." The Empress returns to sipping her tea, pinky claw extended.

Chrissy looks at the others, embarrassed. "I'm so sorry," she says. "I thought she'd gone to bed. I went into the den to read and later when I checked to be sure the house was locked up for the night, I found the front door wide open. I've been driving all over town looking for her. I was so relieved when Autumn called. Thank you for taking her in."

"Of course. What else would we do?" says Smokey.

"I'm sorry to trouble you."

"It's no trouble," Autumn assures her. "We love the Empress."

Tears glisten in Chrissy's eyes for a moment. Then she turns to her great aunt. "Come on, Auntie. It's time to go."

"I have not yet finished my tea."

"There's only a sip or two left. Please finish up. It's getting late and you need to get to bed."

"Oh, is it night now?"

"Here you go, Auntie. Put this on so you won't get wet." Chrissy tries to help her into her raincoat.

"No need, Princess Christina. I decreed against rain." She points to the decree sitting the table.

"But Auntie, you'll get soaked."

"No, dear. Read the decree. I've made the rain stop."

Sighing, Chrissy looks at the others, shaking her head. "I guess I'll just hold the umbrella over her head," she whispers.

Undaunted, the Empress takes the last sip and carefully places the cup back on the saucer "That was delicious. I thank you."

"It was a pleasure to serve you, Your Highness," says Greyson.

"Such a nice young man." She pats his arm. "When did you say the wedding will be?" she asks Smokey.

Smokey starts to reintroduce Greyson as her cousin, but he cuts her off saying, "We'll be certain you get a very special invitation."

"Won't that be nice. I'll look forward to it."

"Come now, Auntie." Chrissy helps her up from the chair.

The entire group make their way to the front door. Greyson reaches for the doorknob as Chrissy prepares to open the umbrella.

The Empress puts out a paw and says, "There's no need for that. I've decreed against any more rain until Autumn needs it for her garden."

As Greyson opens the door, they all stare into the darkening night.

"Well, I'll be," says Greyson.

"It was pouring buckets when I got here," Chrissy says. The rain has stopped and only a light mist is falling.

"Told you," says the Empress. With her head lifted high, she walks regally from the cottage to Chrissy's waiting car.

"Well, that was interesting," says Greyson watching them drive off. "What a hoot that it stopped raining just as she left."

"Well, she did decree it," Autumn reminds him.

"Will you have to get her to write another decree, so you don't have a drought?" he asks.

Autumn laughs. "I hope not. But it does remind me that I should pay her a visit soon. She really does have the most splendid gardens in town."

"So that part she remembered correctly?" he asks.

"Oh, yes. For the most part she lives in a fantasy world now, but what she says about gardening is spot on. She was an avid gardener in her day, and she still retains her memory of it. If you catch her in her garden, you'd never know there was a thing wrong with her. Once you get her talking about gardening, you'll get some great information. I suppose I could look it up online, but I'd rather talk to her. She's a lovely lady and I like to hear her wisdom."

"It's probably good for her, too, to have someone come visit and take an interest in her," Greyson observes. "I've certainly met some fascinating people since I've been here. I can only imagine what wine and cheese at Abigail Fluffington's will be like tomorrow night."

Chapter Thirteen

An Evening with the Fluffingtons

"Welcome, welcome, come right in." Abigail Fluffington, draped in an emerald evening gown, a matching scarf tossed sideways around her neck, waves them into her luxury apartment with a flourish of her paw.

Smokey who is wearing a short, black sequined dress and spiked heels enters, taking in her surroundings. Autumn Amelia smooths her yellow chiffon dress and follows. Greyson has chosen a neat gray suit for the occasion.

Smokey insisted they dress up.

"It's only wine and cheese," Autumn had protested. "And it's only us."

"You don't understand," Smokey explained, rifling through Autumn's closet. "It's an evening invitation to Abigail Fluffington's apartment. No one from the office gets invited to her home. Ms. Fluffington doesn't do anything without a reason. I'm not sure what it is, but it must be important. She's also very…um…I don't know how to express it. Old school, maybe. Not casual. I'm taking no chances. We're going to dress appropriately."

They enter Abigail's living room. A large sofa and two club chairs are centered in the sunken portion of the room. Two silver trays of *hors d'oeuvres* sit on a cherry coffee table along with four wine glasses.

Abigail sweeps her way to the wine rack. "What can I get for you, Greyson? White or red?"

"Ladies first."

"Very well. Smokerina, what would you like?"

"Red, please."

"Autumn?"

"Ice water is fine."

"Are you sure?" Abigail asks. "How about an iced tea?"

"That would be wonderful."

"And Greyson?"

"What are you having, Ms. Fluffington?" Greyson asks.

"I thought I'd break out the Pinot Noir. And please, Greyson, do call me Abigail."

Crossing the room, Greyson takes the bottle from Abigail's paw. "A 2007 Tip Tail. Excellent choice. I believe I'll join you. May I assist?" He picks up the corkscrew.

Abigail smiles, her eyes gleaming. "You certainly may."

Smokey and Autumn, still on the other side of the room look at each other. Smokey clears her throat.

"Oh!" Abigail turns as though she's forgotten them. "Smokerina, dear. A cabernet sauvignon?"

"That would be lovely. Thank you."

"And Autumn, I'll get that iced tea right away. Make yourselves comfortable. Help yourselves to the *hors d'oeuvres*." Abigail goes to the kitchen while Greyson uncorks the bottles and fills the glasses.

"Just look at this place," Smokey whispers to Autumn. "Can you imagine living here?"

They look around at the clean, white walls adorned with exquisite works of art, the rich oriental rugs, and the gleaming white baby grand piano by the wall in the upper living room.

"Look at that," Smokey says as Greyson hands her a filled wine glass. She points towards the gold brocade curtain hanging from ceiling to floor. "I'll bet there's a balcony out there."

Smokey and Autumn sink into the sofa. "It is fancy," Autumn says, "but not what I'd call homey. I like our cottage better."

"Seriously?" Smokey sips her wine. "I'd feel like a celebrity living here. This would be a dream come true."

Greyson eases into one of the club chairs. "Well, Smokey, keep playing your cards right with Abigail and maybe someday your dream will come true."

Smokey leans towards him. "I can't believe she told you to call her Abigail. No one calls her that except for cats like Miguel Gato." She picks up a plate from the coffee table, placing some caviar and a selection of cheese and crackers on it before leaning back into the leather couch.

Greyson winks.

"Here we go," says Abigail, breezing back into the room with a tall glass of iced tea in one paw and a pitcher in the other. "Help yourself to more, if you like," she tells Autumn, indicating the pitcher she's placed on the coffee table. "Do you like the caviar, Smokey? I had Miguel's sous chef whip these up for me. Oh, and I mustn't forget to bring out the *petit fours* that his pastry chef made. Greyson, be a darling and remind me later if I forget, would you?" she asks, inclining towards him from her club chair.

"I'll do my best," says Greyson.

Abigail gestures towards the table. "There are cream cheese and olive biscuits with parsley spread, chicken and bacon satay, pork tenderloin crostini, shrimp martinis with Napa cabbage slaw, mini crab cakes with pineapple-cucumber salsa, and, of course, an assortment of cheeses."

"You had me at the shrimp," says Greyson. "I adore shrimp, though I don't think I've ever had it like this before." He picks up a martini glass fille with coconut shrimp and a lime wedge on a bed of slaw. "Mm…delicious!"

"What a coincidence. Shrimp is my favorite, too." says Abigail.

"It is?" Smokey asks. "I thought crab was your favorite." As soon as the words are out of her mouth, Smokey wishes she could pull them back.

Abigail shoots her a sideways glance. "I do adore crab, Smokerina, but shrimp is my *favorite*," she states, a hint of ice in her voice.

"Oh. I didn't know." Smokey glances down.

"Aren't you going to eat?" Greyson asks Autumn who has yet to fill a plate.

"I'm trying to control myself," Autumn explains. "It all looks so good, I'm afraid if I start eating, I won't stop."

"Eat away, dear!" says Abigail, laughing in a light, breathless manner. "All you like. That's what it's here for."

"Well, in that case…" Autumn picks up a plate and, starting at one end of the table places one of each item on it until the plate is full then begins munching.

"Smokerina, before I forget, I need to tell you that I spoke with Rufus Tailwagger today." Abigail turns her full attention to Smokey. "At Miguel's suggestion he's contacted the Faunaburg News about doing a feature story on the new cat park. They were very interested. They've set up a time to interview him next week and they want you in on it as well. A reporter will contact you first thing Monday morning to arrange an appointment. Be thinking about what you want to say."

"So soon?" Smokey asks. "We've barely begun the project."

"Yes, but it's going to be huge. Miguel is spending an enormous amount of money on this park. He wants early and continuing coverage. I believe he's trying to build excitement in the Faunaburg cat community. I'm certain there will be a spot or two on the local news as well. Certainly, Miguel will have every news outlet covering both the groundbreaking and the grand opening."

"Wow, Schmoke. You'll be on TV."

"Autumn Amelia don't talk with food in your mouth," Smokey hisses.

"How about that," Greyson adds. "Our Smokey will be a star."

"A minute or two on the local news does not make one a television star," states Abigail. "However, if this park comes off as I'm hoping it will, Smokerina could be a rising star in the field of architecture."

"Ms. Fluffington, did Rufus mention to you any of my concerns about the rodents?"

"Rodents?"

"Yes. I'm worried that they may not react well to a cat park going up so close to Rodent Way."

Abigail puts a paw to her cheek, her eyes shifting upwards. "Now that you mention it, I believe he may have said something about it." She waves her paw dismissively. "Don't worry. Rufus will handle that. You just do what you do best and let him worry about the rodents."

"But I'm afraid they'll protest. Maybe it would be better to wait until we're closer to ground-breaking before we go to the news outlets. Otherwise, we might be facing a long, public battle with them."

"With rodents?" Abigail titters. "If Miguel wants to go public now, that's his call, not ours. If it wasn't a good idea, Rufus would have counseled him against it. I doubt the rodents will give us much trouble. What can they really do, after all? Miguel owns the property. Rodents have no say in it. Now, let's forget about them and have a nice evening, shall we?" She crosses her legs, turning sideways in her chair to face Greyson, giving him her most dazzling smile. "Another shrimp?"

"What was that?" Autumn asks. A loud thud had just come from the other end of the apartment.

"Oh dear! That's my sister, Dusty. She must have slipped on her floof again. She's forever doing that. Please excuse me."

"I'd forgotten her sister was supposed to join us. I wonder why she hasn't come out yet," says Greyson once Abigail is out of earshot.

"It's all okay," says Abigail, returning to the living room. "She did slip on her floof, but there's no harm done."

"Isn't she going to join us?" asks Greyson.

"Dusty is terribly shy. She may come out if she can gather up enough courage."

"Didn't you say she and Autumn have something in common?" Smokey asks.

"Indeed, they do. They're both savants. As Autumn is to cooking, Dusty is to be sewing. She made the gown I'm wearing. In fact, she makes most of my clothes."

"Truly, she made your gown?" asks Greyson. "I would have thought it came from a famous designer."

"She makes the clothes you wear to work?" Smokey's eyes nearly pop out of her head. "You're the best dressed cat I've ever seen."

"Nearly all," says Abigail. "I do have a few frocks I've purchased in my travels, including from some of the biggest names in fashion design. Frankly, they can't hold a candle to Dusty's work."

"Why isn't she in business?" Smokey asks. "She could be making a fortune."

"It's that terrible shyness of hers," Abigail explains. "She never leaves the apartment unless she's with me. Even then she can barely let go of me. She doesn't seem to care about going into business or making a lot of money. She just likes to design and make clothes. I order all her supplies so she can spend her days happily doing her thing. I get the most amazing apparel. What I don't keep for myself I give as gifts, so she more than earns her keep."

Hmph! Thinks Autumn. *That's no way to live.*

"I would like to meet your sister. Do you think she'd be more comfortable if I went to her?" Autumn asks.

"That might be just the thing," says Abigail. "Come with me. I'll introduce you."

Abigail leads Autumn down the long hallway. She knocks on a door. It opens a crack. Huge green eyes set in a face flowing with ginger and white fur peek out.

"Dusty, this is Autumn Amelia. She's the cat I told you about. She'd like to meet you. May she come in?"

Dusty doesn't speak, nor does she open the door any further. She simply stares at them, unsure what to do.

"Ms. Fluffington told us you made the dress she's wearing. It's gorgeous! I'd love to talk to you about sewing," Autumn offers.

The green eyes grow a bit wider. "Okay," she mewls. As the door opens, Dusty leans out to peer down the hallway.

"Don't worry, dear. I only brought Autumn Amelia. You two have a good time. Ta! Ta!"

Abigail heads back towards the living room. Dusty opens the door wide enough for Autumn to enter then quickly closes it behind her.

Three of the room's walls have floor to ceiling shelves filled with fabrics of various colors and designs. Crimson velvet is laid out on a large table in the center of the room. Just beyond is a sewing machine. The only wall without shelves has a large cabinet, each drawer labeled with its contents: needles, pins, thread, and so on. Off to one side is a rack filled with clothes.

"What a paradise for a seamstress," Autumn observes.

"You like my sewing room?"

"It's amazing."

"Thanks. Do you sew?"

"A little. Mama Cat taught me a bit, but I can only do basic repairs. I made a dress once long ago, but it was nothing like what you can do. How did you learn to sew so well?"

"Mama Cat taught me. She loved to sew, but I love it even more, so I just kept going and going."

"That's what happened to me with cooking."

"Abby says you know what ingredients are in the food just by tasting it. She said you can make up recipes in your head and they come out perfect."

Autumn nods. "I don't really know how I do it. It's a gift, I guess."

"I'm like that, too. I used to use sewing patterns, but I don't need them anymore. Now I just know how to put everything together without a pattern."

Autumn looks at the sweet little face as fluffy as her own. "It's a joy, isn't it? When you really get into it, it's like everything else in the world goes away. When that happens to me, it's as if all that exists is me, my ingredients, and my pots and pans."

"I know! I know!" says Dusty. "That happens to me, too. Only it's just me, my fabric, and my sewing equipment." She bobs on her toes with excitement. A foot slips and she starts to fall. Autumn reaches out to steady her.

Dusty's face crumples. "Stupid floof!" she says, looking at her feet.

Autumn holds out her paw. "Me, too!"

"But do you ever slip on it?"

"Don't all long furs?"

"Abby never does. She says I should learn to deal with my floof. Being clumsy isn't very catlike."

"Smokey makes fun of my floof, too, only she doesn't have any. She's a short fur. Anyway, your fur is beautiful. You should be proud of it."

"Do you really think so?"

"I do. Just look at your colors. That soft ginger and creamy white. You're adorable! How can anyone keep from hugging you?"

Dusty giggles. "No one hugs me."

"No one?"

"Just Abby sometimes. No one else. Of course, I hardly ever see anyone but Abby."

"Why not?"

Dusty turns away, fingering some fabric on a shelf. Autumn puts a paw on her shoulder.

"Dusty, why don't you ever leave the apartment?" she asks.

"I do, sometimes."

"But only with your sister?"

Dusty nods.

"Why? Are you afraid?"

She nods again. "I don't like to talk about it."

"You don't have to, but sometimes talking helps."

"How?"

"Discussing something can help you see it from a different perspective. Or, sometimes, it just makes you feel better to get it off your chest."

Dusty turns towards her, continuing to stare at the floor. "I have a terrible sense of direction. One day, while Abby was at work, I ran out of thread. I really wanted to finish the project I was working on. I was sure I knew where the sewing goods store was so I set out to buy the thread." She begins to tremble.

"But once I was a few streets from home I got disoriented and panicked. I couldn't find the store or my way back. It was the scariest thing ever."

By now Dusty is crying. Autumn gently wraps her paws around her. "It's okay," she murmurs. "Obviously, you made it home."

"I was gone all night. I left the apartment in the afternoon, but I was so lost I didn't get home until the next morning. That was only after Abby came home, realized I was missing, and called for help. A search party had to look for me."

"You poor thing. You must have been terrified. How far had you gone?"

Dusty shrugs. "Only about five blocks. I thought I was much further. I spent the night under a bush, crying. I didn't think I'd ever see my home again."

Dusty gulps. "The worst part was facing Abby. She'd had to call the Bloodhound League to find me. At first, she couldn't stop hugging me, but after a while she got angry. She said I shouldn't have left the apartment on my own. I've never had a good sense of direction and shouldn't have tried. She even said..." Dusty leans her forehead against Autumn's shoulder and cries harder.

"Autumn pats her back. "What did she say?"

"She said she never heard of a cat with no sense of direction. She said it was disgraceful and I was never to leave the apartment alone again."

"How long ago did this happen?"

"I think it's been about seven years."

"Seven years! You haven't left the apartment in seven years?"

"Not without Abby. And when I do go somewhere with her, I have to hold her tail the whole time, so I don't get lost."

"That's ridiculous! You're a grown cat. You shouldn't be walking around the city holding your sister's tail."

"What else can I do, Autumn? If I go out on my own, I'll get lost. I never, ever want that to happen again. Besides, Abby is right. I've been an indoor cat my whole life, so I never learned my way around outdoors. Still, cats are supposed to have a good sense of direction. I don't, so there must be something wrong with me. Sometimes it makes me think..." She pauses, swallowing hard.

"Think what?" asks Autumn.

Dusty takes a deep breath. "Sometimes it makes me think I might not be a real cat."

Autumn feels her face flush. Another cat who questions her felineness. She'd thought she was the only one.

Autumn cups Dusty's face in her hands so that they are looking eye to eye. "Listen to me Dusty. There is more to being a cat than a good sense of direction. No cat is perfect. We all have our shortcomings. All of us. Even Smokey. Even your sister. Not only are you a real cat, but you are also one of the most beautiful and talented cats I've ever met. Remember that. Okay?"

Dusty drops her gaze. "I'll try. It's hard.

Autumn decides to change the subject. "Would you show me some of the clothes you've made?"

"Sure." Dusty leads Autumn to the rack. "These are mostly dresses, but there are some skirt suits and blouses. And here are some suits for man cats. I can also make slipcovers for chairs and sofas. I do curtains too." Dusty's countenance brightens as she talks.

Autumn looks through the rack of clothes. "These are amazing! They all look like expensive designer clothes. Are these all for your sister?"

"A lot of them are. I make most of her clothes, but she likes to give some as gifts, too, so I make them for her friends as well.

"Don't you make any for yourself?"

"Not much. I don't need fancy clothes."

"What's your favorite thing to make?"

"I like evening gowns. They're fun because they're pretty and I can put in sequins or rhinestones. I like to make things sparkle."

"Me too!" says Autumn. "That's why I put candied dragonfly wings on my cakes. I like how the colors catch the light."

Dusty giggles. "I'd like to see that." Then she says, "My other favorite things to make are miniatures. They're harder, but they're fun and I love to see the babies in them."

"You make clothes for kittens?"

"No. Well, yes, I can, but I was talking about the mice."

Autumn's ears perk up. "Mice? What mice?"

"My mice."

"You have your own mice?"

"Sort of. I don't *own* them, of course. They're the mouse family that lives in my room."

"You're kidding?" Autumn's mouth is agape.

"No." Dusty cocks her head. "Why do you think I'm kidding?"

"Because I've never...I mean I...well...um." *Should I admit it?* She wonders. Looking into Dusty's sweet, innocent eyes, she decides it's safe to say it. "I've never caught a mouse in my whole life."

"Why are you whispering?" asks Dusty.

Autumn swallows hard. "It's embarrassing." She wonders at Dusty's incomprehension.

"It is? Oh, well, I won't tell anyone. Would you like to meet my mice friends?"

"I'd love to. How many are there?"

"There's the mama and papa and eight babies."

"Eight babies!"

Dusty giggles again. "Uh-huh. Mice have lots of babies. They're so cute!"

"And you sew for them?"

"Yes. I made all the blankets for their beds. And I made the family's tablecloth and napkins, the slipcovers for their chairs, the mama's aprons, and, oh dear, I can't even think what else."

"Where are they?" Autumn asks, looking around the sewing room.

"They're not in here," says Dusty. "They live in the wall in my bedroom. Come on, I'll show you."

The two cats hurry to the room across the hall. Dusty leads Autumn to the wall beyond her bed.

"I hope we don't wake the babies," says Dusty. "It's a bit late."

Dusty lightly taps her paw against a tiny arched doorway. The door opens and out pops a nose and whiskers above which is perched a pair of tiny spectacles. A sudden intake of breath so quiet it would have been inaudible if both cats hadn't been utterly silent precedes the immediate slamming of the door. Scurrying feet and scraping noises come from behind the closed door.

"What's that all about?" asks Autumn.

"It's my fault," says Dusty. "I should have warned them first that another cat was with me. They're barricading the door with their furniture. Oh, I feel just awful."

"Why are they doing that?"

"They're afraid of cats. Except for me, of course."

"Why are they scared of cats?"

"Don't you know? Mice think cats eat them."

"Yuck! Why would they think that?"

"Beats me, but they swear it's true."

"That's the strangest thing I've ever heard. I can't imagine eating a mouse."

Dusty eyes Autumn. "You did say you were embarrassed because you've never caught a mouse."

"It's true. I haven't."

"What did you mean by, 'caught'?"

"You know. Cats are supposed to catch mice. That's what makes a real cat." For the first time Autumn wonders if that's really true.

"What do cats do once they've caught one?" Dusty asks.

Autumn thinks a moment. "I'm not sure exactly. I've always assumed that's how you make a mouse friend. You catch one and ask him to be your friend. I think. Isn't that how you got these mice?"

"No. They just showed up one day. It was only the mama and papa mouse then. I think they were looking for a nice place to live because they knew babies were coming. I heard them through the wall.

Plus, I could smell them. They didn't trust me at first. I had to talk to them through the wall."

"How did you convince them to trust you?"

"I started making aprons and tablecloths and other things they'd need for setting up housekeeping. I'd leave them right outside their door, tell them they were there, then go away. After a while they finally got up the courage to open the door. We've been friends ever since."

"So, you didn't actually catch them?"

"No. But I've held the babies. They're soft and cuddly."

"I wish I could see them. I've never even seen a mouse in real life, only in pictures. I'll bet the babies are the cutest things ever. Please tell them I won't hurt them."

"I'll try." Dusty knocks lightly on the door again. "Mr. and Mrs. Mouse? It's me, Dusty. I'm sorry I didn't warn you that I'd brought a friend. Her name is Autumn Amelia. She's a very nice cat. I promise she won't hurt you. Could she just peek in, please? I'll be right here the whole time."

Autumn feels sick at the idea that another creature thinks she'd harm them.

Hushed voices come from inside the wall.

"It sounds like they're moving the furniture away from the door," Dusty whispers.

Autumn's heart races. She's finally going to see a mouse for real.

Dusty whispers into Autumn's ear. "Keep one paw in front of your mouth when you talk. They get frightened if they see your sharp teeth."

Autumn nods. There is so much she doesn't know about mice.

Slowly the door opens. The nose reappears along with the whiskers, but this time the whiskers are trembling.

Poor things, Autumn thinks. *Where did they get such a terrible idea about cats?*

"Good evening, Mr. Mouse," says Dusty. "I'm terribly sorry to have frightened you. I just wanted you to meet my new friend, Autumn Amelia."

Keeping one paw against her mouth lightly enough so that she can speak clearly but careful to cover her teeth, Autumn says, "It's a pleasure to meet you, Mr. Mouse."

He nods but looks suspicious.

"Mr. Mouse, may Autumn take a quick peek at the babies?" Dusty asks.

"No! Not my babies!" The voice, a feminine squeak, comes from inside.

Autumn can see Mr. Mouse clearly now. He's gray from nose to tail. He has the tiniest feet she's ever seen. His whole body is about the size of her paw. He's wearing a little red vest with gold stitching across its one pocket. She's about to ask Dusty if she made it when she realizes Mr. Mouse is shaking.

"I'm so sorry," Autumn says. "We shouldn't have disturbed you. We'll go now. It was very nice to meet you. I hope we'll be friends someday, but right now is obviously not a good time for you. Good night, Mr. Mouse."

"Good night." The words come out in a high-pitched squeak as he shuts the door.

"I hope I haven't ruined your friendship with them," Autumn tells Dusty.

"I don't think so. They just get nervous easily. I'll talk to them in the morning and work it all out. You handled it very well. Since you didn't insist, they'll be more likely to trust you in the future. Let's go back to the sewing room so they can calm down."

"Dusty, wouldn't you like to meet my sister, Smokey, and my cousin, Greyson?" she asks as they leave the bedroom.

"Um…maybe. I guess."

"Don't you like other cats?"

"It's not that I don't like them. They're all so perfect, especially the ones Abby brings home.

They're nice to me, but I'm certain they can tell I'm not a real cat like them. They're probably laughing at me behind my tail."

"I'll bet they're extremely impressed at how talented you are." Autumn leans in close. "And maybe some of them are jealous."

Dusty's eyes grow big. "Jealous? Of me?"

"Absolutely! Just look what you can do." Autumn points towards the sewing room. "I know Smokey would be amazed at your work. She adores beautiful clothes. Come on, I'll introduce you."

In the living room they find that the gold brocade curtain has been opened to an expansive view of the city. The sun has set. The city lights shine like stars. Abigail and Greyson stand at the balcony railing, talking quietly. Smokey stands off to one side looking out at the city lights, then around the room, then back out. Relief washes over her face when she sees Autumn and Dusty.

"What's going on?" asks Autumn as Smokey joins them in the living room.

"I'm not sure," says Smokey. "Ms. Fluffington asked if we'd like to see the view. She opened the curtain, and we all came out on the balcony. We were talking about the city and Ms. Fluffington's favorite shops. Then I suddenly realized she and Greyson weren't talking to me anymore. They seemed to forget I was here. I've been feeling like a fifth paw ever since."

"I love that view," Dusty's eyes look dreamy. "Whenever I'm not sewing, I sit on the balcony and look out at the city."

"It is a lovely view," Smokey agrees.

"You'd like to be out there, wouldn't you?" Autumn whispers to Dusty.

Dusty nods. "But I can't." A single tear trickles down her face.

Autumn stands up straight, gathering all her determination. "Oh, yes you can! I'm going to teach you how to find your way around without getting lost."

"No, Autumn. I can't do it."

"We'll only go around the block to start. I just thought of a little trick we can use to help you. Please bring me a square piece of fabric and a pair of scissors."

While Dusty heads back to her sewing room, Autumn Amelia steps onto the balcony. "Ms. Fluffington, if it's all right with you, we'd like to take a quick walk around the block for a little exercise. You wouldn't mind if we left you two alone for a few minutes, would you?"

A smile spreads across Abigail's face. "Of course not. Take all the time you want." Abigail turns back to Greyson who draws her attention to the full moon.

Dusty returns with a felt square and scissors. Smokey starts to ask what it's for, but Autumn hushes her. The three cats slip out of the apartment. Once in the hallway, Autumn explains.

"Dusty needs a little help getting her bearings and I think I've come up with a way to do it."

Autumn cuts a curved section from the center of one side of the square. Then she makes one snip in the first corner, two snips in the second corner, three in the third, and four in the fourth.

As they ride down in the elevator, Dusty nudges Autumn. "Can I hold you your tail?" she asks, a pained look in her eye.

"Of course, you can. We'll make a train. I'll be at the head. You hold my tail and Smokey will hold yours."

"What?" asks Smokey. "Why are we holding each other's tails? That's ridiculous."

Dusty puts both paws over her eyes. "I can't do this. I have to go back to the apartment."

"No, you don't," says Autumn. "Smokey just said that because she doesn't know the whole story."

"What story?" asks Smokey.

"Don't take this the wrong way, Smokey, but the story isn't your business. Just help us out and hold Dusty's tail."

Smokey looks incredulous. "Autumn, this is—"

Autumn puts her paws on her hips. "Smokey you hold her tail and not another word about it!" She commands as the elevator door opens on the lobby.

They stand on the sidewalk in front of the building. "Dusty, you take the felt square. See where I cut the curved part? That represents the main door. It's where we're standing right now." Autumn points to the left. "That end of the block is represented by the square with one snip cut from it. When we get there, we'll turn the felt and walk to the next corner. That'll be the end with two snips. We'll keep going until we come back to the curved cut, and we'll be back here at the front door. Got it?"

"I think so." Dusty looks unsure.

"It'll be easy. You'll see. I'll go first. You take my tail in one paw and hold the felt in the other. Smokey will hold your tail, so you'll always be between the two of us. You can't possibly get lost that way so all you have to do is concentrate on matching the turns in the block with the snips in the felt square. Ready? Let's go."

They reach the first corner. "Okay," says Autumn. "Now look at the square. See the corner with only one snip? That's where we're standing now. And look," she points to the street sign. "We're on First Street. You can remember that the street you come to when you arrive at the first corner is First Street, don't you think?"

"Yes. That's easy," Dusty agrees.

They continue down the sidewalk on First Street until arriving at the next corner.

"Now look at your square," Autumn instructs.

"I get it," Dusty says. "It's the second corner of the block so it matches the corner of the square with two snips, right?"

"That's right. Now what's the name of this street?"

"Doubletree Avenue," says Smokey.

"I can remember it's the second corner from the word *double*," Dusty announces. "Let's keep going."

The street at the third corner is called Parker Street.

"Hmm…" says Autumn. "How can you remember that Parker is the third street?"

"I know!" Dusty exclaims. "I have a cousin named Parker. He's my third cousin."

"Good for you!"

They reach the fourth corner of the block.

"This one's easy," says Autumn. "It's Lincoln Avenue. Your street. As you turn the corner here, you'll be walking back to the front door."

"And here we are," says Smokey as they arrive at the apartment building's main entrance.

"Let's try it again," says Autumn. "Only this time, let me hold the felt square. See if you can figure it out by the street names."

Dusty hands the square to Autumn. "I can still hold your tail, right?"

"Of course. And Smokey will still hold yours. Let's go."

They make it around the square again. Dusty identifies all the corners by the street names with no problem. When they return to their starting point, Autumn asks Dusty, "Do you think you can do it on your own?"

"Without you?" Dusty's smile fades.

"You can use the square." Autumn hands the piece of felt to her. "You know all the street names. You just did it yourself. We didn't say a word."

"I know, but I felt safe because you were with me."

"I'll tell you what. I'll stay here and Smokey will stand about halfway down Doubletree. That way when you see her, you'll know you're doing it right."

"I don't know," says Dusty.

"Trust me, Dusty. You can do it. Just follow the felt square. Think of it as a sewing pattern. I know you don't use them anymore, but you still know how."

"Seriously? You don't use sewing patterns?" Smokey asks. "You make Ms. Fluffington's clothes without a pattern? Are you kidding me?"

A smile spreads across Dusty's face. "I haven't used a pattern in years."

"Ladies, let's stay on topic, please!" Autumn claps her paws. "Smokey, go wait halfway down Doubletree. We'll give you a few minutes to get there, then I'll send Dusty on her way. Dusty, I'll be waiting right here when you get back."

They give Smokey a head start. Autumn goes over the felt square and street names with Dusty once more then sends her off. She watches as Dusty heads towards First Street. She stops every few seconds to look at the square. About halfway down the street she turns back. Autumn waves a paw and calls, "I'm still here and Smokey is waiting for you. Turn around and keep going. You can do it!"

Dusty stands still for a moment, then turns around and heads down the street. Autumn looks around at the cars passing by the buildings lining the street. More time goes by than she thinks is necessary. *Maybe she stopped to talk to Smokey for a minute*, she thinks.

Autumn says, "hello" to a few residents alighting from a cab to enter the apartment building. She looks down the street. Still no Dusty. *Please don't have gotten lost.* She wonders if she should go looking for her. *But if I'm not here when she gets back, she'll really be confused. What should I do?*

"Autumn Amelia! Autumn Amelia!" Dusty has just rounded the corner.

"I did it! I did it!" Dusty says when she reaches her.

"Good for you! I didn't doubt you for a minute." Autumn hugs her.

Smokey returns a few minutes later.

"Do you want to try it completely by yourself this time?" Autumn asks. "Smokey and I will both wait for you here."

This time Dusty nods vigorously. "Yes, I really think I can do it."

"You go, then! We'll be right here waiting for you."

Dusty heads off down the street, not stopping at all this time.

"Okay, Autumn, now tell me what's going on? Is there something wrong with her? How come she can't find her way around her own block?"

"There's nothing wrong with her, Smokey. At least nothing that can't be fixed. She got terribly lost once several years ago. The Bloodhound League had to rescue her."

"Oh, my catness!"

"She was traumatized. And that silly Ms. Fluffington, instead of teaching her how to get around, just made her stay inside from then on unless she goes with her which only deepened the trauma. Now Dusty's convinced that she has no sense of direction and that she's probably not even a real cat. That's why she's so shy."

"Oh? She thinks that?" Smokey looks at the sidewalk.

"Yes. It could have all been avoided if her sister had taken some time from her busy schedule to teach her to find her way around. Instead, she turned her into a recluse with no self-esteem. She'd be a very different cat if it weren't for Abigail Fluffington. Oh, I could just bite that cat's tail!"

"Autumn!"

"Well, I could."

Smokey gasps. "Oh dear!" She claps a paw over her mouth.

"What?"

"Were we not supposed to take Dusty out with us?"

"Probably not, but who cares?"

"I care! Autumn, Ms. Fluffington is my boss. She'll be furious with me. We have to get Dusty back into the apartment right away."

They hear Dusty calling. "I did it! I did it! I did it all by myself!"

Autumn giggles. "Just look at her. She's skipping like a kitten."

Other cats and dogs turn to look at Dusty. Some smile. Others move cautiously away.

"She looks a little nutty if you ask me," Smokey whispers.

"No one did. I think she looks deliriously happy."

"Whatever. Let's just get her back inside."

"Here I am. I did it." Dusty prances up to them. "I want to go around again. And then again and again!"

"Well, actually, Dusty," says Smokey. "We need to go back inside. Your sister and Greyson will wonder what's happened to us."

"My sister! I forgot all about her. I hope Abby won't be mad at me."

"So what if she is," says Autumn. "You have every right to go outside. Besides, you didn't go alone. You were with us. Don't let her bully you."

"Autumn Amelia!" Smokey exclaims.

"Smokey's right, Autumn. We should go in."

"Thank goodness." Smokey opens the door and leads them to the elevator.

"There you are! Where have you been? I've been a wreck!" Ms. Fluffington rushes towards them as they enter the apartment.

"We went for a walk around the block, Abby. Autumn Amelia taught me a trick so I can do it without getting lost."

"You did what?" Abigail looks as though she might faint.

"Calm down, Abigail," says Greyson. "Everyone's back safe and sound. I told you she probably went with Smokey and Autumn."

"But she knows she's not supposed to leave the apartment."

"Ms. Fluffington, I assure you, I had no idea Dusty wasn't supposed to go out. I would never have taken her with us if I'd known." Smokey fidgets with her paws. "I'm terribly, terribly sorry."

"I'm not," Dusty announces. "I had a great time. I'm going to walk around the block every day."

"Dusty!" Abigail exclaims.

"It's okay, Abby. Look at this." She holds up the felt square, explaining Autumn's teaching method.

"Well, that is rather ingenious," Abigail admits. "But that's only for going around the block. Nowhere else. Understand? Absolutely, nowhere else."

"At least not yet," Autumn interjects.

Every cat looks at her.

"If you want, Dusty, I'll teach you to read a map. Your cell phone probably has GPS, but it's best if you can do it on your own just in case."

"I don't have a cell phone," says Dusty.

"Then buying one will be our first errand."

Dusty's face lights up.

"Oh, no. That's kind of you to offer, Autumn, but I simply can't allow it," says Abigail.

"Why not? She's not a prisoner, is she?"

"No. Of course not. It's just that…well… she had a very frightening experience once. It's left her unable to find her way around. She gets disoriented too easily. I'm afraid it's out of the question."

"Dusty told me all about it. She can find her way if she has someone to teach her how to do it. You know how to get around outside because you went out all the time right from kittenhood."

"Autumn, please." Smokey hisses, but Autumn ignores her.

"She's been an indoor cat her whole life. How could anyone expect her to know how to get around outdoors when she's had no experience?"

Smokey steps in front of Autumn. "Ms. Fluffington, I'm very sorry. Please excuse my sister. She doesn't mean any harm. She just doesn't understand the situation."

Greyson stands in the midst of the ladies, looking bemused.

"Excuse me, Smokey! I understand very well." Autumn takes Dusty's paw. "Dusty, do you want me to teach you how to get around outside?"

"Autumn!" Smokey wails.

"For goodness' sake, Smokey. Dusty's not a kitten. She's older than you. She can make her own decisions." She turns back to Dusty. "It's up to you. Would you like me to teach you?"

"Yes! Yes! Yes!" Dusty jumps up and down in the middle of the living room, executing a perfect back flip on the last bounce.

Abigail gasps. "I didn't know she could do that!"

"I'll bet she can do a lot of things you don't know about," states Autumn.

* * *

Smokey rests her head against the window glass on the passenger side of her car. Saying she felt a bit frazzled, she'd asked Greyson to drive home.

"That was an interesting evening, wasn't it?" he says.

"Hmph!"

"Oh, come on, Smokey. Abigail agreed to let Autumn teach Dusty to get around. All's well that ends well."

"I think she only agreed so she wouldn't come off sounding like a prison warden. I don't think she's happy about it. I hope I don't get thrown off the cat park project."

"Nonsense," says Greyson. "She's hesitant because she worries about her sister, but I get the feeling that if Abigail Fluffington doesn't want something to happen it's not going to. Since she agreed, albeit reluctantly, she must have realized it was the right thing to do."

"I suppose. By the way, what's up with the two of you? You got awfully cozy out on the balcony."

The corners of Greyson's mouth turn up. "That we did. Let's just say that while I may be leaving tomorrow, I'll probably be back sooner and more often than originally expected."

Smokey looks directly at him, her eyes growing wide. "Well, well, well. It's like that, is it?"

"We'll see."

"Smokey?" Autumn speaks up from the back seat.

"What?"

"You and I need to talk later."

"About what?"

"Mice."

Smokey leans her head against the window glass. "Great."

Chapter Fourteen

Interviews

What a day! Smokey thinks as she tosses her purse on the nearest chair, kicks off her shoes, and collapses on the couch.

"Smokey! Smokey!" Autumn's call from the kitchen is followed by the smooth patter of floofed paws on the floor. Smokey opens her eyes just as Autumn skitters across the living room, slides into the sofa arm, grabs hold with her claws, and makes a swinging landing on the end opposite Smokey.

"How did the interview go? Did they take your picture? When will it be in the paper?"

"Slow down. One question at a time." Smokey props herself up.

"I've been waiting all day to hear about it. Come on, tell!"

"The interviewer was a springer spaniel named Bettie Lou."

"I know that name. She writes the arts and entertainment section in the paper. What was she like? Was she nice? Did she ask good questions? What did she think of the cat park idea?"

Smokey chuckles. "It's really not that big a deal, Autumn. It was just an interview in the newspaper. It's not like I'm going to be on the cover of Catmopolitan. And no. No pictures were taken."

"Phooey. Oh well, your name will be in the paper. What questions did she ask? What did she say? What did you say? I want to know the whole thing."

"You'll be able to read it this weekend. The interview will be printed in Saturday's paper. Don't forget, Rufus Tailwagger was there, too. He did most of the talking."

"I still want to hear it from you. What was it like to be interviewed?"

"It was just answering a bunch of questions and explaining what we're planning."

"Like what?"

Smokey sighs, realizing she's not going to get any rest until Autumn gets a full account. "The three of us met at Sylvester's for lunch."

"Sylvester's? Have I been there? I don't think I've been there. What did you have? Was it good? What did Bettie Lou and Rufus have?"

"I had a chef salad. Bettie Lou had a Rueben, and Rufus had some sort of burger with a bunch of stuff on it."

"Mushrooms? Onions? Cheese? What kind of cheese? What about sautéed peppers? I like sautéed peppers on burgers. Oh, and sautéed apples, too. They really finish it off."

"Honestly, Autumn, I don't know what was on Rufus's burger. Do you want to hear about the interview or not?"

"Oh, that's right. I forgot. Yes, tell me about the interview."

Smokey shakes her head and rolls her eyes. "At first it was just small talk so Bettie Lou could get to know me. She's interviewed Rufus before, but it was the first time we'd met."

"What questions did she ask when the interview actually began?"

"She started with the basics — who came up with the idea and who is working on it, where will the park be located, what will be in it, when will we break ground, when is the expected opening, why does Faunaburg need a cat park, how will it benefit the community. Stuff like that."

"Did you tell her about the slide?"

"The slide?"

"You know. Greyson suggested a slide when we were at the lighthouse on Niptucket Island."

Smokey laughs. "Oh, that. I did mention that a lookout tower was being considered. I don't remember saying anything about a slide."

"You will put one in, won't you? It would be such fun. But remember, no plastic. I hate static in my fur."

"If we do build a tower, I'll be sure to include a non-plastic slide."

"Good!"

"Rufus talked a lot about a restaurant. Apparently, Miguel was serious about having one in the park. He's been taken with the idea ever since we had lunch with him, and you one-upped his chef."

"I did not! At least, I didn't mean to. I was just helping."

"I know. Don't worry about it. Gustav needed it anyway."

"Will Gustav run the restaurant at the cat park?"

"That's not his style. Actually, Rufus said that Miguel insists you be the head chef at the park's restaurant."

"Me?"

"Yes. He was quite impressed with you. He did mention it that day at lunch, remember?"

"Yes, but I didn't think he was serious. At least not about me running the restaurant."

"He was serious, all right. Would you like to do it?"

"I'd really have to think about it. I'm honored that Miguel wants me as head chef, but it's a huge undertaking. Would it be full-time?"

"Definitely."

"Then I couldn't work for Furry's anymore."

"Probably not."

"I love working for Furry's."

"I know, but this is a great opportunity, Autumn. It would be a big step up for you."

"You know that kind of stuff isn't important to me. I'm happy doing what I'm doing now."

Smokey sits up straight and takes Autumn's paws. "Just think, Autumn. You'll have your own restaurant. The kitchen will be enormous, filled with state-of-the-art equipment. The finest ingredients will be at your clawtips. You'll have a full staff to help you. You can hire whomever you want. You can experiment with all sorts of recipes and cook and bake to your heart's content and it would be all yours. Wouldn't you be in your glory?"

A dreamy look passes over Autumn's face. "My own state-of-the-art kitchen. I'd hire at least one floofless cat just to get things off the shelves for me."

Smokey laughs. "And it would be a kitchen from which you could never be banned."

Autumn drops her gaze to her lap.

"What's wrong?" asks Smokey.

"What you just said. A kitchen from which I could never be banned. That might ruin everything."

"What are you talking about?"

"It wouldn't really be my restaurant, Smokey. It would be Miguel's. He's putting up the money for it. I'd just be the head chef. He insists on that now, but he could change his mind later. I'd be devastated if he told me to leave."

"Why would he do that? There's no better chef than you. Even Gustav had to admit you improved his recipe. Miguel would never fire you."

"He might if I eat so much of the inventory that the restaurant starts losing money. I could ruin the place as easily as I could make it a success. Besides, every day in a place like that, before long I'd be so big, I couldn't waddle through the door." Autumn takes her paws out of Smokey's. "No. I'd better stick with what I'm doing. I'm sure there are lots of great chefs who'd love that job. Miguel won't have any trouble finding one."

Smokey leans forward. "You don't have to decide right now. I'm sure there's some way we could work around your problem. Just promise you'll think about it, okay?"

Autumn shrugs. "Sure," she says, but the excitement has left her voice. Suddenly, her nose twitches. She lifts her head. "It's ready," she announces.

"What is? Smokey asks.

"The cream of tomato soup I've been simmering. Can't you smell it?"

"Sure. I smelled it when I came in the door."

"But at this very moment it has reached perfection. Can't you smell the perfection?"

"No. It smells the same as when I came in."

"Don't be silly. Finish telling me about the interview while we eat." Autumn gets up and heads for the kitchen.

Smokey follows, silently mouthing the words *and that's why you should be the head chef at the cat park's restaurant* behind Autumn's back while fighting the urge to kick her in the rump for being so obtuse.

Smokey sits down while Autumn ladles soup into her bowl. She fills her plate from the big bowl of potato salad. Autumn pulls fresh rolls from the oven. Smokey can hardly wait to smear them with butter and sink her teeth in.

"It was such a hot day today, I thought we should have a light supper. Want a glass of ice water?"

"I'll get it." Smokey pulls the pitcher from the refrigerator and fills a glass for each of them.

"Finish telling me about the interview. What did you tell Bettie Lou would be in the park?"

"I told her we're still in the planning stages. We don't know everything that's going to be there yet. Besides the lookout tower, I told her about the tree bridges, the catnip garden, and a possible brusselball court. And, of course, Rufus talked about the restaurant.

"Sounds like the interview went well, then."

Smokey hesitates. "Yes, to a point."

Autumn looks up from her soup. "What happened?"

"We were nearing the end of the interview when Bettie Lou asked if we thought the park's location would be a problem because it's so close to Rodent Way. She asked if the rodents know about it yet."

"Do they?"

"Nothing's been publicly announced, although Rufus and I have been out to the site a few times. Of course, Miguel and Ms. Fluffington have been there. I'm sure some of them overheard us talking. They know something's up even if they don't know precisely what." Smokey rests her head on her paw. "I have to admit I'm very nervous about this."

Autumn puts down her spoon. "Why would the rodents be upset about it?"

Smokey watches Autumn break open a roll, steam wafting out in wispy curls. A little square of butter placed on one half of the roll slowly melts into its white interior. Autumn puts down her butter knife and looks expectantly at Smokey.

"Lots of cats being so close to Rodent Way, spending a lot of time in the same vicinity so near to where the rodents have their homes and schools. I honestly wish the park was going to be in a different location. It's the only thing about this project that really bothers me. Of course, I couldn't say that in the interview, though."

"Smokey?" Autumn's voice is low, almost hesitant. "Something happened recently that really upset me."

"Oh? What?"

"That night when we were at Ms. Fluffington's Dusty wanted to introduce me to her friends, Mr. and Mrs. Mouse. They were terrified to meet me. It was because I'm a cat."

"Who are Mr. and Mrs. Mouse?"

"They're the mice who live in the wall in Dusty's bedroom. They have eight babies. I didn't get to see them, though. I only met Mr. Mouse."

"Get out!" Smokey exclaims. "Are you kidding me? Abigail Fluffington has mice living in her apartment?"

Autumn nods.

"I can't believe it! Does she know?"

Autumn shrugs. "Dusty's friends with them, but they sure don't trust cats in general, so probably not."

"I can't get over this! Mice in Ms. Fluffington's apartment. Right under her nose! I'll bet you anything she'd doesn't know. I can't imagine what she'd say if she found out."

"Why?" Autumn demands. "What's wrong with mice?"

"Well they're, you know, mice. And Ms. Fluffington is, well, Ms. Fluffington. I mean, really. Mice in *her* apartment. Oh, this is too much!" A snort escapes as Smokey laughs.

"I don't see why it's funny. In fact, after my encounter I see nothing funny about it at all. You can't imagine how terrified they were of me. Of me! No creature's ever been afraid of me, and I didn't like how it felt one little bit!"

Smokey takes a long drink of her ice water. "How did you think they'd react? Why do you think I'm so worried about the cat park going in so close to Rodent Way?"

"That's what I don't understand, Smokey. I want you to tell me the truth about something." Autumn puts both front paws on the table. She leans forward to look Smokey dead in the eye. "I'm very serious, Smokey. I want an honest answer."

Smokey puts down her fork. She's never seen this look from Autumn before. "Okay. What is it?"

"Dusty said the mice were afraid to meet me because they think cats eat mice. I was appalled. Dusty said she didn't know where they got that idea, but they swear it's true. Now I know Dusty has been very sheltered and there's a lot about life in general she doesn't know. I've been sheltered in some ways, too, but at least I knew that cats catch mice. She didn't even know that. I did not, however, think that cats ate mice. I've never seen a cat eat a mouse. I've never heard of any recipes with mice as ingredients. So where exactly did this idea about cats eating mice come from?"

Autumn's stare into Smokey's eyes never wavers. Smokey looks away and twists her napkin in her paws. It never occurred to her that Autumn had missed this particular fact of life.

"Just something they heard, probably. You know, urban legend kind of thing." Smokey's voice sounds unconvincing even to her.

"Smokey!" Autumn's paw pounds the table. "I know when you're lying. I want the truth. Do cats eat mice or not?"

Smokey feels tears welling up. She looks towards the ceiling, then at the walls, anywhere but at Autumn. "Only when they're desperate," she whispers.

"What does that mean?" Autumn's voice sounds startled.

Smokey looks down at her lap. "I suppose you might as well know. Yes, cats have been known to eat mice, but only when they have no choice. Well-fed cats don't. They don't need to, don't even want to. But homeless cats, ones who can't get anything else to eat, they hunt for survival. They eat mice, moles, birds, bugs, frogs, whatever. When you're starving you eat what you can catch if you want to live."

Smokey looks up at Autumn. The shock on her face is like a knife in Smokey's heart. She knows what's coming. In a hoarse whisper, Autumn says it. "You've eaten them."

Smokey has to look away from Autumn. She's not sure what emotions she's seeing. Shock, anger, confusion, hurt, betrayal, they all seem to be passing over Autumn's face in a desolate parade. She hears a little gasp. "Mama and Papa Cat, too?" Autumn's question has a tone of desperation. Smokey knows how badly Autumn doesn't want this to be true, but she can no longer deny it. Smokey pushes her plate out of the way and drops her head into her paws on the table, sobbing.

She doesn't hear anything from Autumn. When Smokey finally looks up through her tears, she sees Autumn sitting still, her food untouched, staring blankly ahead.

"Autumn, please understand," she begs. "We had no home. We had no food. We would have died if we hadn't hunted. Would you have wanted us to die? To starve to death? There was no other way."

Autumn looks down at her own lap. A tear drips slowly down her cheek. "Mama Cat," she whispers.

"Yes. Mama Cat," Smokey answers. "To keep us alive."

"She taught you to hunt?"

"She had to. We didn't know then that things would turn around for us. I had to know how to survive on my own."

"She didn't teach me. She didn't even tell me."

"By the time you were born, Papa had a good job. We had this cottage. We could buy all our food. We didn't need to hunt anymore, and we never did it again. That's why she taught you to cook instead."

Autumn nods and swallows hard. She pushes away her dishes. "I can't eat," she says. "I'm going to my room. Thank you for explaining."

Smokey sits staring at the table. She no longer has any appetite, either. After a while, she scrapes the untouched potato salad from their plates back into the bowl and dumps the soup they've barely touched down the sink. She washes the dishes, wipes the table and stove, mechanically going through the motions all the while wondering if she has shattered Autumn's memory of their Mama Cat beyond repair.

The thought makes her choke. She sits down and cries so hard her throat and ribs ache.

Once the kitchen is cleaned, Smokey goes to her room. She gets into bed, but the pounding in her head won't let her sleep. Hours go by while she stares at the wall. Memories of the old days, of hunting for survival, of going days with no food, the fear of not knowing when or if another meal would appear play over and over in her mind.

A soft knock at the door pulls her back to the present. "Come in," she says, her voice barely audible.

Autumn sits on the end of her bed.

"I want you to know that I understand." Autumn's voice is soft, but stronger than it was at supper. "I know what if feels like to be hungry, but I don't know what if feels like to starve. I can only think of hunger pangs and multiply them a hundred times. I know what it's like to wonder what to make for dinner, but I don't know what it's like to wonder if there will be dinner. I don't know what it's like to have babies and watch them go hungry or worry that they will die because I couldn't feed them or that I will die and leave them with no one to take care of them. Thinking about it makes me so sad for Mama and Papa Cat. And for you. I just want you to know that I don't blame them or you. I can't fully understand what it was like, but I do understand that it wasn't what any of you wanted. I just wanted to be sure you know that, so you don't worry that I think less of you."

Smokey sits up in bed and reaches her arms out towards Autumn. "Thank you, Autumn," Smokey whispers as they hug and cry together."

Chapter Fifteen

Sukey

"I'll bet you thought I'd never come," says Sukey as Autumn opens the front door.

"Oh, I knew you would eventually. Come in."

It's been weeks since Sukey was supposed to come over to bake with Autumn, but she had to keep rescheduling.

"It's that ridiculous Gustav," Sukey explains. "He's been making us work tons of overtime, even pulling us in on our days off. I've been dying to bake with you, but every time I think I'm going to make it I get a call from him and have to go in."

Autumn ushers Sukey into the kitchen. "It's just a regular kitchen," she says. Not like what you're used to."

"Believe me, it's fine. Anything is better than being in the kitchen with Gustav. He's always difficult, but lately he's been worse than ever." Sukey looks around. "Your cottage is adorable."

"Thanks. You can set your stuff down anywhere. I'm all set up on the table and over there." Autumn points to the counter space to the right of the stove. "I put an extra table up for you and you can have the counter space to the left of the stove. I hope it's enough. I know you're used to more room."

"Oh, I can bake anywhere." Sukey puts down her bags, pulls out her ingredients, baking dishes, and implements and sets them on the counter.

"Why is Gustav working you so hard? Have there been a lot of big events?"

"There was one, but that's not the reason he's working us to death. You are."

Autumn stares at Sukey. "What do you mean?"

Sukey laughs. "Ever since you showed him up in his own kitchen, he's been determined to create new recipes. He wants to come up with some new creation to show he's still the world's greatest chef. As if! I mean, he is a great chef. In the top ten, maybe top five, but that doesn't make him *the* number one greatest chef. He just thinks he is and wants everyone else to think so, too." The speed of Sukey's words increases as she continues to talk. "Ever since an unknown chief, that would be you, a chef who never even went to cooking school, who was taught only by her Mama Cat, improved his world-famous sauce, well, oh my whiskers, he's been a positive dragon to work for. Not that he wasn't already. He's always been a pain in the paws, but now it's worse than ever."

"Oh dear. Smokey said those same words. I mean about me showing him up. I didn't mean to do that. I was just trying to help. I feel terrible."

"Don't. His ego needed deflating. Despite the extra hours, Sally and I are relishing his discomfort."

"Sally? Oh, the Beagle. She's the sous chef, right?"

"Uh-huh. Poor thing. She gets it worse than I do. He drives me up the curtains, but he's even worse to her. Ordering her around, yelling at her all the time, blaming her when something doesn't turn out the way he wanted, even though she did everything right. But I'll tell you something I've noticed. Sally used to cry in the corner on her breaks whenever Gustav had been particularly nasty to her, but ever since your visit, I see her sitting on a stool at break time with a dreamy look in her eyes and a big smile on her face. I was confused at first, so I asked her about it. Turns out whenever he acts like that, which now is nearly all the time, she spends her break reliving your visit." Sukey laughs. "I always know when she's thinking about it. She's positively beatific looking!"

"I'm glad I gave her something to smile about," says Autumn, "but I still feel bad that I made Mr. Gustav upset, especially since he's taking it out on the two of you."

"We'll deal with it. Eventually, he'll come up with some amazing new recipe and all will go back to normal, or at least what passes for normal in Gustav's kitchen."

Once set up, Sukey gets to work mixing ingredients in a bowl while Autumn continues kneading dough.

"It sounds like a terrible work environment. If it's so awful, why do you work there? I wouldn't stand it for a minute."

"Well, he is one of the world's greatest chefs so it's an honor to work in his kitchen. Not just anyone can get a job with a great chef like Gustav. He is temperamental, but I hear that all the great chefs are, though he might be the worst. Still, if you aspire to greatness in the culinary arts getting a job in the kitchen of a world-renowned chef is a major coup, so you've got to be willing to put up with the tantrums."

"I guess I don't aspire to much," says Autumn. "I'd leave in a tail flip."

"There's also the fact that Miguel pays us well. He knows we're good too. Maybe not Gustav good, but good, nonetheless. I think he pays us a little extra just for putting up with Gustav. We do appreciate that."

"I'd say you deserve it, but no amount of money would be enough for me to deal with that. Gustav would never get away with it in my kitchen."

"Your kitchen? Do you mean you're going to do it?"

"Do what?"

"Take the job as head chef at the cat park's restaurant."

"How do you know about that?"

"I heard Miguel say it the day you were there, and he's mentioned it several times since. I think it's one of the things that's sending Gustav over the edge."

"Does Gustav want the job?"

"Oh, my whiskers, no! He'd think it was beneath him. It's just the way Miguel goes on about what a great chef you are. He relates the story of how you improved Gustav's sauce to every guest he has in his private dining room. Then they all request it made your way and Gustav has to cook it up using your recipe and it's driving him catnip crazy!"

"Oh dear. That's terrible."

"Sally and I think it's hilarious. At least as long as we stay out of the way of the flying pots and pans. So? Are you going to be head chef?"

"Smokey asked me to, but I don't know. I really like what I'm doing now. I know it doesn't seem like much, but it's fine with me. I don't need to be a great chef and I like working for Furry Confections. Tabby Furry has been very kind to me. I owe her my loyalty."

"You say you don't need to be a great chef, but guess what, you already are. It's just that no one knows it yet. Well, except for the pawful who've had your food." Sukey almost doubles over with laughter. "And Gustav. He knows! Oh, my whiskers, does he know!"

Autumn giggles from Sukey's infectious laughter. "I don't care who knows. I just like to cook and bake, and I like others to enjoy what I make. That's what makes me happy."

"Then you'd make a lot more cats very, very happy if you were head chef at the cat park."

Autumn thinks for a moment. "I suppose that's true. But still, I'd have to quit working for Furry's."

"Think it over. Maybe you could do some baking for Furry's on the side."

Sukey pulls some oranges from her bag.

"What are you making?" Autumn asks.

"An orange layer cake with cream cheese frosting."

"Sounds delicious. I have lots of moth flour if you need any."

"You use moth flour?"

"All the time. It makes everything light and airy. I love it. Don't you use it?"

"We never used in pastry arts school. I've heard of it, but I've never cooked with it. Gustav won't allow it in his kitchen. He says it's pedestrian."

"Are you baking for him right now or for yourself?"

"This one's for my Mama Cat. It's her birthday today. I'm having dinner with her tonight, and I wanted to make a special dessert for her."

"Would she mind moth flour?"

"Probably not."

"Then I'll get you some." Autumn goes to the pantry and returns with a jar and a scoop. "Two scoops should do it. Mix it well and you'll be all set. How do you plan to decorate the cake?"

"I'm going to swirl the frosting and lightly toss some orange peel strips over the top."

"Hmm..." says Autumn. "Does your Mama Cat like praying mantises?"

"I think so. I know she likes crickets, so probably."

"I've got some catnip drenched praying mantises you can set into the frosting if you think she'd like them."

"I bet she would."

"I'll go get them." Autumn heads back to the pantry and returns with a large jar.

"I've never had these before." Sukey dips a paw in the jar. "Mm. Delicious!"

"Have another," Autumn offers. "Just be sure to leave enough for the cake."

"I knew baking with you would be fun," Sukey says as she crunches another bug. "I'd better be careful, or I'll eat them all."

"I know all about that," says Autumn, then relates her own misadventures in munching her way through her cooking supplies. The more Autumn talks, the more Sukey laughs. By the time Autumn has finished, Sukey is laughing so hard she can barely pour the batter into the cake tins.

Once the tins are in the oven, Sukey takes a seat at the table with Autumn. "I can see why you feel you owe Tabby your loyalty. Oh, my whiskers, that is just so funny."

"I suppose it is if you're not the one living with it. For me it's a bit of a handicap. You haven't even heard about what happens when I go to restaurants."

"I have to tell you, Autumn, it's so nice to be here with you. I love being able to talk while I bake."

"Can't you talk at work?" Autumn asks, as Sukey takes two more praying mantises from the jar.

"Not really," she says, munching away. "These are great. The combination of catnip and mantis is perfect."

"Be careful. They're strong."

"Uh-huh. Anyway, Gustav doesn't like it when we talk. He wants all our attention focused on our work. Only he can talk and that just means giving orders." Sukey's voice drops low to imitate Gustav's. 'Chop those carrots faster! More rolls, we need more rolls. Hurry up! Where's the Dijon? I had it right here. Who moved it? Sally, grate the cheese. NOW! Sukey, why aren't the mini cheesecakes out yet?" Then back to her own voice, but in an under-her-breath whisper, she says, 'Because it's not time for dessert yet, dumbtail!"

"He really is a tyrant, isn't he?" says Autumn.

"Oh, you don't know the half of it. If Sally and I talk at all, even if it's about what we're cooking, he yells, 'Enough chit chat! I hate chit chat!' I remember when he hired me, he said, 'I'm hiring you because you're supposed to be one of the best pastry chefs around here, but I know you Siamese have a reputation for talking a lot. I don't like a lot of talking so keep your mouth closed while you're in my kitchen.' Can you believe it? What a thing to say and honestly, I don't talk that much. I mean, I do sometimes, like when my friend, Tamarind, and I get together, she's a Tonkinese, she owns Tonk's Treasures, a little boutique in Faunaburg, have you been there? Well, you should go. It's great. She's got everything. But as I was saying, I know we Siamese are known for talking a lot, can't help it, it's in our genes, so when I have to spend all day keeping my meows inside it about drives me up the curtains, that's why it's so nice to be here where I can bake and talk, and, oh my whiskers, these catnip mantises are good, I've never had them before, well, I've had praying mantises, but not ones soaked in nip, where did you get them or did you do it yourself because it wouldn't surprise me, you're so talented, like what you explained to me about how you make candied dragonfly wings, hey would you teach me to make those, they sound awesome..."

Autumn slides the jar of mantises off the table, sidles across the room and shuts the jar into the upper cabinet all the while wondering if Sukey has forgotten there's such a punctuation mark as a period.

"I'll be happy to teach you, but we'll need a whole day just for that. It's a long process."

"I don't mind. It sounds like fun. Hey, maybe you could bake things to sell at the cat park. It wouldn't be as good as if you were head chef at the restaurant, but it would be better than nothing. I filled out the online form asking what I'd like to see at the park. I checked off restaurant. I should go back and add a bakery. The form lets you check off stuff already in the works, but you can type in things you think of that aren't on the list, so I could add that in. Have you filled it out yet? I love the idea of the lookout tower. Maybe at the top instead of a light they could have a barbecue pit. That would be fun, don't you think?"

"Sure. I haven't been on the website. Does it mention anything about a slide?"

"Slide? No. I didn't see anything about a slide."

"Drat! I'll have to call Jasmine myself and tell her to add it. I really want a slide."

"What fun! Oh, I know, how about a spiral slide? It could go around the outside of the lookout tower. Oh, and there can be one inside, too, in case it's raining. That makes me think, it won't be a water slide, will it? I hate getting wet. What am I saying? Of course there wouldn't be a water slide in a cat park. Are dogs going to be allowed in the park? It's okay if they are, I don't mind dogs. It's just that they like water. And mud. They like to get wet and roll in mud. I don't know why. It's a dog thing, I guess. Anyway, I don't want a water slide. Did Smokey ever put a water slide in the dog parks she's designed? I'd bet they'd love one, especially if they landed in mud at the bottom. But not in the cat park. And no plastic. I hate static. But not metal. It will get too hot. Oh, I know! Wood. Yeah, a wooden slide. A wooden spiral slide. Keep it polished so it always goes fast. My friend and I…did I mention Tamarind? I did, didn't I? She owns the boutique, Tonk's Treasures. Yeah, I mentioned her. Anyway, we'd both go down a slide, each facing the opposite direction, tails linked, and slide down together. That would be a blast! Who's Jasmine?"

Autumn's head is spinning. *How does she talk so fast?*

"Jasmine is Smokey's best friend. She built the website you mentioned."

"Oh. I know a Jasmine who's a web designer. She plays on the same brusselball team as Tamarind and me. I wonder if it's the same one."

"It must be. She plays brusselball. She's really good."

"Yeah, she's the best player on the team. Tam and I, Tam is Tamarind, I call her Tam sometimes, or Tammy, I call her Tammy, too, but mostly either Tam or Tamarind, anyway, she and I think Jasmine is the best. I'll tell Jasmine at the next practice that we want a wooden, spiral slide. I wonder if Tam has filled out the form. I'll ask her. I'm going to her store when I leave here to pick up Mama Cat's birthday gift. Have you been to her store? You should go. It's great. It's in Faunaburg. Tonk's Treasure's. Tam's a Tonkinese, did I mention that?"

Autumn nods. *Does she ever take a breath?*

"You'd love her store. It's the cutest little boutique. It's small, but it's got everything. I mean everything! I don't know how she fits it all in. And so many different things. Most are gift items, really nice perfumes, fur conditioners, claw polish, decorative items, jewelry, and now she's starting to sell clothes. What are you baking? I shouldn't just be sitting her while you work. Let me help you. After all, it's my cake that's holding up your oven."

Autumn goes to her recipe box and pulls out the card for raspberry anchovy popovers. She hands it to Sukey along with the ingredients and pans. "Thanks," says Autumn. "If I can get everything prepped, I can get it all into the oven when your cake comes out."

"My pleasure." While getting right to work on the popovers, Sukey dives back into her monologue.

"Oh! I almost forgot. How could I forget this? Tam sells herbs and spices. You've got to check them out, they're really exotic. They come from all over the world. I'll bet she's got some you've never heard of. Just imagine how you could use them once you get to know their flavors. I can only imagine what you'd do with them. What else does she have? Oh, yes, miniatures, some nice china dishes and—"

"Miniatures?" Autumn interrupts. "What kind of miniatures?"

"I think they're mostly things for doll houses. Do you like miniatures? I had a doll house when I was a kitten. I loved it, but I'm not into them anymore.'

"What about miniature textiles?"

Sukey cocks her head, silenced for a moment, staring at Autumn.

"Does she sell miniature bedspreads and curtains? Or miniature clothes?"

"Um, I don't know. I think it's mostly doll house furniture, but I'm not sure. If that's something you want, she might be able to special order it for you."

"Actually, I know a cat who makes miniature textiles. I think it would be great if she could find a place to sell them. Does Tamarind sell on consignment?"

"Not a lot, but I think a few things she does. If she thinks it's something that will really sell, she could probably be persuaded. What's the market for miniature textiles?"

"Mice."

"Mice?" Sukey laughs. "I don't think she gets many mice customers in her store."

"Why not?"

"Why do you think? I mean can you imagine mice daring to go into a store owned by a cat?"

"They shouldn't be afraid to. Tamarind wouldn't harm them, would she?" Autumn's eyes narrow.

"No, of course not. It just isn't something that happens."

"Maybe it should start happening."

"Hmm…well, it would open a new market. That is, if you could convince the mice to shop there. Does your friend sew for mice now?"

"She does. She made all the curtains, tablecloths, dish towels, and bedding for the mouse family that lives in her bedroom wall."

"And they're not afraid of her?"

"They were at first, but after a while they realized there was no reason to be afraid. She just wanted to be friends. And now they are."

"Oh. That's nice. Who's your friend?"

Autumn smiles. "Dusty Fluffington."

"Fluffington? She's not related to Abigail Fluffington, is she?"

"She's Abigail's younger sister. They live together in one of those fancy Faunaburg apartments."

"Are you serious?" Sukey jumps out of her seat. "Abigail Fluffington has mice living in her luxury apartment? And her sister sews for them?"

"Not only that, but she makes all of Ms. Fluffington's clothes, too. She can sew just about anything. She's so good she doesn't even use a pattern. She just knows instinctively what to do. And they look better than most of those fancy designer clothes."

"You must take her to meet Tamarind. Take her to Tonk's Treasures. I'll tell Tam about her. If she's that good, maybe she could sew for the new clothing line Tam wants to add. She's only just started that, and she wants it to grow. It's mostly for cats, but some for dogs, too. It's a more viable market than mice, I'm sure."

Autumn thinks for a moment. "I'll tell Dusty. We can make going to Tonk's Treasures one of our outings. I do wish Tamarind would consider the mouse line, though. I think it would be one way to bring cats and mice together. It's time to start building better relations between us, don't you think?"

"I've never thought about it."

"Why not?"

Sukey shrugs. "I guess I never saw a need."

"Mice are terrified of us. That really bothers me. I'd never hurt a mouse and I don't like it that they're afraid of me." Autumn hesitates for a moment. "I do understand why, but I still don't like it and I want it to change."

"You're an interesting cat, Autumn. I've never heard a cat say anything like that before. I've never even given it a thought. I mean, I don't hunt mice and, unless, I was starving and had no choice, I never would. But I never thought about how they feel. You're probably right, but I don't know if we could ever change the way things are. Mice are afraid of cats. That's how it is."

"But why does it have to be? I hate that any creature lives in fear. Just because something is a certain way, doesn't mean it should stay that way. Your friend, Tamarind, could help start the change. Do you think she'd at least consider it?"

Sukey thinks for a moment. "I don't know. She's a businesscat so she's not going to want to lose money on it. I suppose she could sell the textiles as dollhouse miniatures if the mouse thing doesn't work. It can't hurt to talk to her about it. If it worked and added to her client base she'd be delighted."

"And if mice did start shopping at the store it could begin to build better relations," Autumn adds. "Wouldn't she like to be part of that?"

"Tam is well-known in that section of Faunaburg. Everyone loves her boutique. She knows all of her customers by name. They tell her everything like she's their best friend. That's just her personality. Everyone loves her. If mice did start shopping there and she got to know them I'll bet they'd fall in love with her, too. When she knows two customers have something in common, she always introduces them if they happen to be in the store at the same time. She loves putting friendships together. Maybe she could start some friendships between cat and mouse customers.

Autumn feels excitement build. "I can't wait to tell Dusty."

"Don't get your hopes up too much, Autumn. I can't speak for Tam. You'll have to convince her first that it's a good idea."

"You're her best friend. Will you mention it to her? See if she might go for it?"

"Sure. But I can't promise anything."

"I understand." Images of mice and cats shopping together, comparing prices, exclaiming over great finds, whirl in Autumn's head.

The buzzer rings.

"My cake's done." Sukey pulls two tins from the oven. "Perfect!" she announces. "Now let's get your tarts in. I'll put this on the rack to cool while I start making the frosting. Hey, where did those praying mantises go?"

By late afternoon, all the baking is finished. Autumn gives Sukey a box for her cake and packages up all her own creations. She calls Tabby to send the Squirrel brothers for a pickup. After washing her pans and utensils, Sukey repacks her bags.

"I had a wonderful time, Autumn. I hope we can do it again soon."

"I'd love to," says Autumn. She's had fun, too, but knows she'll need time to recover from Sukey's high speed conversation before she can handle another baking session with her new friend.

The Squirrel brothers arrive on their tandem bikes as Autumn walks Sukey to her car.

"Who are they?" Sukey asks.

"Simon and Sam. They're Tabby's couriers. Autumn turns to the squirrels as they dismount from their bikes. "Boys, this is my new friend, Sukey. She's a baker, too."

"Hello, Miss Sukey," says Simon.

"Pleased to meet you," says Sam.

"Pleased to meet you, too."

"Everything's stacked up in the kitchen, boys," Autumn tells them. "Go ahead in and get it while I see Sukey off."

The squirrels scamper through the front door.

"Oh, my whiskers, they're adorable!" says Sukey.

"They are, but they're a pawful. They mean well, but they get distracted easily. If they don't come out right away, I'll have to go after them. It will mean they've smelled seeds and nuts in my pantry and lost all thought of loading my baking into their cart."

"Oh dear! And you let them go in alone?"

"They don't mean any harm. They just get carried away. Considering what happens to me when I bake, I can hardly complain about them. I always give them some seeds and nuts before they leave, anyway."

"You know, Autumn, you talked about eating unconsciously while you bake, but I never saw you eat once all day. We didn't even stop for lunch."

Autumn's eyes widen. "I must have been so caught up in our conversation that I didn't even think of it." Astonishment is suddenly replaced by guilt. "Oh dear! I'm sorry I never offered you any lunch. How thoughtless of me!"

Sukey waves a dismissive paw. "Don't worry. I skip lunch half the time anyway. Gustav rarely gives us time to eat, so I'm used to it. Besides, I did munch those praying mantises. They held me over."

The Squirrel brothers return carrying stacked trays of baked goods. They load them in the cart and jump back on their bicycles.

"Wait a minute, boys! Don't leave before I give you some seeds and nuts," Autumn calls.

"That's okay, Miss Autumn," Simon replies. "You're busy with your friend. We'll catch you next time." The two speed off down the driveway.

"Well, that's a first," says Autumn. "Today is full of surprises."

Sukey finishes packing her equipment into her car. Autumn places the boxed cake on the passenger seat. "Please wish your Mama Cat a happy birthday from me."

"I will. And don't forget to check out Tonk's Treasures."

"I'm looking forward to it."

Just before Sukey climbs into her little yellow sports car, she turns to Autumn. "I should warn you about something. When you do go to see Tamarind, be prepared. That cat is a chatterbox!"

Chapter Sixteen

First Response

"Drat!" Smokey exclaims.

"What's wrong?" Autumn asks, plopping down on the couch next to her.

Smokey hands the newspaper to Autumn. "Read this letter to the editor." She taps her paw on the paper.

A cat park has been proposed in the city of Faunaburg. Its location is directly adjacent to Rodent Way. For generations rodents have lived in that section of the city. It's the one place we feel safe. We've scurried in the nearby fields for years. Our children play there. We've held school outings and Creator worship in those fields.

Two weeks ago, this newspaper ran an article describing plans for a cat park in what we consider our fields. While we do understand that the fields fell under the authority of city property, at least until they were purchased by Miguel Gato, they've been a part of Faunaburg's rodent culture for decades. It is disturbing to the rodent population that cats, of all creatures, feel it necessary to encroach on our space. If cats need a park in which to gather, could they not have found another location? One that would not destroy the feeling of safety and security we rodents have worked so hard to create for ourselves in an often-hostile world?

It is enough to make this rodent wonder if an ulterior motive exists. I've been assured by many that I am not alone in this speculation. Miguel Gato, the most wealthy and powerful cat in Faunaburg, somehow persuading the city to sell him that parcel so that a clowder of cats may suddenly descend upon the very edges of Rodent Way seems more than a little suspicious. It is all too believable that hiding behind the façade of an idyllic park lies a sinister monster. Rodent Way is now on high alert. Perhaps it begins with an innocent game of brusselball, but will it end in an organized mouse hunt? Will the clowder find strength in numbers for bigger game? You'll read of no such plans in the Faunaburg News, *but they now lurk in the back of every rodent's mind.*

We will not sit idly by while our one safe haven is invaded by marauding felines! I offer fair warning. The rodents of Rodent Way stand united. If the cats are sincere in their desire for a gathering place that has nothing to do with bothering rodents, we strongly urge them to consider another location. Otherwise, we will fight the creation of this park with every ounce of strength we possess. We've nowhere else to go and, therefore, nothing to lose.

> *Respectfully,*
> *Jerome J. Ratley, President*
> *Rodent Action Taskforce*
> *(R.A.T.)*

"Oh dear, this is a pickle!" Autumn folds the paper on her lap. "That reminds me. I need to add pickles to my grocery list."

"Autumn Amelia!"

"What?"

"Can't you see how disastrous this is? Why are you going on about pickles?" Smokey paces the living room floor.

"Sorry. What are you going to do?"

"I can't do anything. Miguel and Rufus will have to decide about changing the location. But this is exactly what I feared would happen. I tried to tell Rufus that the first day we walked the site together."

"Can the location be changed?"

"I don't know. Miguel's invested a lot of money in this project."

"You're still in the planning process. Nothing's actually been built yet."

"True, but he's also hired Fluffington's and a construction company. What if he can't find another location? What if the city won't buy it back?"

"Miguel is an astute businesscat," says Autumn. "I don't understand why he didn't foresee this."

Smokey stops pacing. "That's what bothers me. He should have known, yet he chose the property anyway."

"You don't think Miguel really has sinister plans, do you?"

"No. I mean, I don't know him that well, but his reputation has never been in question. He's very friendly with Ms. Fluffington and I know she'd never risk her business or her reputation on anything nefarious."

Smokey is quiet for a moment. "I do understand why Miguel likes this land parcel. It's ideal, except for being so close to Rodent Way. That's the only drawback, but it's a big one."

"If I remember right, the idea for a cat park came from Rufus Tailwagger, not Miguel. Rufus is a dog so the rodents can't blame the idea on cats."

"Yes," Smokey agree. "But Rufus didn't choose the location. That was Miguel."

Autumn picks up the paper. "Have you ever heard of this Jerome J. Ratley or the Rodent Task Force?"

"Ratley, yes. The R.A.T., no. They probably organized that as soon as they read about the park."

"So, who's Ratley? I'm assuming he's a rat, but what does he do?"

"He runs the Rodent Placement Agency. They help rodents find jobs. The organization does good work, but I hear he tends to be overzealous, not to mention a bit paranoid when it comes to cats, hawks, eagles, and the like."

"Can you blame him?"

"No, I suppose not." Smokey sighs. "On the other paw, he tends to assume we're all bad and won't think of giving any fur or feather a chance."

"How effective is he?"

"Very. He's one tough rat. And he's great at organizing. I'm sure he's got all of Rodent Way behind him. If Miguel won't change venues, we're in for a real fight."

Smokey's cell phone rings. It's Abigail Fluffington.

"Smokerina, have you read this morning's paper?"

"Yes, Ms. Fluffington. Autumn and I were just discussing Jerome Ratley's letter to the editor."

"I've called Miguel. We're meeting at his private club for lunch this afternoon along with Rufus Tailwagger to discuss this matter. Please arrive promptly at noon."

Smokey glances at her watch. It's already ten thirty. "I'll be there," she says. "Ms. Fluffington, what did Miguel say about the letter?"

"Not much. He didn't even want to meet until Monday, but I insisted. He told me I'm overreacting. Can you believe that? See you at noon. Don't be late."

"What was that about?" Autumn asks.

"I'm to be at Miguel's club for a lunch meeting with Abigail, Rufus, and Miguel at noon. I'll have to hurry. This is not exactly the way I planned to spend my Saturday afternoon," Smokey says as she runs upstairs to change.

* * *

"We must discuss damage control. Miguel, how do you plan to handle this?" Abigail's claws make tiny holes in the tablecloth.

Already nervous, Smokey feels ready to jump out of her skin at the sight of her boss's anxiety.

Miguel leans back in his chair. "Maxwell," he says to the Greyhound bartender. "We'll need drinks here." Looking at the others, he asks, "Niptini's for the cats and, Rufus, an Anisini for you?"

"Whatever," snaps Abigail. Rufus and Smokey nod.

"Miguel eyes the claw marks in the tablecloth. "Bone dry, if you please, Max."

Returning his attention to his guests, Miguel says, "I don't see why we're all so worried over one letter to the editor."

"Because it's a letter from Ratley," Abigail answers. "You know as well as the rest of us that he's already gone into activist mode. He's organizing right now."

"What if he is?" Miguel spreads his paws in a *so what?* gesture. "He can't do anything. That parcel is now private property. Mine."

Maxwell sets large glasses down at each place. Smokey takes a sip, then another. The knot in her stomach loosens a tad.

"That's not the point, Miguel," Abigail argues. "Even if he can't win, he can create a horrible problem. The PR will be bad. There will be backlash. We'll come out looking terrible. You know what he's like."

Miguel nods. "I've seen him work before."

"Then why aren't you worried?" Abigail stares at Miguel.

"I think you should try that niptini, Abigail. It will calm your nerves."

"If I may," Rufus interrupts. "Smokerina foresaw the likelihood of this very problem the first day we walked the grounds together. I didn't think much about it then, but now that I've seen Ratley's letter, I must confess I am concerned."

Miguel turns his attention to Rufus. "Does Ratley frighten you, Rufus?"

A low yelp escapes him. "Frighten me? Well, no, not exactly." For once Rufus's tail is perfectly still. "But the situation. Yes, the situation does concern me."

"And why is that?"

"It's bad PR. Very bad PR."

"So, you think we should forget it then?" Miguel asks. "Drop the whole idea because a rat said so?"

"Well, I…um…I don't know. I suppose we can't do that, but we must think of something. Suppose we found another location?"

Smokey has never seen Abigail or Rufus so distressed. The knot in her stomach begins to tighten again. She grabs her glass and downs half.

Miguel reaches across the table and taps her paw. "Easy, Smokerina. Maxwell makes those quite strong." Then he looks towards the bartender. "Max, would you pop into the kitchen and see how soon lunch will be served?" Turning back to his tablemates he says, "I hope you don't mind. This meeting was called so quickly I had to pull the staff in at a moment's notice, so I asked Gustav to make his salmon supreme. I hope that's to everyone's liking."

Murmurs of "of course," "it's fine", and "anything will do," pass around the table.

"Good," says Miguel. "I'm sure you'll all enjoy it. It's certainly one of my favorites, though I do wish your sister was here, Smokerina. I wonder how she'd improve it."

"Miguel, could we please get back to the issue at paw!" Abigail's tail, now wrapped around her body, thumps the table's edge.

Miguel sighs. "Very well. Frankly, I find it rather disappointing that one letter from Ratley has you all so agitated. I thought you were tougher than this.

Smokerina, you haven't said anything yet. What are your thoughts.?"

The butterflies in Smokey's stomach seem to have passed out thanks to the half-finished niptini. "There's something I'd like to ask you, Miguel."

"Ask away."

"You are a brilliant businesscat. You must have known putting a cat park so close to Rodent Way could cause a huge problem."

Miguel cocks the whiskers above one eye in a gesture of agreement.

"So, why did you do it? Were you purposely trying to antagonize the rodents?"

Rufus's eyes widen. Abigail kicks Smokey under the table.

Miguel laughs. "You are a very astute cat, Miss Smokerina."

Smokey is taken aback. "Is that a yes?" she asks.

"Not entirely," he answers. "I'm not out to antagonize anyone. Quite the opposite, actually."

"I don't understand." Smokey wishes she hadn't drunk half the niptini so fast.

Abigail's eyes narrow. "What exactly are you up to, Miguel?" she asks.

Returning from the kitchen, Maxwell whispers in Miguel's ear.

"Ah. Lunch is served," Miguel announces.

The waiter emerges from the kitchen. The mingling scents of salmon and lemon waft to Smokey's nose as the waiter sets a plate before her. Braised string beans with tomato and garlic take the place of the usual asparagus pairing.

"We're waiting?" Abigail stares at Miguel, barely seeming to notice the food in front of her.

"Wait no longer, my dear. Lunch is here." Miguel puts a forkful in his mouth, chews, and swallows. "Mm...and it's delicious!"

"You know what I mean, Miguel. What's going on?" Abigail demands.

"Your lunch is getting cold," Miguel tells her.

"I don't care about lunch!"

"Don't let Gustav hear that. Especially not after I made him come in on his day off." Miguel's eyes twinkle. "Smokerina, you seem to be enjoying your meal. Do tell Abigail not to let hers go to waste."

Smokey stops mid-chew. She'd sooner tell Gustav his salmon is spoiled than order her boss to eat her lunch.

Miguel laughs. "All right, all right. I'll answer your questions." He turns his attention to Abigail. "First of all, nothing is 'going on' as you put it. At least it wasn't at first."

He takes another bite before continuing. "After Rufus first proposed the cat park idea to me, I started looking at land parcels. I found a few that were okay, but not quite what I wanted. Then, one afternoon, I happened to be driving past the parcel in question. Funny, I wasn't even thinking about the cat park at that particular time."

He takes another bite. "Really, Abigail, you must eat before it gets cold."

"Very well, but you keep talking and stay on topic," she says before putting a piece of salmon into her mouth.

"As I passed that parcel of land, it struck me like a thunderbolt. I pulled over and walked around. Perfect size, excellent tree spacing, plenty of room for structures, fields stretching into the distance, good drainage so no mud puddles — no offense, Rufus. I thought, 'this is it! This is the perfect spot for the cat park.' The next day I went to the City and started negotiations. And that's all there is to it."

Abigail puts down her fork. "And while you were out there being inspired by this perfect piece of land, you never noticed the close proximity of Rodent Way?"

"Don't take me for a fool, Abigail," his voice grows stern and his eyes narrow, surprising Smokey. "I've lived in Faunaburg my entire life. I know precisely where Rodent Way begins and ends.”

Abigail leans forward, her blouse just a furs’ breadth from dipping into the sauce on her plate. “And it never occurred to you that that could be a problem?”

“Of course, it occurred to me. I fully expected it.”

All forks drop to their plates.

Smokey is the first to find words. “You *wanted* this to happen?

Miguel finishes the last bite of his lunch and takes a sip of his niptini. “Yes and no.”

“I’m sorry. I don’t follow. Am I missing something?” asks a flustered Rufus. “I thought…I mean you told me originally…that is, I understood that we’d have no problem building on that land. I’m not a cat. It must be that I don’t fully understand the situation.”

“None of us fully understand this situation and I, for one, would like a complete explanation, right now!” Abigail’s paw slams the table making the silverware jump.

“Careful, Abigail, you nearly spilled your niptini,” Miguel purrs.

“Miguel!”

Smokey grabs her own glass and downs the rest of it. “Miguel?” she asks.

His gaze leaves Abigail’s to rest on Smokey.

“I truly would like to understand,” Smokey keeps her tone even. She hardly believes she has the courage to ask her next question. “Are you looking for a fight?”

“Not a fight, Smokerina, though I’m sure that’s what we’ll start out with in one form or another. No, what I’m looking for is a resolution.”

“A resolution?” Abigail asks. “To what?”

Miguel leans back in his chair. “Abigail, how long would you say cats and rodents have been at odds with each other?”

"Forever, I suppose."

"Don't you think it's time that ended?"

Stunned silence engulfs the room.

"How...what?" Abigail stammers.

Miguel sighs. "My first thought upon recognizing the perfection of that land for a cat park was to dismiss the idea precisely because of the location. I almost did, too. Then I got to thinking. The only way cats and rodents are ever going to get along and learn to trust one another is if we begin interacting. I've tried over the years to engage Ratley, but he's impossible. However, other rodents have been much more responsive. The problem is that Ratley is their leader, so in the end they go along with whatever he decides."

"Excuse me. If I may?"

Miguel turns his attention to Rufus.

"So, you thought that a cat park, butting right up against Rodent Way would be a good idea?" Rufus shakes his head in confusion. "Again, I'm not a cat. I don't quite understand."

"It's like dogs and rabbits, Rufus," Miguel offers.

"Oh, yes. That I understand. That I quite understand. A dog park close to Rabbit Warren would never do, never do at all."

"That's just the point," Miguel continues. "A dog park next to Rabbit Warren would force the two together. The dogs and rabbits become neighbors. They get to know each other. They become friends."

"I don't know about that," says Rufus. "I don't think it would work."

"Why not? Rufus, would you do anything to harm a rabbit?"

"Me? Heavens no! I mean, of course, when they hop, I want to chase. It's an instinct thousands of years old. But it only lasts a second. I've no need to chase so the instinct passes almost before it begins and all's well."

"Why is that?"

"Hm…I suppose because I don't need to chase rabbits. Just look what I have to eat." He points to his plate. "It's not part of my survival. I believe the instinct is just an echo of long ago."

"Exactly," Miguel agrees. "But when a rabbit sees you, what happens?"

"Hop! Oh, they hop away fast. Disappear in the underbrush or down a warren, I suppose."

"Why?"

"They're afraid. They think I'm going to chase them."

"Does it hurt to think they fear you when you'd never do a thing to harm them? Do you wish you had a different relationship with rabbits?"

"It would be nice, I suppose, but I don't see how. I understand why they're afraid. It makes perfect sense. How are they to know I'm not going to chase them?"

"Do you have any rabbit friends at all?"

"No. None."

"Why not?"

"I told you. They don't trust me."

"Do any rabbits work in your office?"

"Not in my office, *per se*, but a few work in the building. They keep their distance, though."

"What would happen if you went out of your way to start a conversation with them?"

Rufus looks dumbfounded. "What would I talk to them about?"

"Work. The weather, Whatever. It doesn't matter. Just get the conversation going."

"I think they'd be suspicious."

"At first. But once you got to know one another you might become friends."

"Maybe." Rufus sounds anything but certain.

"Do me a favor. When you go to work on Monday, give it a try."

Rufus shrugs. "Okay."

Abigail clears her throat. "Miguel, could we bring this conversation back to the issue at paw. It seems we've gotten off topic again."

"Actually, we haven't. Those rabbits aren't going to come to Rufus because they're afraid of him. If he wants better relations with rabbits, he'll have to initiate it. It's the same thing with cats and rodents."

Smokey thinks this over as the waiter clears away their dishes and replaces them with key lime bars and whipped cream.

"Miguel, I think I understand where you're going with this," she says. "I'm just not sure that forcing the issue in this manner is the best idea. I mean, I would be terrified if coyotes took over the land that abutted my cottage. Frankly, I don't know what I'd do. Move away, probably. And it would only fuel my anger and bitterness towards them." Then in a very low voice she adds, "They killed my father, you know."

Miguel reaches across the table to take her paw. "Oh, Miss Smokerina, I didn't know. I am so very sorry."

"Thank you," she replies.

He continues softy. "You know that if coyotes did move in near you, they wouldn't be the same ones that killed your father."

"I know, but they're all the same. Coyotes kill cats. Period. Even if there are some who wouldn't, I couldn't take that chance. I couldn't stand to have them near me."

Miguel's tone remains soft. "I don't mean to be indelicate, but you are friends with many dogs, Smokerina. Coyotes belong to the canine family. Clearly, you have managed some level of tolerance."

Smokey glances at Rufus who stares down at his untouched key lime bar.

"It was coyotes. Not dogs. They may be in the same family, but they are not the same. It would be like blaming me for something a mountain lion did."

She reaches over and pats Rufus's paw. A tear slides down his nose.

"It's okay, Rufus. Really." She tries to assure him.

"I understand what you mean, Smokerina,' Rufus admits. "And I appreciate it, but the fact remains that coyotes and dogs are related. Even some cats and dogs still don't get along."

"But here we all sit at this table sharing a meal and a conversation," says Miguel. "I want all animals to be able to do that."

"Miguel, I applaud your altruism. Truly, I do," Abigail interjects. "But I am very concerned that this is not the appropriate way to go about it. While your heart was certainly in the right place, I cannot fathom where your head was when you made this decision. It will be nothing but a PR nightmare and may bring about far more problems than it solves."

"Abigail, I admit it is a very unorthodox approach, but sometimes those are the ones that work best. If you worry that I'm losing my business edge, don't. I didn't get where I am by fearing to take risks. I realize this is a big one, but one I believe is worthwhile."

Smokey picks up her key lime bar, licking at the powdered sugar. "Miguel, if you want to do something to improve feline and rodent relations, couldn't you come up with another method, that isn't quite so...in your whiskers?" she asks.

Miguel chuckles. "I would have loved to, Smokerina. The problem is that we are dealing with Ratley. Every effort, every overture I've ever made has been squashed by that rat."

"So, you are doing this to spite him?" Smokey asks.

"Hardly. When I decided on that parcel of land it wasn't with the idea of riling up Ratley even though there was no question in my mind that it would. I didn't do it to spite him. I did it to win him over."

"How?"

"By proving that cats and rodents can peacefully coexist. Make no mistake, we are in for a fight, but we're not fighting for our rights as cats to have a park wherever we want one. We're fighting for kinship with our fellow creatures. And we've got a lot of work to do to make that happen. Now, if everyone has finished their dessert, I think it's time to adjourn this meeting and get on with our Saturday afternoon."

Abigail puts up a paw. "Just one question, Miguel. Why didn't you tell me or Rufus any of this before we started this project?"

"If I had, would you have agreed?"

"Oh, Great Creator in Heaven, no!"

"That's why." He smiles. "Now, we all have lots of thinking and planning to do. We will need other meetings to decide how to proceed, but I'd prefer they be scheduled during regular business hours."

All the way home Smokey keeps replaying the lunch conversation in her mind. As she pulls into the driveway the thought occurs to her, *I'm not just designing a cat park. I'm now an activist in interspecies relations. Oh my catness, how did I ever get into this?"*

Chapter Seventeen

A Day Out

No sooner had Smokey left the house for her lunch meeting, than Autumn Amelia was on her way to take Dusty on her first outing.

As they step outside the apartment building, Dusty wraps both paws tightly around Autumn's tail.

"What are you doing?" Autumn asks.

"Holding on. I can't go anywhere if I don't hold on to you." Dusty's voice quivers. "If you won't let me hold your tail, I won't go."

"But we just went over this." Before leaving the apartment, Autumn had spread out an enlarged street map of the section of the city they would cover this afternoon. Dusty had no problem understanding the map. The two had already discussed pitching Dusty's miniature textiles to Tamarind. When Autumn realized that Tonk's Treasures was within walking distance she decided to make that their destination. Dusty was to find her way using the map.

"I thought I could do it, but now that I'm outside I'm scared." She scrunches the map in her paws as they grip Autumn's tail, her handbag hanging from the crook of her arm.

Autumn turns to face Dusty, her tail wrapping her body as Dusty does not let go. "That will defeat the purpose," she explains. "The only way you'll overcome your fear is if you can find your way around yourself. You can follow that map. I'm going to stay with you so there's nothing to worry about."

Dusty begins to shake. "I can't do it, Autumn. Please don't make me let go."

"I have an idea," says Autumn. "Give me the map."

"It's right here. Take it." Dusty shakes Autumn's tail indicating the crumpled map under her paws.

"Autumn sighs. "Dusty, you can let go long enough to give me the map. Besides, you're starting to pull my tail and your pocketbook keeps bumping me."

"Sorry." Dusty releases one paw. "Can you grab it? Once you take hold of it, I'll put my paw back on your tail and then let go with the other paw so you can get the map without tearing it."

Oh, for catness sake! Autumn thinks but agrees in order to extricate the map. She smooths out the creases against the side of the apartment building.

"What's gotten into you, Dusty? Don't you remember the evening you were able to walk the whole block by yourself? You were so excited. What happened?"

"The more I thought about going further on my own, the more nervous I got. I started having nightmares about getting lost again."

"But you must still want to do it. You didn't cancel."

"I do, but I'm scared. Besides, I made a promise."

"What promise? To whom?"

"Abby."

"What promise did you make to her?"

"Before she left for her lunch meeting, she made me promise that while I'm out with you I'll hold your tail the whole time."

"She did?"

"Uh-huh. She said she has some very complicated problems with a work project and the last thing she needs is to have to call the Bloodhound League again."

"Hmph! As if we'd need the Bloodhound League. Doesn't she think I know what I'm doing?"

"I'm sure she didn't mean anything against you, Autumn. Anyway, she made me say these exact words before she left: 'I, Dusty Fluffington, promise not to physically detach myself from Autumn Amelia the entire time we're out."

"You must be joking." Autumn pictures Dusty standing with one paw raised, the other over her heart with a stern Abigail Fluffington staring her down while she repeats the silly oath.

"No, I'm not. I had to say it. She made me."

"And I thought Smokey was bossy!"

Dusty looks wide-eyed at Autumn. "Smokerina bosses you around?"

"She tries. Honestly, I used to think Smokey was the bossiest cat the Creator ever made, but your sister takes the tuna!"

"Autumn, do you see why I have to hold your tail? I promised. And I'm scared."

Autumn straightens up to her full height. Paws on hips, she says, "I'll tell you what we're going to do. You're going to take this map. You're going to hold it in *both* paws. And you're going to find your way to Tonk's Treasure just like we discussed in your kitchen."

"But Autumn—"

"And" Autumn continues. "I will hold your tail the whole time. That way you can keep your promise of not detaching from me." She rolls her eyes. "And learn your way around at the same time. Does that solve the problem?"

Dusty thinks for a moment. "You won't let go?"

"Nope."

"Not even for a second?"

"Absolutely not."

"What if I get lost?"

"I'll let you know if you start going in the wrong direction. But you'll have to figure out how to get back on track on your own. It's the only way you'll learn and gain confidence."

"But you won't let go? No matter what?"

Autumn raises her right paw. "I, Autumn Amelia, do hereby promise I will not let go of your tail for any reason whatsoever, even if my very life depends upon it."

Dusty laughs. "Okay."

"Good. Now take the map. Figure out what direction to go and start walking."

Autumn hands the map to Dusty and takes hold of her tail.

Dusty studies the map, looks around, then points down the street. "This way?"

"That's right. Let's go."

They move slowly at first as Dusty stops often to consult the map, check street signs, and ask Autumn if she's still going in the right direction. Though it takes about fifteen minutes longer than necessary, they finally arrive in front of Tonk's Treasures. The little storefront is one of several quaint specialty shops that line the city's side streets.

"We're here! We made it!" Dusty bounces on her toes in excitement.

"I told you, you could do it," Autumn says. "You didn't even need my help. All you needed was the map and your own perfectly capable brain. Take that, Abigail Fluffington!"

Dusty giggles.

"Before we go inside, let's go over what we talked about," says Autumn.

"I'm going to introduce myself to Tamarind," Dusty states. "You're sure your friend told her about me?"

"Positive. I talked to Sukey on the phone yesterday. She said she told Tamarind all about our conversation and she's looking forward to meeting you. Just tell her about your work and show her your samples."

Dusty pats her handbag containing the miniature textiles she's brought with her. "How do I look?" she asks, smoothing her long Persian fur.

"Extremely silly with me holding your tail."

"Oh. I guess you don't have to do that now that we're here."

"Thank goodness!"

Once inside the shop Autumn's senses immediately overload.

"There certainly is a lot of stuff in here," Dusty whispers as they enter. "It's awfully small and crowded."

Autumn wonders how to make her way around the shop without knocking over anything. Shelves are stacked high as are freestanding displays. The limited floor space offers only narrow paths to maneuver through.

Though the shop is congested, Autumn notices that everything is perfectly organized. Scented lotions, perfumes, and soaps are in one area, clothing, and accessories in another, treats and decorative household items sit on a display table in the center of the store.

"Those? Oh, I just got those in. They're flying off the shelves. I can tell already I won't be able to restock fast enough." The voice across the room comes from a cream-colored cat with a chocolate face and big blue eyes.

"That must be Tamarind," Autumn whispers to Dusty, motioning towards the cat behind the counter who is talking to a Cornish Rex holding a black felt pocketbook with colorful embroidery.

"And just look at those wallets on the table next to them. Funky cool, huh? You can find one to match the pocketbook. Here, I'll show you."

Tamarind comes out from behind the counter. She strides towards the Rex, easily negotiating the twists and turns around the displays in her path.

"She's gorgeous!" Dusty whispers, a little too loudly.

Tamarind's head turns in their direction. "Oh, hi, ladies!" She waves a paw at them. "I didn't see you come in. Take a look around and let me know if you need any help."

Autumn and Dusty peruse the store, taking it all in, but don't actually move.

"I'm afraid to budge," Autumn admits. "With all my fur, I'm sure to knock something over."

"Don't worry," they hear Tamarind call, though they can no longer see her as she's obscured by a display. "It's very crowded. Stuff gets knocked over all the time. I just put it back up and go on, so no worries," she assures them.

"Oh, you've just got to get this one. Look how the colors match the embroidery." Tamarind's attention is back with her wallet-shopping customer.

The door opens behind Autumn and Dusty.

"We'd better move," Dusty whispers as a German Shepherd couple enters. The cats step to the side as the dogs move in behind them.

"I wish she'd do something about the lighting in here," the male Shepherd mumbles.

"Hush, dear. The low lights add to the atmosphere."

"You can tell a cat owns this place. They don't need much light, but I can hardly see where I'm going. It's so crowded I'm surprised I haven't knocked anything over yet."

"It's exotic and the lighting helps create the ambiance. And it's only crowded because there's so much wonderful stuff," his wife explains. "You don't seem to mind the dim light in that stinky cigar shop down the street."

"Yoo-hoo! Hi, Hildegard! Nice to see you." Tamarind is back behind the counter ringing up the Cornish Rex's purchases. "And you, too, Otto."

"Hello, dear!" Hildegard calls back. "Otto, why don't you go down to the cigar store and I'll meet you outside in a bit," she says to her husband.

"Don't mind if I do."

The Cornish Rex brushes past them as she leaves. Autumn notices her bag has much more than just a pocketbook and wallet.

"Tamarind's certainly a good salescat," she whispers to Dusty. "That bodes well for you."

"I'll bet you're here for that special shampoo you like so much," Tamarind says, once again coming out from behind the counter.

"You know me too well," says Hildegard. "But I'd also like to get a little something for my niece. She just had her first litter. Four pups."

"How exciting! Have you seen them yet?"

"No. We'll be going tomorrow, and I want to bring something special for them."

"I've got the perfect thing. They just came in last week. Look at this." She grabs a small squeak toy from a bin. "I know they're too young to play with them yet, but it won't be long, and you know how puppies love to chew. These are tough enough to handle all the chewing a pup can give. Plus, they are totally safe, no small parts or toxic colorants. And look, you can choose from a variety of shapes so you can get a different one for each pup."

"They're so cute!" exclaims Hildegard. "I'm going to look through the bin and find four I really like."

"You go for it, honey. Oh, and if you want to get something for the new mom, I've got a wonderful cream. You know how sore you can get from nursing? Well, she just puts this cream on after the puppies are done feeding and all that soreness magically disappears. She'll love it."

"Really? I wish they'd had that in my day."

"I'll get it so you can take a look. The ingredients are all natural so there's nothing to worry about for mom or the pups." Tamarind sweeps around two displays, grabs a tube of cream, and brings it to Hildegard. "Here you go."

Autumn is mesmerized by watching Tamarind. She moves around her store with precision, easily locating every item. Her cheery voice and infectious laugh boost the spirits. *She's a living shot of catnip* Autumn thinks.

The idea of catnip suddenly makes Autumn's nose twitch. She sniffs the air. Following the scent, she weaves in and out of tightly packed display stands until she stops at a shelf in a corner of the store. Dusty taps her on the shoulder.

"What are you doing, Autumn?"

"I smelled cooking spices. Look, a whole shelf of them."

"Can I help you, ladies?" They turn to see Tamarind standing beside them.

"My name is Dusty Fluffington. This is my friend, Autumn Amelia."

"You're the seamstress Sukey told me about, right?"

"Yes."

"I'm so glad you stopped in. I've been hoping you would."

"I'm going to take these four toys," Hildegard calls from across the store. "And the cream."

"Hold on," Tamarind says to Dusty and Autumn. "Let me take care of this customer and I'll be right back." Grabbing a bottle from the shelf on her way back to Hildegard, she says, "Don't forget your shampoo."

Once the German Shepherd is rung up and out the door, Tamarind returns. "Sukey said you make miniature textiles. I'd love to see them."

"I do, but I also make regular size clothes." Dusty says, eying the clothing hanging on the opposite wall. "I made the outfit I'm wearing."

"No way!" Tamarind looks her over. "I would never have dreamed that was handmade. You're certainly talented. I'm starting to grow my clothing line. I just started about a month ago and it's proving very popular. I'm hoping to talk the landlord into knocking out part of that back wall so I can have a little changing room. As you can tell, it's far too crowded in here. But things just fly off the shelves and I can't say no when I find something great that I want to share with my customers."

"You do have a lot of interesting things. I could spend all afternoon just looking," Dusty says.

"Thanks. That's so sweet. But I want to hear about what you have to offer. Why don't I show you the miniatures I have for sale, and we'll see if they're a good fit?"

"If you don't mind, I'm going to continue looking through your spices," says Autumn as Tamarind ushers Dusty to another part of the store.

At first Autumn can hear their conversation. Dusty exclaims over the miniature furniture. "Just look how well my little tablecloth and napkins would go. They're a perfect fit for that table." Autumn hears the click as the clasp on Dusty's handbag opens and knows she's pulling out her samples.

"Adorable!" she hears Tamarind exclaim.

Before long, their voices blur until they're gone completely. All of Autumn's senses are focused on the spices lined up before her. She recognizes most of them, but there are a few that are new to her. *Hmm…*she thinks. *I know truffle oil, but truffle salt? And what's this? Fennel pollen? Asafetida? Urfa biber? I have to find out about these.* She picks up each jar, reads the labels for origins and recommended uses. Her head starts spinning with recipe ideas.

But something keeps nagging at Autumn's nose. Another aroma she's unfamiliar with smells intoxicating. Yet it doesn't seem to be coming from any of the spices on the shelf. She tries to block the other scents so she can follow the one she's singled out. She crouches down. It grows stronger the lower she goes.

Autumn jumps when she feels a tap on her shoulder.

Dusty and Tamarind have returned to find her on the floor with her nose pressed against the base of the display case.

"It's in here," she says.

"What's in there?" Dusty asks.

"I don't know, but whatever it is, it's definitely in there. I can smell it."

"Autumn, that's amazing!" It's Tamarind's voice behind her. "Sukey told me what a culinary genius you are; how you can tell the ingredients of a dish just by one taste or even a sniff, but I would never have believed this if I hadn't seen it with my own eyes."

"What are you talking about?" Dusty asks.

"Autumn, you smell an herb you don't recognize, don't you?" Tamarind asks.

"I smell something edible. Yes, I'd say it's an herb. It reminds me of catnip, but, somehow, it's different." Autumn's nose is still pressed against the case.

"That's because..." Tamarind walks behind the case sliding herself into the small space between the display and the wall... "it's where I keep the matatabi."

"What's matatabi?" Dusty asks.

"It is..." Tamarind's voice trails off again as she disappears below the display shelf. Hearing keys jangle they realize she's unlocking the stand from the other side. "...a very potent herb, similar to catnip, but much stronger." Tamarind pops up holding a tray. In it lay several clear packages. Some hold long sticks, others a powdered substance, and still others little bits that look like fruit pits.

"That's it!" Autumn exclaims. "That's what I smelled. What are they?"

"Matatabi. Another name for them is silvervine. They originate from the other side of the world, though you can grow them here, too, if you know how."

"Why do you keep them locked up?" asks Dusty. "Aren't they legal?"

"Oh, my catness, of course they're legal. I wouldn't dream of risking my business selling anything that wasn't legal. I keep them locked up because if I don't, they'll disappear on me."

"You mean they get stolen?" Dusty is aghast.

"I honestly don't think any cat means to steal them. It's just that they are so potent and so attractive, cats can't seem to resist. I lock them up as much to keep myself from diving into them. Besides, I sometimes have kittens in here and I don't want them getting into it. Though, they might not even be interested. It's like catnip — not particularly attractive to really young kittens. But once they start to reach adolescence, watch out!"

"It's that good?" Dusty asks.

Tamarind nods. "But strong. I mean really strong."

"They're not dangerous?"

"No, Dusty. But I wouldn't eat any and then drive a car or try to make an important decision."

"Can you use them in cooking?" asks Autumn.

"Sure. I think they're best in desserts but be warned. A little goes a long way. You could sprinkle a bit of the powder into a cake, poke a fruit — that's what the ones that look like pits are called — into a muffin, or my favorite, shave some from the sticks into a cup of hot chocolate. I'm certain you'd come up with some really great ways to use them, Autumn."

"I sure would like to try them."

"Since no one else is in the store right now, I'll give you a teensy taste. Then you can decide if you want to buy some."

Tamarind puts the tray on the counter and unties one of the bags of powdered matatabi. She sprinkles a miniscule amount onto the counter. "Wet your paw with your tongue to pick up the powder, then lick it," she instructs.

Immediately upon licking the matatabi Autumn's tastebuds dance. A poof of air seems to pop in her brain. "Wow!" she says. "That's amazing!"

"Pretty good, huh?" says Tamarind. "Now you know why I keep it locked up."

"How long does it last?" asks Autumn.

"An amount that small, only a minute or so."

"Any aftereffects?"

"Not from that much, but if you used it in a dessert, you'd use more. Then you'd get that euphoric feeling for a bit longer. I tend to get the giggles. Later I fall asleep, but I always wake up feeling refreshed. It's actually quite healthy for you. As long as you use it in moderation, of course."

"Dusty, you've got to try it," Autumn urges.

"Want to?" Tamarind asks her.

"You're sure it's safe?"

"It's as safe as catnip, just stronger. You've had catnip before, haven't you?"

"Only a few times. My sister doesn't like me to have it. She's afraid it will make me forget what I'm doing and leave the apartment."

"That's it, you are definitely trying some," Autumn insists. "Don't worry. I can already feel it wearing off."

"Well, okay," Dusty agrees, though there's a note of uneasiness in her voice.

"You'll love it," says Tamarind as she pours out the same amount.

Dusty licks her paw, places it on the matatabi powder then tentatively brings it to her mouth. She sticks out her tongue just enough to barely touch her paw, but a little of the dust dances onto her tongue. Her eyes widen. She stares at her paw with most of the dust still sticking to it. "That's good," she says, giving her paw a thorough lick. "Really good!"

Autumn and Tamarind laugh. "Told you," Autumn says.

"Wow! I feel great! I think I want to dance!"

"Not in here," says Autumn. "You'll knock the whole place down." The three of them dissolve in laughter. Within moments, the effects have worn off and Dusty is back to normal.

"What do you think, Autumn?" asks Tamarind. "Do you want to buy some?"

"Absolutely! I'll take a bag of powder, a bag of fruits, and a bag of sticks. I'm also going to get a jar of each of your spices. I need to restock my spice cabinet and I found a bunch I've never heard of. I can't wait to try them."

Tamarind grabs a wicker basket. Handing it to Autumn she says, "Fill it up with whatever you want."

As Autumn piles up her basket, she asks, "What did you two decide about Dusty's miniature textiles?"

"I love them and think they'll sell so I'm going to take some on consignment. I'm just not sure about the idea of selling to rodents. I do think my regular customers who buy miniatures will love them, though."

"Why don't you want to sell to rodents?" Autumn asks.

"It's not that I don't want to. It's just that none shop here. I mostly get cats and dogs, with the occasional rabbit. Once a great blue heron stopped in, but she was vacationing from out of town."

"Would you welcome rodents if they came?"

"Of course. I welcome every customer. But I think it's unlikely. They're afraid of cats so they really don't want to shop at a cat-owned store. Besides most of them are nocturnal. I'm only open late two nights a week. Even then it's still light out when I close except for in winter."

"Squirrels and chipmunks are rodents. They're out in the daytime," Autumn points out.

"True. But I've never had any stop in."

"What if you advertised that you have something of interest to rodents? Wouldn't that help?"

Tamarind cocks her head. "Maybe, but I honestly can't see spending money on advertising that I don't think will work. I have to think of what makes good business sense."

"If you developed a rodent clientele, that would boost your sales, wouldn't it?" asks Dusty.

"I'll tell you what," says Tamarind. "If you can talk any of your rodent friends into shopping here maybe they'd start spreading the word. If I start to get enough rodent customers to make advertising to them pay off, I'll seriously consider it. Meanwhile, I'm afraid I'll have to market the miniature textiles to collectors and kittens and puppies for their dollhouses."

"That seems fair enough," Dusty agrees.

Tamarind finishes ringing up Autumn's order. "It was so nice to meet you ladies," she says, a wide smile lighting up her face. "I can't wait for next week!"

"What's next week?" asks Autumn.

"I'm going to bring in some stock for Tamarind to put on display," Dusty tells her.

"Don't forget to bring a few outfits for cats and dogs to add to my new clothing line, too," Tamarind calls as they head out the door.

Standing outside the shop, Autumn asks Dusty, "When are you coming back with your textiles?"

"Tamarind said to come on Tuesday. It's her slowest day so we should have time to set things up."

"How are you going to get here?"

"Well…I was hoping…" A pleading look appears on Dusty's face. "Would you come with me?"

"Tuesday's a workday for me."

Dusty drops her gaze to the ground. "I know. I shouldn't have asked."

"You can do it yourself. You followed the map to get here. There's no reason you can't do it again."

"But I'd be alone. What if I get lost? Besides, Abby will never let me. Oh, Autumn, what am I going to do?"

"You're going to bring your textiles here on Tuesday."

"How?"

"The same way you got here today. As for Abigail, don't tell her. She'll be at work, so she won't know."

"You mean lie to her?"

"I mean keep your business to yourself. You're a grown cat, Dusty. She doesn't have to run your life. It will be good for her to find out that you're perfectly capable of doing things on your own."

"I don't know."

"It's either that or lose your chance at selling your stock. It may be a tiny store, but that cat sure knows how to sell. You shouldn't let this opportunity slip through your paws."

"I'm still nervous about finding my way."

"The only way to overcome that is to do it. Where's that map, anyway? Let's see how you do getting us back to your apartment."

While Dusty searches her pocketbook for the map, Autumn rummages through her shopping bag looking over her spices. "I can't wait to try these," she says. "Especially the matatabi. They remind me of cinnamon sticks. I think the shavings would be great in hot chocolate, but they'd also go well as a decoration on cakes."

Autumn pulls out the bag of matatabi sticks, undoes the twist and pulls one out. "They smell a little different from the powdered version. The aroma is stronger."

"Here it is," Dusty says, pulling the map from her purse. She points to a spot on the map, then looks up the street. "We came from that direction," she says, indicating the street they'd come down. "We should go back that way, then take a left at the end of the street, right?"

"I could use it like chocolate shavings on a cake. I wonder what else I could do with it," Autumn says, absent-mindedly popping the end of the stick in her mouth.

"Autumn, please look."

"What? Oh, yes. That's the right way to go. You know the stick tastes a little different from the powder. Here, try a bite." She breaks off a piece and hands it to Dusty.

"Do you think we should?"

"I'm sure that little bit won't hurt."

"It really does taste good," Dusty admits. "Don't forget to hold my tail."

"Uh-huh," says Autumn, one paw on Dusty's tail, the other holding her shopping bag. With no free paw she pops the matatabi stick in her mouth and continues to suck on it while ruminating on possible recipes.

"You know what, Autumn," Dusty announces, glancing again at the map. "There's more than one way to get back. Let's go home a different way."

"Matatabi lava cake!" exclaims Autumn around the stick as they head down the street in the opposite direction.

"I like Tamarind, don't you?" Dusty asks.

"She's super friendly," Autumn agrees.

"I wish I was sleek and floofless like her. It's supposed to be glamorous to be a Persian, but for me it's just a lot of fur to un-mat every day and floof to slip on."

"Did I tell you about the time I slid off the shelf in my pantry?" Autumn asks.

"You did," Dusty says, with a giggle.

"It's funny now when I think about it." Autumn giggles too. An image of herself sliding around the pantry shelves comes to mind. Suddenly, she can't control her laughter.

"It's not that funny, Autumn," says Dusty.

"Yes, it is. Have some more of this and you'll see." She breaks off a piece of another matatabi stick and gives it to Dusty. Within a moment, she too is laughing uncontrollably.

The two cats wander down alleyways and sides streets, nearly tripping over each other all the way.

When she can catch her breath, Dusty checks the map again. "Up this street?" she asks, pointing to a dirt path across from them.

"Sounds good to me," Autumn says, giving neither the map nor the path a glance.

They are quiet for a moment as they walk, but suddenly Autumn starts to laugh again.

"What's funny now?" Dusty asks.

"Do you know Rufus Tailwagger?"

"Sure. He's been to the apartment a few times."

"I just pictured him in Tonk's. Imagine what his tail would do to that store."

"I can't."

"Close your eyes."

Dusty stops walking and shuts her eyes.

"Now picture it," Autumn instructs.

Dusty's closed eyes scrunch up tight. Within seconds she's doubled over with laughter.

"See what I mean?" says Autumn.

"Hey, where did all these trees come from?" Dusty asks as they continue to walk. "I don't remember this many trees on the way to Tonk's."

"We're taking a different route home, remember?"

"Oh, yeah. I'd better check the map." Dusty stops walking, but sways on her feet. "I can't figure this out. There are no trees on this map."

"Maps don't have trees. Just streets."

"Then how do I know if I'm going in the right direction? If the trees are on the street, they should be on the map."

"Oh, wait," says Autumn. "I see the problem. The map is upside down."

Dusty looks around. "It can't be."

"Why not?"

"Because the trees aren't upside down. If the map is upside down, shouldn't the trees be upside down, too?"

"I told you trees don't have maps."

"That's right. They only have wings."

"Wings? You've had too much matatoborbi."

"Too much what?"

"Mastafusi."

"Oh. That. What should we do now?"

"You wanna climb a tree?"

Dusty tips her head back, looking up to the top of the nearest tree. "Wow! That's really tall. That's the tallest tree in the world. It goes all the way to the clouds." She points a paw skyward. "I don't think I could climb all the way to the clouds," she says and falls over backwards.

"Are you sleeping?" Autumn asks.

"I don't think so."

"Then why are you lying down?"

"The tree pushed me."

"Trees can't push. They don't have arms. Oh, wait. Maybe they do. I can't remember. You'd better get up."

Dusty, flat on her back, continues to stare at the treetops. "I can't," she says. "The trees won't let me."

"I'll help you," says Autumn. She bends over Dusty, loses her balance, and falls on her face.

"Oops. That didn't work," Autumn says. "I'll try again."

"Whatever you do, don't look at the trees. They'll hold you down."

"Okay," says Autumn. Keeping her focus on the ground, she pushes herself up onto all fours. A light breeze ruffles the fur on her back.

Dusty starts laughing hysterically, kicking her feet in the air.

"What now?" asks Autumn.

"The leaves are tickling me," Dusty gasps.

Autumn tries to stand, but tips over backwards. Gales of laughter pour forth. "They're tickling me, too," she says. Both cats laugh uproariously, waving their paws helplessly in the air.

Once their fits subside, Autumn pushes herself to a sitting position. After looking around she says, "Dusty, I'm very sorry to tell you this, but I think we're lost."

Dusty, still on her back, responds, "Autumn, I'm very happy to tell you this. I don't care."

The two dissolve into laughter again until tears run down their faces.

Dusty nudges Autumn. "I think we need the bloodhounds."

"You're right," says Autumn. "Let's go get them."

After much tripping over each other, they struggle to their feet.

"Where do they live?" asks Dusty.

"Who?" asks Autumn.

"The bloodhounds."

"This way," says Autumn as she leads Dusty off the path, into the woods.

After wandering for a while, they hear barking in the distance. Coming into a clearing, they see a group of dogs playing in a park.

"See. Told you," says Autumn.

"They don't look like bloodhounds."

Emerging from the woods, they're nearly knocked over by a Rottweiler jumping to catch a Frisbee in his mouth.

"Sorry," says the Rottie. "Didn't see you there."

"Are we invisible?" Dusty whispers to Autumn.

"I hope not, or the bloodhounds will never find us," Autumn whispers back.

A pit bull runs over to join his friend. "What's with the cats?" he asks.

"I don't know. They just came out of the woods."

"Can we help you?" asks the pit bull.

"We're looking for some bloodhounds," Dusty answers.

"What for?" asks the Rottweiler.

"We're lost and we want to see if they can find us," Autumn says.

The dogs exchange glances. "Nipsters!" says the pit bull, shaking his head. "Where's a Police Dog when you need one?"

"We are not nipsters," Dusty asserts. Indignant, she attempts to straighten up, but only staggers into Autumn.

"That's right," Autumn agrees. "We're matawbasters."

"We're what?" asks Dusty.

"Mabatabasters? Mustawfeters? Matabistifers? What's that stuff called again?"

"What stuff?" asks Dusty.

"I don't know. You asked."

"That's it," says the pit bull. I'm calling a Police Dog." He reaches for his cell phone but is stopped by a yell from across the field.

"Autumn Amelia! Dusty!"

"Another cat?" says the Rottweiler, catching sight of a Siamese running towards them. A Jack Russell terrier joins in beside her.

"Autumn. Dusty. Thank goodness I've found you."

"Sukey!" Autumn exclaims. "What are you doing here?"

"Don't you know this is a dog park?" asks the Rottweiler, annoyance in his voice.

"Hey! My sister designed this park. She designed dog parks all over this city." Autumn pokes his shoulder. "So, you'd better be grateful because if she'd never been born, your Frisbee wouldn't even exist."

The terrier cocks his head in wonder.

"Come on, girls. Let's get you home. My car is over there in the lot." Sukey puts an arm around each cat, guiding them across the field. "Sorry, fellas," she calls to the dogs. "Just a little misunderstanding. We'll get right out of your way."

"How did you find us?" Autumn asks as they climb into Sukey's car.

"Tamarind called me. Luckily, she glanced out the store window in time to see the two of you chewing matatabi sticks and heading towards the dog park. She was afraid something would happen. Since she couldn't leave the store, she got on the phone to me. I'm glad I found you before you wandered off in some other direction."

"You didn't need to worry," says Dusty. "The trees wouldn't let us go anyway."

"Uh-huh," says Sukey. "Let's get you home fast. I hope you can remember your address."

"Um…" Dusty thinks for a minute. "Nope. Oh, wait. Big apartment building. That's it."

"Great."

"Don't worry. It's in my phone," says Autumn. She fiddles with her phone for a moment then hands it to Sukey.

"Autumn, that's your address."

"Do you want me to find yours?"

Sukey pulls over, "Give me your phone." She scrolls until she finds what she's looking for. "Got it," she says.

Once inside the apartment, Autumn and Dusty collapse on the couch, barely able to keep their eyes open.

"Autumn, I can't stay so promise me you won't drive home until you've completely slept it off." Autumn hears Sukey's voice as if it's coming down a long tunnel.

"I promise," she says. That's all she remembers until she awakens just as the sun is beginning to set.

Autumn sits up. Her head is clear. She feels as though she's had the best rest of her life.

"Dusty?" she calls.

"Right here," says Dusty, coming down the hallway. "I woke up a few minutes ago. Tamarind was right. You do wake up feeling very refreshed."

"Is your sister home?" Autumn asks.

"No, but there was a message from her on the voice mail. She went into the office to work after the lunch meeting. She'll probably be home anytime now."

"I think I'd better go. But first I want to do something. Do you have a little bag?"

"What do you want it for?" asks Dusty coming out of the kitchen with a small paper bag.

"I'm giving you some ammunition." Autumn pours half of the matatabi powder into the bag. "The next time Abigail starts bossing you around or saying you can't do something, slip her some of this."

Chapter Eighteen

The First Meeting

"Are you ready, Smokerina?" Abigail pokes her head into Smokey's office.

"Ready as I'll ever be." Smokey takes a deep breath, pushing herself up from the desk.

Abigail steps inside, shutting the door behind her. "Smokerina, a word, please."

"Yes, Ms. Fluffington?" The stern expression on Abigail's face worries her.

"You look nervous."

In minutes Smokey will be the main presenter in a meeting with Abigail, Rufus, Miguel, and Jerome J. Ratley.

"A little," she admits.

Abigail steps closer, nose to nose with Smokey. Her fur billows out as though forming a fluffy shield. "Don't let it show," she commands. "I don't mean to be rude, but you are the neophyte here and Ratley knows it. He'll do everything he can to unsettle you. You're playing in the big leagues now. If you expect to take over this firm when I retire, you'll need to prove your mettle. Let's see what you've got."

With that Abigail heads for the door. If she meant that as a pep talk, it failed. Now Smokey isn't only afraid of Ratley, she's afraid of not living up to Abigail's expectations, maybe even losing her chance at obtaining her dream.

Abigail has been miffed ever since Autumn's outing with Dusty. Talk about their matatabi adventure circulated through Miguel's club staff eventually reaching Miguel himself who apparently related it to Abigail, thinking the whole thing hysterical. By the time it reached her it bore little resemblance to what really happened. Abigail was not amused and became concerned that Autumn was not a good influence on Dusty. Abigail tried to forbid Dusty from anymore outings with Autumn, but Dusty astounded her by asserting that she had every right to go where she wanted and with whomever she pleased.

"She's an innocent. She doesn't understand the dangers of the world," Abigail had told Smokey. "Your sister means well, I'm sure," she said in a tone indicating she might well think otherwise. "However, she has rendered a change in Dusty that greatly concerns me. Do you know she left the apartment one day with a suitcase full of clothing? She said she was taking them to sell at some boutique. And she walked right out the door. By herself. In front of me!"

"But isn't that a good thing?" Smokey had asked.

Abigail's eyes grew big. "You don't simply understand. She knows nothing of business. I don't have time to check into this so-called boutique to make sure she's not being taken advantage of. I hope she doesn't come to ruin."

"Perhaps she'll be a success. She is an amazing seamstress."

"That's true but she is not a businesscat. She could easily be exploited. I so wish your sister hadn't filled her head with unattainable dreams. I don't want Dusty to get hurt."

"She could learn business. Autumn could help her."

Abigail held up a paw. "I think Autumn has done enough. I'd rather they not associate with each other anymore. Please tell her so."

Smokey felt as though she'd been slapped. She realized the shock and hurt must have shown in her face prompting Abigail to pat her shoulder and say, "It's nothing personal, dear. I'm just looking out for my sister." Then she added, "This situation will have no bearing on our work relationship."

That comment had caused a lump to rise in Smokey's throat. She knew sometimes words were used to mean their opposite. If she didn't convince Autumn to relinquish her friendship with Dusty, would it put her future with Fluffington's in jeopardy? It all seemed so unfair. Smokey wondered if Abigail was beginning to regret the idea of relinquishing the reins to a younger cat.

Smokey tries to concentrate on her presentation as she follows Abigail to the meeting room.

"Our lead architect has arrived." Miguel stands as they enter, taking Smokey by the paw. "Mr. Ratley, I'd like you to meet Smokerina. She's the cat in charge of this project. Smokerina, Jerome J. Ratley."

Smokey extends a paw. Ratley hesitates, then reluctantly gives it a quick squeeze.

"It's very nice to meet you, Mr. Ratley. I've heard much about the work you do with the Rodent Placement Agency. You've made a wonderful difference in the community."

"Thank you." Ratley clears his throat as if accepting praise from a cat is hard to swallow. "Shall we get down to business?"

"Absolutely," says Miguel. "We thought it would be best to begin by explaining our plans for the park, put it all out in the open. To that end, we've asked Smokerina to give a presentation. Smokerina?"

Smokey walks to the front of the room, hits a key on the laptop already set up for her and begins.

"This, of course, is a picture of the lot to be used for the cat park. As you can see, I've marked off the perimeters. Though the edge of the parcel does abut

Rodent Way, we thought that in light of our desire to be good neighbors, we'd add a buffer zone."

"What do you mean?" asks Ratley.

"The parcel is more than large enough for all that we want to do so there's no reason why we have to use all of the space. We plan to leave a section around the entire parcel which will not be used. It will put a bit of distance between the park and Rodent Way. You can see it here." Smokey moves to the next slide, showing the buffer zone.

"I see," Ratley sneers. "So, the rodents get a little strip of land and that's supposed to appease us? What's to keep you cats out of that so-called buffer zone?"

"We're thinking of a fence. A pretty one that will look lovely from either side." Smokey flips to the next slide showing a few fence samples.

"A fence? You think a fence is going to stop marauding felines? I'm pretty sure your species can climb fences. Last I knew you all still have claws. Besides, those are picket fences. Most cats could squeeze right through. How does that protect us?"

"Well, Mr. Ratley, the issue isn't really one of protection. At least not the way we see it. We want the rodent community to feel comfortable with the cat park, but we don't want to create insurmountable barriers. Our goal is to bring the cat and rodent populations together. The ease of getting through the fence is actually meant for the rodents.

Stunned, Ratley's mouth falls open. "You can't be serious! You truly expect rodents to want to cross over into the cat park? Do you think we enjoy being mauled and eaten? Are you insane?" Ratley gets to his feet as his voice rises. "This is preposterous!"

Smokey takes a deep breath, reminding herself to stay calm. "Please, Mr. Ratley, if you'll allow me to continue, I think you'll gain a better understanding of what I mean as the presentation unfolds."

Ratley resumes his seat, tapping his paw on the table.

"As you noted in your letter to the editor, rodents have used the fields in the area for years. The fence will serve as a boundary the cats aren't to cross, but it will also let the rodents come through to get to the fields. The park will be closed at night, and since many rodents are nocturnal, the entire area will be available to them all night. Of course, they are welcome any time and, we hope that eventually, cats and rodents will share the park."

Ratley leans back, folding his arms across his chest. "Really?" His whiskers twitch. "You honestly expect me to believe that you think cats and rodents will someday share the park?"

"Yes. Why not?"

"I daresay, Ms. Smokerina, that you are aware of the history between cats and rodents." His long whip of tail thumps the floor below his chair.

"I am very aware of it, Mr. Ratley. I'm also aware that it's time for a change. Thankfully, we now live in a time when most cats no longer hunt for their food. I don't know a single cat who actually wants to eat any rodent. I understand perfectly why rodents are reluctant to trust us, but we want that relationship to change. We want to coexist peacefully, build strong bonds, become one community. We see this park as a step in that direction."

Smokey watches the look of calculation on Ratley's face. The room is silent. Smokey's not sure if she should go on with her presentation or wait for someone to speak. Before she can decide, Ratley gets to his feet and moves towards her. He comes too close, invading her personal space. Smokey fights the urge to take a step back. Instead, she stands straighter and juts out her chin.

Looking her directly in the eye, Ratley states, "You're lying."

Furious at the accusation, Smokey remains silent. Everything she wants to say will only cause more anger, so she holds her tongue. But she never looks away, never blinks.

"If this is so," continues Ratley, "If the cats truly want to improve feline-rodent relations, then why not come to us first and propose we build this park together? Why must the cats do it on their own? As if only cats can resolve the problem and we rodents need your help because we're incapable of helping ourselves. More than a little condescending, is it not, Ms. Smokerina?"

The realization that Ratley is right hits Smokey like a punch to the gut, draining the fight from her. All her focus now is on keeping her whiskers from trembling. Suddenly, she is aware that Miguel is at her side.

"I believe I am the appropriate one to answer that question as I chose the park's location." Miguel has a paw on Ratley's shoulder and is guiding him back to his chair.

"I'm afraid I am the one to blame for that misstep and for that I truly apologize. When Rufus came to me with the idea of the cat park, I began to look for land. I settled on this particular parcel for its many desirable attributes, but I, admittedly did not take the feelings of those living on Rodent Way into account. That was poor judgment and lack of consideration on my part and I wish to sincerely express my apologies to the rodent community. I will take the first opportunity to do so publicly. However, the land has been purchased and plans for the park are underway, so why not make the best of it? Though I was wrong to do it the way I did, I'm coming to see it as a valuable opportunity to make great strides in improving feline-rodent relationships. An opportunity that should not be lost."

Rufus, seated beside Ratley taps his arm. "Mr. Ratley, I must say, your idea of the cats and rodents working together on the park is an excellent one. It should have been approached that way from the beginning. You are right about that, of course, but as they say, better late than never. I'd like to hear more of your thoughts about how the cats and rodents could work together on this."

Once Miguel had redirected Ratley's attention, Smokey had sunk into a chair, trying to regain her composure. Now she watches in fascination as the scene continues to unfold.

"What? I have no ideas for cats and rodents working together on this project!" Indignation sounds in Ratley's voice. "I merely asked why you cats decided it all on your own without taking us into account."

"I'm a dog," Rufus mumbles under his breath.

"And that's another thing. How did a dog come up with the idea of a cat park? Don't we have enough trouble with cats and raptors? Do we need to start worrying about dogs as well?"

"You don't have to worry about any of us," Abigail announces. "We've admitted we made a mistake in the way this project began, but Miguel is right. This is a tremendous opportunity for fostering better relations. Why not embrace it?" Abigail's tail sweeps up to wrap around her, the fluffy tip resting on the table. "Mr. Ratley, you have great influence in the rodent community. Your support would go a long way in building a better future for all. We would love to have you as part of our team."

"My support? You want my support?" Ratley is aghast.

"I can't think of anyone better suited for the job," says Miguel. "This is a perfect opportunity for you to use your standing in the rodent community to make an even greater difference than you already have in so many ways."

"You must all be daft! I came here to insist this park be stopped. I still insist on it. If I was to change my position the rodent community would disown me as a traitor and rightly so. I know what you're doing. You're trying to use me as a dupe. You think if you've got me on your side, making promises of better relations, then the rodents will let their guard down. The next thing you know we'll become easier pickings for the hundreds of rodent-hunting cats climbing your ridiculous fence and overrunning Rodent Way!"

Ratley is on his feet, whiskers twitching wildly, tail whipping from side to side so fast Rufus has to jump onto the table to keep from being hit. "I WILL NOT betray my fellow rodents by allowing myself to be used as a pawn in your wily feline scheme," he bellows.

"Please calm down," Miguel urges. "I assure you there is no wily scheme, and we are not trying to use you."

"Why should I trust you? Give me one good reason."

The room goes silent. Smokey has an idea, but unsure, she hesitates.

"Hmph! Just as I thought." Ratley starts towards the door. "This is not over," he says, crossing the room.

Smokey jumps from her chair. "Mr. Ratley, before you go, may I ask a question?"

He stops, turns towards her. "What?"

"When was the last incident of a rodent being harmed by a cat on Rodent Way?" Smokey has no idea what the answer is. Asking this question is a risk.

Ratley rocks back and forth on his feet. "I see where you're going, Ms. Smokerina, and it won't work. There have been no such recent incidents, but that is not because cats have changed their ways. It's because we rodents have worked for years to create a safe environment. We have a vigilant neighborhood watch. We've taken every precaution possible to ensure the safety of the rodent community. If we let our guard down for one second, we'd be in trouble.

We protect ourselves and each other. That's why there have been no recent incidents. And I'll not see a cat park destroying the security we've worked so hard to build."

"It must be exhausting," says Smokey. "All that vigilance. The constant looking over your shoulder. Living in fear. I know what that's like. When I was a kitten, my family was feral. I'm the only one of my litter who survived. It's a terrible way to live and I thank the Creator every day that it's over for me. I want it to be over for you, too. For all the rodents. Isn't that what you want, too?"

Ratley's eyes narrow. "You were feral?"

Smokey's stomach lurches. Why had she said it? The implication is obvious.

"When I was young. Very young. Fortunately, things changed for us. By the time my sister was born, we were in a cottage and living a totally different life."

"So, you hunted. You, yourself, have killed and eaten rodents. And your parents, too. They taught you to do it."

Smokey feels shame wash over her.

"What did they say?" Ratley's voice changes to a mocking singsong. "Just watch us, sweet kitten. This is how you stalk your prey. This is how you grab a mouse. This is where you sink your teeth in."

"Stop! Stop!" Smokey yells, her eyes filling with tears. "How dare you talk to me like that? You know nothing of what my life was like!" Smokey hears her voice growing hysterical. She fights to regain control, purposely evening her tone. "My parents never spoke like that. Yes, they taught me to hunt because it was the only way to survive. They also taught me to be as swift and merciful as possible. They hated it. They hated the fact that they had to hunt and that they had to teach me to do it. That's why they never taught my baby sister. You never saw cats so happy as my parents were the day they knew we'd never have to hunt again."

Ratley blinks. He looks away for a moment, then returns his gaze to Smokey. "Yes," he says. "I suppose hunting is hard work and there's no guarantee of a kill. I'm sure they were happy to be relieved of the burden."

Smokey strides towards him. "Of all the unmitigated gall!"

"Smokerina!" It's Abigail's voice, but Smokey ignores her.

"You know what I think, Mr. Ratley?" Smokey continues, staring him down. "I think you don't want good relations between cats and rodents. I think you like keeping fear and enmity between us. It gives you a sense of power and fuel for your hate. You could be a wonderful agent for change, but instead you choose to keep the status quo. You, with all your influence in the rodent community, are a traitor to your fellow rodents, after all, because you perpetuate their fear instead of working for change. Here you've been offered the perfect opportunity and you throw it away. Perhaps you should take a good look at your own motives."

"Well, I never!" Ratley turns toward the rest of the room as does Smokey. All have come to their feet. Dumbfounded looks line all three faces. *What have I done?* Smokey thinks.

Miguel, Rufus, and Abigail rush toward them.

"I apologize for my employee, Mr. Ratley," says Abigail. "I'm certain she didn't mean to say those things." Abigail glares at Smokey.

"I think she did mean it and I'm glad she said it," Miguel counters.

"What?" Smokey, Abigail, and Ratley all say at once.

"She called you out, Ratley. I have a feeling if you really think about it, you'll see she hit the mark whether you want to admit it or not." Miguel chucks Smokey under the chin. "Good job, Smokerina."

Smokey doesn't know how to respond. She's never felt in such a muddle in her life. Abigail is furious and Miguel is praising her. She feels she must say something.

"Mr. Ratley, I apologize for getting so worked up. I may have spoken out of turn, but it's only because I am so passionate about this subject. I really do believe in fostering the best relations possible between cats and rodents. I know cats who have rodent friends. My own sister works for a bakery whose delivery boys are two squirrels. My sister just adores them. My best friend, Jasmine, lives next door to a family of beavers and they are wonderful neighbors. Cats and rodents can live peacefully, even joyfully, together. I really want to see that happen. Why, even Ms. Fluffington has a family of mice living in her apartment."

"She does?" This time it is Miguel, Rufus, and Ratley who speak at once, all turning to look at Abigail.

"I do?" says Abigail.

Suddenly, Smokey remembers that Dusty has never told Abigail about the mice. Realizing it's too late to backtrack, Smokey continues, "She does. They live in the wall in her sister's bedroom. My sister has met them. Ms. Fluffington's sister, Dusty, sews for them. She makes clothes, tablecloths, and bed linens for them."

"She does?" asks Abigail.

Smokey nods. "They've even let her hold their babies. She adores them and would rather die herself than let the slightest harm come to them."

Ratley looks Abigail up and down. "You seem surprised. Didn't you know a family of mice was living with you?"

"Of course, I know it," Abigail bluffs. "I just didn't know about the sewing part."

"It shows that we can coexist. It proves it," Smokey insists.

"It proves nothing," says Ratley. "It's an extraordinary occurrence with a rare cat and an even rarer, not to mention stupid, mouse family."

"Not so stupid," Smokey replies. "They're getting great clothes and household goods from one of the best seamstresses you'll ever see. Dusty's now selling her miniature clothing and linens in a successful Faunaburg boutique called Tonk's Treasures. Tonk's is owned by a cat who is more than willing to welcome rodent customers. So, you see, Mr. Ratley, whether you're on board or not, Faunaburg is already moving ahead with mending relations between cats and rodents. Rather than trying to stop it, why not join us and be part of the positive change that's coming to this city?"

Ratley is quiet for a moment as the others wait expectantly.

"Well?" asks Miguel, losing patience.

Ratley appears uncharacteristically indecisive. He looks from one face to the next, finally stopping at Smokey. "Ms. Smokerina, you've told me something about your youth. Now let me tell you something about mine. When I was a young rat, my baby sister and I were out for a stroll in the field. Suddenly, out of nowhere, a huge feral pounced. He grabbed my sister, crushing her in his jaws and ran off with her." His body begins to shake. "So, you'll excuse me if I have a difficult time trusting cats."

Chapter Nineteen

A Strange Night

"Mama Cat, I wish you were here." Autumn strokes the glass pirate ship as she wipes a tear off her whiskers. At supper she told Smokey she planned to ask Dusty to go shopping with her on Saturday.

"You can't do that," Smokey had said, looking alarmed.

"Why not?"

"Autumn, I'm so sorry. I should have told you this right away, but I couldn't bear to. Now I have no choice. Abigail heard about what happened when you and Dusty went out. The whole matatabi thing. She was very upset about it."

"How silly. Everything turned out fine." Autumn waved a dismissive paw.

"Abigail doesn't see it that way," Smokey said. "She said to tell you you're not to associate with Dusty anymore. She thinks you're a bad influence."

"What!" Autumn threw her napkin on the table. "Dusty has made great strides since that day. She's got a whole line selling at Tonk's. She walks there and back all the time. She's even ventured to a few other places. She told me so herself."

"I know, Autumn. I don't blame you for being angry, but there's nothing I can do about it. I'm sorry."

"Dusty is not a kitten and Abigail has no right to tell her what she can and can't do. If Abigail told you that, she must have told Dusty too. But I've spoken with Dusty on the phone several times. She's never mentioned it. She even talks about getting together again. I don't think she's taking it seriously so I'm not going to either."

Smokey looked aghast. "Autumn, please! You have to."

"You're siding with Abigail? Against me?"

"No! I think Abigail is way out of line."

"So why are you telling me to cut ties with Dusty?"

Smokey's gaze dropped to her lap where her paws fiddled with her napkin.

"It's your job, isn't it? You're afraid if I continue my friendship with Dusty, Abigail will take it out on you."

"She's been acting strangely towards me lately," Smokey said without looking up. "Maybe if you just wait a while, it will blow over. Just give it time, okay?"

Autumn heaved a huge sigh. "This really rubs my fur backwards."

"I'm sorry. I'm sure it won't last forever. We're under a lot of stress right now because of the rodents. Once that's settled, I'm sure things will be okay."

"I suppose. But next time Dusty calls me I'm going to explain why we can't get together. I hope she understands."

"I'm sure she will. Abigail's her sister, after all."

"And what if Dusty says she doesn't care what Abigail thinks and wants to get together anyway. Then what do I say?"

Smokey squared her shoulders. "You know what? It's up to you, Autumn. I'm not going to tell you who you can be friends with."

Autumn looked intently at Smokey. She saw both fear and defiance flicker in her eyes.

Now Autumn sits in the little arc of light on the closet floor. In her mind, she sees herself and Dusty on the deck of her pirate ship, cutlass in paw. Abigail stands on the shore calling Dusty to come back. She and Dusty shake their swords at her and yell, "We're off to plunder and pillage and fill our stores with matatabi. See you in a year, Abigail. If you're lucky!"

As Autumn comes out of her revere, her thoughts turn to Mama Cat, as they always do when her pirate ship is in view. Her tears are born of frustration as well as anger. She wishes she knew what Mama Cat would tell her to do.

Autumn's attention is suddenly drawn by strange noises in the cottage as though furniture is being dragged across the living room floor. Leaving the closet, she is surprised to see the clock by her bed reads 11:00 p.m. She knows Smokey went to bed right after Evening Chant, tomorrow being a workday. A bang from below sets her fur on end.

The door to Smokey's room is open, her bed empty. The bathroom is also empty. Autumn creeps to the banister to peek over the rail. She catches a glimpse of the living room where Smokey is darting frantically from window to window.

"Smokey, what are you doing?" Autumn asks, descending the stairs.

"Shh! They'll hear you," Smokey whispers.

"Who?"

"The coyotes."

"What coyotes?" Autumn leans over Smokey's shoulder to peer out the window. "I don't see any coyotes."

"Me either. But I hear them. They can't be far away."

Autumn looks around the room. An easy chair has been pushed against the front door. All the shades have been pulled and the tie backs on the curtains undone adding an extra layer of darkness.

Smokey drops the curtain on the last window. "Help me secure the back door," she whispers.

"We locked it when we came in," says Autumn.

"Shh!"

Autumn follows Smokey into the kitchen. "Help me move the refrigerator in front of the door."

"I will not. We'd have to unplug it and all the food will go bad. Honestly, Smokey, what's gotten into you?"

"I'm trying to protect us. We need to barricade the cottage so they can't get in." She drags the kitchen table across the floor, shoving it against the door. "Now for the basement." Smokey races down the stairs, Autumn following.

"What are you going to do in the basement?"

"We can hide here," she says.

"I don't want to stay down here," says Autumn.

Smokey glances up at the small windows. "You're right," she says. "We can't cover those windows. They could look in, see us, and break the windows. I'm not sure if they could fit through them, but let's not take the chance. Come on." She grabs Autumn's paw, rushing her back up the stairs. Closing the cellar door behind her she asks, "What can we put against it in case they do get in through the cellar windows? I know! The couch. Help me push it over here."

"I'm not dragging the couch anywhere, Smokey. It's too heavy."

"Fine. I'll do it myself." Smokey heads for the living room.

Smokey grunts as Autumn moves a curtain and lifts a shade at one of the living room windows.

"Autumn, what are you doing?" Smokey yells, forgetting her own instructions to be quiet.

"Just looking," says Autumn. "I've never seen a coyote before. Except in pictures. I don't see anything."

Before she knows what's happening, Autumn feels a painful tug on her fur as Smokey snatches her from the window, lowers the shade and drops the curtain. "Do. Not. Do. That." Smokey is glaring at Autumn.

"What is wrong with you?"

"What's wrong with me? What's wrong with you? Don't you realize there are coyotes out there? If they find out we're in here, they'll come in and eat us."

"Why would they do that?"

"Because it's what they do."

Autumn rolls her eyes. Smokey stamps her paw. A howl in the distance grabs their attention.

"See! I told you," says Smokey. More howls join in.

"They sound hungry," says Autumn.

"Of course, they're hungry," Smokey's voice pitches high with exasperation. "They're hunting. Don't you get it?" Another howl. "And they're getting closer."

"Maybe I should cook something for them. What do they like to eat?"

"Us, Autumn. They like to eat us."

Autumn stares at Smokey, taking in her words and the look of terror in her eyes. Autumn is frightened, but not by the coyotes. She's never seen Smokey look so wild.

"Smokey," she says gently petting Smokey's arm. "Let's sit down for a moment." Autumn leads her to the couch which is now sticking halfway into the hall.

Smokey sits, but her body twitches, eyes darting in every direction.

"Smokey, please relax. You can't even think straight in this condition." Autumn keeps her tone soft. She cuddles close to Smokey hoping to calm her.

"Why aren't you scared, Autumn?" Smokey asks, tears choking her voice.

"Because we're safe. The house is locked. The shades are pulled. The lights are off. We can't be seen. We're perfectly safe."

Another howl. Smokey shakes her head. "Don't you understand? Those are coyotes. They killed Papa Cat."

"Those were different coyotes, Smokey. That was too long ago to be the same ones."

"It doesn't matter. They all eat cats."

"Why do they eat cats?"

"Because they're hungry. They are hunting."

"Just for cats? Don't they eat anything else?"

"They eat whatever they can find. They're desperate. That's why they're so dangerous."

"Then we're much safer than all the animals that live outdoors, aren't we?"

Smokey hesitates. "I guess," she says, finally. "But I'm still scared."

"Then we'll just stay here together until they go away."

They sit silently on the couch hugging each other. After a while, Autumn falls asleep. When she awakens, slivers of sunlight peek through the edges of the shades.

"Smokey. Smokey, wake up." She shakes Smokey's shoulder.

Smokey jumps, instantly roused, fur standing on end.

"Calm down, Smokey. It's morning. They coyotes are gone."

"Oh. Okay. Did I fall asleep? I must have. I didn't mean to."

"Why don't you go up to bed. You didn't get much sleep."

Smokey looks at the clock. "No. It's time to get ready for work."

"Call in sick. You need to rest."

"I'm fine," Smokey mutters as she stumbles her way up the stairs.

Autumn drags all the furniture back into place. Just as she opens the last window shade her cell phone rings. It's Tabby Furry.

"Autumn, we've had a disaster," says Tabby. "Coyotes broke into the bakery last night. They ate everything and made a huge mess."

"That's wonderful!" Autumn exclaims.

There is silence for a moment, then Tabby asks, "Autumn did you hear me right?"

"Yes," says Autumn. "Coyotes broke in and ate everything."

"How is that wonderful? I've lost all my inventory, there's shattered glass all over the floor, some of my shelves are broken. It's terrible!"

"I'm awfully sorry about the mess. But if coyotes ate all of your stuff that means they didn't eat any animals. That's what's wonderful!"

"Oh. Well, I guess."

In the background Autumn hears a cacophony of broken glass being swept, voices shouting orders and asking questions, and what sounds like a mountain of cake tins toppling to the floor.

"Autumn, I have to go. A Police Dog wants to talk to me. I just called to tell you what happened. We're going to be closed for a while so don't do any baking. I'll let you know when we'll be ready to reopen."

"Can I help clean up?"

"Maybe later. Right now there's too much commotion in here as it is. I'll call you later."

"Smokey! You'll never guess what happened!" Autumn calls, racing up the stairs. She bursts into Smokey's bedroom to find her sister face down on her bed, snoring.

Poor thing, she thinks. Autumn picks up Smokey's cell phone from her bedside table. Looking up Abigail's direct line, she leaves a message saying that Smokey doesn't feel well and will not be in today. She lays down next to Smokey, suddenly realizing how exhausted she is. She wonders what brought the coyotes to their neighborhood. *And if they come back*, she thinks, *what could I feed them?*

Chapter Twenty

The Protest

Smokey is still on edge when she returns to work the next day. Talk of the coyote break in at Furry Confections is big news in Wild Whisker Ridge, but no one in Faunaburg has heard about it. Smokey stares at the work on her drafting board, unable to focus. It's almost lunchtime and she's done nothing yet. She nearly jumps out of her fur at the sound of a knock on her office door.

Abigail enters, holding her cell phone. "Smokerina, there's trouble."

"What is it?"

"Look." Abigail hands the cell phone to her. "Rufus just sent it to me."

Smokey looks at the image on the phone. It shows a crowd of rodents holding signs that read NO CAT PARK NEAR RODENT WAY! and STAY AWAY, CATS! And even one that reads, FIND SOMETHING ELSE FOR SUPPER!

"Scroll to the next one," says Abigail. "It's a video."

Smokey taps the triangle and the video plays, showing sign-carrying rodents picketing in front of City Hall. They scurry around the sidewalk chanting, "No cats near the rats! No cats near the rats!"

"Is this going on right now?" Smokey asks.

"Yes. As you'll notice, it's mostly squirrels and chipmunks with a few gerbils and hamsters. It's daytime so most of the rodents aren't out now, but Rufus said the mice, rats, porcupines, and other nocturnals were there all night. Ratley's got them working in shifts."

"This is awful," says Smokey. "Have you spoken with Miguel?"

"Yes. He's on his way to City Hall and wants us to meet him there. Let's go."

"Wait. What? He wants us there. Why?"

"He plans to address the situation head on."

"He doesn't expect us to speak to that crowd, does he?" Smokey's heart hammers at the thought. She's in no condition to force an appearance of confidence.

"I've no idea what he's planning, but we'd better get going. Ride with me. One the way, you can give me an update on your design plans."

When they reach City Hall, they find a horde of television and newspaper reporters taping the protest. Several are conducting interviews.

"Where's Miguel?" Smokey asks, scanning the crowd.

"There," says Abigail pointing towards a group on the steps of City Hall. Just as she says it, the group disperses and Miguel steps away. Seeing the two cats, he heads in their direction.

"Well, that was something," says Miguel, adjusting his tie.

"An interview?" asks Abigail.

"Yes."

"It must have gone well. You look pleased," says Abigail, looking anything but.

"I am. Very."

"What did you tell them?"

"I apologized for not bringing the rodents in on the planning from the beginning, then rhapsodized about what a great opportunity this park will be to improve feline-rodent relations. The reporters ate it up."

"Miguel!" Abigail crosses her arms over her chest.

"Sorry. Poor word choice."

Smokey notes that Miguel appears energized, more as if he's enjoying a carnival than attempting damage control at a protest.

"That's not what I meant. Miguel, you can't possibly think this is a good thing," says Abigail. "You do understand this is a disaster?"

"No, it isn't. It's an opportunity."

"You can't be serious."

"Look, Abigail, I know you'd rather everything run smoothly with none of the fuss, but the truth is that this forces attention on the issue. I'm glad Ratley staged this protest. I think it's time we listened to what the rodents have to say. They should have an equal part, maybe even a greater part, in solving the feline-rodent problem. This type of thing," he gestures towards the protesters, "is painful, but necessary. This has become much bigger than just a cat park. In fact, I'm not so sure we should be calling it a cat park anymore. Maybe we need to come up with another name."

"Like what?" It's obvious to Smokey by Abigail's tone that she has not been won over.

"I don't know. Roline Park? You know, a combination of rodent and feline."

"You have got to be kidding."

"Okay, that's not a great name, but you get my drift. Now, what I want you two to do is get to those reporters and start talking up the benefits of a park shared by cats and rodents. And Smokey," he says, turning towards her. "I'd like you to start thinking about design ideas with rodents in mind. Maybe go talk to some of the protesters. Ask them what they'd like to have in the park."

Smokey takes a step back. "You want me to talk to talk to them? Now? When they're all riled up? They don't even want a park. Why would they give me ideas of things to put in it?"

"Hold on," says Miguel, a spark leaping in his eyes. "I've got an idea. Don't go anywhere."

Smokey looks at Abigail as Miguel hurries off. "What do we do now?"

"Wait. What else can we do?" Abigail's whiskers push forward. Miguel has located Rufus Tailwagger and is shouting into his ear to be heard over the noise of the protesters. Abigail's eyes never leave him. Neither do Smokey's.

Within moments, Rufus is racing up the steps into the building. Miguel is gathering the reporters.

"What is he up to now?" asks Abigail. The irritation in her voice sends shivers down Smokey's spine.

Rufus and a few helpers return with a podium and microphone. As they set up at the top of the stairs, more television vans pull up near the curb. Miguel looks towards Abigail and Smokey, motioning for them to join him. Smokey's stomach flips.

Abigail heaves a heavy sigh. "Let's go," she says, heading towards Miguel. Smokey follows, wishing she could be anywhere else.

By the time they reach the top step, the podium is set up.

"What's going on, Miguel?" Abigail asks.

"You'll see in a minute, Abby. I know you think quick on your paws. Smokey, I hope you do, too."

What does that mean? Smokey wonders. *He's not going to ask me to address this crowd, is he?*

"We're ready," Rufus calls.

"Just follow my lead," Miguel says as he steps up to the podium.

Smokey and Abigail stand slightly behind and to the left of Miguel. Looking out at the crowd, Smokey sees several television cameras pointed towards them. Still unnerved over the coyotes, and now this, she knows she looks anything but her best. She tries taking several deep breaths to calm herself, but it feels as though there's a wall in her chest preventing air from getting through.

"Could I have your attention, please!" Miguel's confident, commanding tone booms through the microphone. "I have an important announcement to make."

Within moments the noise of the crowd dwindles until there is silence. All eyes turn in their direction.

"Thank you. First of all, I'd like to thank all the rodents here today as well as those who came out last night. I am also deeply grateful to Mr. Jerome J. Ratley for organizing this protest. Mr. Ratley has been a staunch advocate for the rodent community for many years. His work in rodent activism is unparalleled. Last night and today are no exception."

"Get to the point or get out!" yells one of the protesters.

"I will do that right now," Miguel continues. "As you all know, plans are in the works for a new park to be built that abuts Rodent Way. It is most unfortunate that I — and I take full responsibility for this — I did not consider asking the rodent community to partner with us on this endeavor. I humbly apologize for that error. I completely understand why rodents are unhappy about the prospect of a cat park in the proposed location. You have every right to be unhappy about it. You also have every right to be frightened given the history of rodents and felines. However, I want to make perfectly clear that while you have a right to be frightened, you have no need to be.

"At first this project was conceived as a cat park, but things have changed. They've changed because rodents have spoken. We hear you. I stand here today to tell you that there will be no cat park in the lot adjacent to Rodent Way."

A roar goes up from the assembled protesters. They throw their signs in the air, jump up and down, hugging one another, and shouting, "We've won! We've won!"

Smokey looks at Abigail who stares in horror at Miguel. Then she drops her gaze to the cement steps. It's over. Her dream assignment has ended before it hardly started. She feels the reigns of Fluffington ArCATecture slipping through her paws. She wants to cry but she's not sure if it's from disappointment or relief that this nightmare is about to end.

Miguel gives the rodents a few minutes to celebrate, then begins again to speak.

"I have a question for you," he says, regaining the crowd's attention. "Have you really won if you still live in fear? Wouldn't it be a greater win if rodents and felines and all furs and feathers live peacefully together? I'm not talking about simply not harming one another, but actively helping one another, recognizing each other as equals, becoming true friends? I ask you to think about it. Would that not be the greater victory?"

A murmur passes through the protester as well as the reporters and camera crews. Miguel gives them a moment to process what he's said, then continues.

"So, I propose something new. I propose that rather than a cat park, the parcel of land in question be used for a park that can be enjoyed by all furs and feathers. But it will only happen — and I want to make this perfectly clear — it will *only* happen if all are in agreement and if we all work together on it. Otherwise, that land will sit there just as it is — a huge space that had the potential to change the world, or at least our little corner of it — but didn't."

Miguel turns towards Abigail and Smokey. "I've brought with me today, Ms. Abigail Fluffington of Fluffington ArCATecture and her lead designer, Smokerina. They are going to say a few words about how you can all help if indeed you agree to this project. Ms. Fluffington."

Smokey sees Abigail purse her whiskers in irritation for a split second before she sucks in her breath and strides to the podium.

"Thank you, Miguel. My dear friends, a reconciliation between rodents and felines is long overdue. Miguel Gato is right. A cat park right next to Rodent Way was a poor idea because we didn't take the feelings of the rodents living in the area into consideration. For that, I am deeply sorry. But now we have a chance to right a wrong and to create something unique. It could be the start of a movement for all of us. Everyone here today could be in on the beginning of it. We have the chance to create something for which our descendants, rodent and feline alike, will thank us. Something that will change things so dramatically they will hardly believe it was ever any other way.

"Just imagine for a moment, a roomful of rodents and felines celebrating Great Creator Day together, laughing, playing, having a wonderful time, their children all the best of friends. One of the adults overhears the children talking. 'I heard that a long time ago rodents and felines didn't like each other.' And another child says, 'that can't be true. You're making that up.' The knowing adult smiles, not correcting them, not wanting them to think that life could be any other way. Ah, but that adult's heart swells with gratitude. Gratitude towards us." Abigail makes a sweeping gesture with her paws to include the entire crowd, "for making life so different. So much better."

Wow! Thinks Smokey. *How did she come up with that so fast? She should run for office.* Then the thought hits her that she is expected to speak. What will she say?

The rodents are staring at Abigail. Many look as though they are picturing the image she's just laid out for them and liking it.

"Now, I'd like to turn the microphone over to Smokerina. She's Fluffington's lead designer on this project. Or should I say what was this project. If you agree and we go forward with a new type of park there will be co-leads, fully equal. But right now, I'm going to ask Smokerina to tell you how you can become involved should you choose to do so. Smokerina."

As Abigail steps away from the podium, Smokey takes a deep breath. This is it. *Oh, Great Creator*, she prays. *Please put the right words in my mouth because I have no idea what to say.*

Smokey steps up to the microphone, looks out at the sea of furry, expectant faces. Cameras roll, bulbs flash, reporters hold their microphones towards her.

"Good afternoon. I'm so happy to have the opportunity to address you. As you know, plans have been in the works for a cat park. With the change, we'd like input from every fur and feather on what you'd like to have in a park that includes everyone."

The air seems to grow thin. Breathing becomes difficult. She doesn't realize how hard she's gripping the podium until she realizes her claws have sunk into the wood. She's not sure where to go from here. There's nothing in the works for anyone other than cats. What's she supposed to say? To buy time, she turns away, pretending to cough. Rufus Tailwagger is suddenly at her side with a cup of water. She takes a few sips, then turns back to the microphone.

"Excuse me," she says. "I guess my throat is a little dry." *What would rodents want in a park?* She asks herself. She has no answer. And that is the spark she needs. She sets her cup aside. Instead of gripping the podium, she rests her paws atop it.

"I would not presume to imagine that I could come up with ideas for what rodents would like in a park. Whenever I've designed dog parks, I've always talked with many canines first to find out what they desired. So, as Ms. Fluffington has indicated there is no way I could possibly be the sole lead on a park that is to include all furs and feathers. But I do believe this is a much better idea. I am eager to work with others. I'm sure we have a tremendous amount to learn from one another. I so hope you'll consider this idea. I can only imagine it would be the most incredible, amazing park the world has ever seen. I would be honored to be even a small part of it.

"My dear friend, Jasmine, has created a website about the proposed cat park with a form that cats have been completing to let us know what they want in the park. I am prepared to ask Jasmine to redesign the website and the form to reflect the new plans, if indeed they will be implemented. I just know Jasmine will be delighted about this change and I'm sure she will welcome rodent web designers to work with her. Getting in touch with Jasmine will be my first order of business upon returning to Fluffington's. So, once the website has been redesigned, I hope you'll all fill out the form. Meanwhile, if anyone would like to speak with me personally, I'll be happy to meet with you as soon as we are finished here. Thank you."

Smokey steps from the podium feeling a mix of exhilaration and trepidation. After listening to Miguel and Abigail and then after speaking herself, she's suddenly enthused by the new concept for the park. Her trepidation comes from the realization that she has spoken for Jasmine, perhaps even undermined her by saying that Jasmine would be happy to relinquish complete control of designing the website. Web design is her profession, after all. It all poured out of Smokey so fast, she didn't have time to think it through before she spoke. She prays Jasmine won't be angry and if she is, that she'll forgive her.

* * *

"What's all this?" asks Abigail as she and Smokey enter the lobby of Fluffington's to find the entire staff assembled and staring at them.

"We saw it all," says Paulie Pomeranian. "It was live streamed."

"Well, then?" asks Abigail. "How did we do?"

"Amazing," says Louie. "Did you know? I mean the change seemed like it came about pretty quickly. No one ever mentioned it."

"It did come about quickly," says Abigail. "On the spot, as a matter of fact. Miguel got the idea and ran with it. The next thing we knew, we were at the podium talking about a project that doesn't exist."

The mouths of the staff hang open.

"Really? You spoke like that off the tops cf your heads?" asks Paulie.

Abigail heaves a sigh. "We did. You never know what you're going to be asked to do when you're working with Miguel Gato. Never a dull moment. Well, Smokerina," she says, turning to Smokey. "I guess you'd better go make that call to your friend."

Smokey enters her office and shuts the door. She pulls out her cell phone, brings up Jasmine's number, paw hovering over it. She can't bring herself to press the phone icon. Before she can make up her mind, the phone rings. It's Autumn.

"Smokey, is it true?" Autumn blurts out as soon as Smokey answers.

"I assume you mean about the cat park. Or whatever park it is now. If it will be one at all."

"Yes, yes. It was on TV. It's all over the news. I wish I had the TV on, but I don't watch it while I'm baking. I hope they show it again. I want to see you on TV."

"How did you find out?"

"Dusty called me. She saw it. She thinks it's a great idea and I do too. She said she's going to talk to Mr. and Mrs. Mouse and see what they think. She's pretty sure they saw it too."

"That would be great. I hope they're for it. It would be helpful to have some rodents on our side."

There is a pause. Then Autumn says, "um…Smokey. Maybe you should stop thinking in terms of sides. I mean that's what the new park is supposed to be about, right? No more us and them. We're all one."

Smokey sighs. "You're right, Autumn. Everything happened so fast. It's hard to change gears so quickly. My whole mindset has to change. I hope I can do it."

"Of course, you can. I'll bet once you start collaborating with other furs and feathers it will become easy."

"If they go for it. If they don't, there won't be a park at all."

"That would be a shame. This is such a great opportunity. Oh, it just has to happen!"

Smokey hears a buzzer in the background.

"My cake is done," says Autumn. "I've got to go. We'll talk more when you get home."

After disconnecting from Autumn, Smokey is determined to get the call to Jasmine over with.

"Hi Smokes," says Jasmine. "I know why you're calling and I'm already on it."

"Oh, thank goodness you're not angry. I realized as soon as I said it that I shouldn't have spoken for you."

"Don't worry. I could tell you got thrown up at the podium on a moment's notice. I'll bet you didn't even know any of this was going to happen until the last minute."

"You saw then?"

"Yup. It's been streaming all afternoon. They're still showing it."

"How could you tell it was last minute?"

"Are you kidding me? How long have we been best friends? Forever. I could tell. But you did great. Really, Smokey, you did. After you drank that water, it was like something came over you, and you went from a nervous wreck to the queen of calm. Um…it was just water, wasn't it?"

Smokey laughs. "I thinks so unless Rufus puts something in it I don't know about. So, you don't mind doing a redesign?"

"Of course not."

"And working with rodents?"

"Are you serious? This could be history-making. I am all in!"

"Thanks, Jasmine. You're the best!"

Smokey hangs up, leans back in her chair. Filled with relief, she suddenly realizes she's skipped lunch and is ferociously hungry. As she's about to head for the lunchroom, Abigail knocks on her door, bursting into the office without waiting for an answer.

"We've got trouble," she announces.

"We do?"

"Oh, yes. I just got a blistering voice mail message from Jerome J. Ratley." She holds her phone out to Smokey. "Listen to this."

Chapter Twenty-One

Dusty's Defiance

Autumn Amelia wipes her paws on her apron as she answers the doorbell to find Dusty on her doorstep.

"Hi, Autumn. I hope you don't mind that I stopped by."

"Of course not. Come in," says Autumn. She sees a cab leave the driveway as Dusty steps into the living room.

"I hope I'm not disturbing you. I knew you'd probably be baking, but I thought you wouldn't mind the company."

"Not at all. I'm just surprised. Why didn't you call first?" Autumn asks, ushering her into the kitchen. "Does Abigail know you're here? Smokey told me she doesn't want you associating with me anymore."

Dusty drops into a chair by the kitchen table. "Nope, she doesn't know. That's why I didn't call first. I was afraid you'd tell me not to come. Abby went on a tirade about the matatabi saying that you were a bad influence on me. It made me so angry I told her to stuff it in her litter box."

"That must have helped matters."

Dusty laughs. "She stood there with her mouth hanging open. Honestly, Autumn, my whole life has changed since I met you. Tamarind called this morning for more inventory. She says it's flying out of the store. Both the miniatures and the adult clothes. I go for a walk every day while Abby's at work. Sometimes I even go on the weekend when she's home. It freaked her out the first time I said I was leaving. She started haranguing me, so I made her a glass of iced tea."

"How did that help?"

"I slipped a little matatabi powder into it. She never noticed I was gone."

"Seriously? You did that?"

"You gave it to me, remember? You called it my ammunition."

"I forgot about that. Did she get mad when she found out?"

"She didn't find out. I've been slipping it to her whenever she gets on my nerves."

"I shouldn't have told you to do that. I was probably still feeling the effects. What if she does something under the influence? Like drive. She wouldn't even realize she shouldn't do it."

"Hmm…I hadn't thought of that. I would feel terrible if she got hurt. It's just that ever since the day you and I first went to Tonk's everything in my life has changed for the better. I can't understand why Abby isn't happy for me. It makes me angry to think she doesn't want me to be a normal, happy cat."

Autumn sets a glass of lemonade before Dusty then continues her baking. "Some furs don't like change. There's a lot going on in her life with the protests over the cat park. Maybe she can't handle having you change so much at the same time."

Dusty looks crestfallen. "You think I should go back to hiding in my room all the time?"

"No! I think you should keep going. You're doing great and you deserve success. I'm just trying to think of a reason for your sister's behavior. I know she loves you. I can't believe she doesn't want you to be happy."

"Whatever it is, I hope she gets over it soon. I've got a lot of lost time to make up for."

Hearing that makes Autumn's heart swell. "Have you tried talking with her, letting her know how you feel?"

"I tried once, but she didn't want to hear it. I don't know how to make her listen to me."

Autumn sighs. "I suppose you'll just have to go about your life as you see fit and hope she comes around. It can't be easy living with her at this point."

"It's not and I don't think I want to anymore."

Autumn lifts her eyebrow whiskers. "Are you going to move out? Can you afford it?"

"Not yet. But I've started looking into other places to sell my clothing. I've got some good leads. I'd love to open my own store. I said that to Abby, but she told me I can't do it because I have no capital and don't know anything about business so even if I did manage to get a loan the store would go bankrupt in no time because I wouldn't know what I was doing."

A low growl escapes Autumn. "Sorry," she says, seeing Dusty's startled look. "It just makes my fur crawl to know she said such cruel things to you."

"I was angry at first, but when I thought about it, I realized she was right. I don't know anything about business so I probably would fail."

"Dusty —"

Dusty holds up a paw. "That's why I've enrolled in the business program at Faunaburg Community College. I start in September with Introduction to Business. My professor will be an owl named Hugh Woodney. I've heard he's an excellent teacher."

"Oh, Dusty! I'm so proud of you! Does Abigail know?"

"Not yet. I was afraid she'd attempt to talk me out of it, and I refuse to let her even try. She'll find out when I leave for my first class. If she doesn't like it, I plan to tell her she can stick that in her litterbox too."

Autumn can't help but giggle. "Your sister must feel like she's living with a stranger."

"In a way, she is. Pretty soon she won't recognize me as the Dusty she's always known. I just hope she comes to accept it. She really is a brilliant businesscat. I could learn so much from her if she'd only believe in me enough to share her knowledge."

"I think you'll have to prove yourself to her first. She strikes me as the kind of cat who prefers action to words."

"That's true. I'm going to give this everything I've got with or without her help. In a way, I like the idea of doing it on my own. That way she can't say I couldn't have done it without her."

Autumn notices a low rumbling noise coming from Dusty's tummy. "Hungry?" she asks.

"Yes. I haven't had lunch."

Autumn looks at the clock. It's after one. "Neither have I. Let me pop this into the oven, then fix us something to eat."

Autumn and Dusty continue to chat over lunch. After cleaning up, Dusty helps Autumn pack her baking for delivery.

"I've got to bring this to Furry's. Want to come with me?"

"Sure, but I thought the Squirrel brothers pick up your stuff."

"They do, but with the break in the other day, I want to see how things are going. Tabby says it's still a mess. She's not open for business, except for furs coming by to pick up special orders. So once this is delivered, I'll have the rest of the day free."

"Doesn't it make you nervous?" Dusty asks. Autumn had told her about the coyote break in at Furry Confections over lunch.

"No, but I do feel bad that Tabby's bakery was damaged, and she lost a lot of inventory."

"It sounds as though Smokey was scared out of her wits."

"That's putting it mildly. But I take it as a good sign that the coyotes went for biscuits, cookies, and cupcakes rather than other animals."

"What does Smokey say to that?"

Autumn rolls her eyes. "She said, 'how do you know they didn't eat any furs of feathers? Maybe they just went to Furry's for dessert.'"

"It really bothers me," says Dusty. "I was sure Rodney and Darlene were mistaken."

"Rodney and Darlene?"

"Mr. and Mrs. Mouse. We're now on a first name basis. Anyway, I really thought they were wrong about cats eating mice. Now with the protests on television and the interviews with rodents, especially that Mr. Ratley, I have to accept the truth. I guess it's true about coyotes too. I hate it, though."

"I do, too. I was heartbroken when I asked Smokey and she finally told me the truth. That's why I think changing from a cat park to an all furs and feathers park is a great idea. I just hope the rodents go for it. What do your mouse friends think?"

"They love the idea, but they still aren't sure about it. Darlene says she's always prayed for a day when her babies wouldn't have to fear for their safety, yet she can't help but wonder if it's too good to be true."

"I wish there was a way to prove our good intentions."

After dropping off the baked goods, Autumn and Dusty return home. "What are you planning to do this afternoon?" Dusty asks.

"I thought I would take a walk to my friend, Chrissy's, house and see if her Aunt Holly will show me around her garden. Would you like to come? Holly Berry is a very interesting character, though you must be sure to address her as Your Highness."

Dusty's eyes grow big as cat bowls. "Is she really royalty?"

Autumn laughs. "No. She just thinks she is. I'll explain while we walk."

When they reach the house, they find Chrissy weeding the flower bed next to the front steps. She tells them her aunt is taking a nap but should be up soon. "I'll take you around back and show you the gardens," Chrissy offers.

When they reach the back yard, Dusty gasps and lets out a loud "MEWOW!"

"Spectacular, aren't they?" asks Autumn.

From the front, the house appears like the many other cottages, capes, and bungalows in the neighborhood — a small front stoop with neat flower beds on either side, a well-manicured front lawn split down the middle by a flagstone walkway leading to the front door, and a driveway to one side of the lawn ending at the garage. But once they round the corner, it's as though they've stepped into another world.

The back porch leads down to a flagstone patio with a white iron table and chairs in the middle, a huge umbrella growing like a tree from the center of the table. The barbecue grill, neatly covered, is pushed against the house. Next to it are folded lawn chairs and a chaise lounge. Ordinary enough, but where the flagstones end is where the magic begins.

Autumn and Dusty gaze in wonder at the impeccable gardens. Not one garden, but several, weaving throughout the yard, circles of flowers with pathways between. Brilliant colors bloom everywhere. For a moment Autumn closes her eyes, letting the light breeze waft the scents of roses, honeysuckle, and butterfly bush under her nose.

"This is magnificent!" Dusty exclaims. "I've never seen anything like it."

"You're welcome to stroll the paths," Chrissy offers. "I'm sure when Aunt Holly wakes up from her nap, she'll be happy to tell you about every flower out here."

Just then a figure emerges from one of the circles, stepping onto the path. "I thought I heard voices," it calls, waving at them.

"Auntie!" calls Chrissy. "I thought you were taking a nap."

"I was dear, but I woke up. You were busy and I didn't want to bother you, so I came outside to tend my gardens." The regal figure seems to glide towards them.

"But you're not supposed to do that. You need to tell me. I need to know where you are at all times."

"Balderdash! You needn't be such a prison warden."

"I'm only trying to keep you safe."

"I'm quite capable of keeping myself safe. Now do show proper manners and introduce me to your friends, please."

Chrissy sighs. "Auntie, you already know Autumn Amelia."

"Good afternoon, Your Highness," says Autumn as she curtsies.

"Lovely to see you, dear," says Holly.

"And this is Autumn's friend, Dusty."

"It's a pleasure to meet you, Your Highness," says Dusty, following Autumn's lead by bobbing a curtsy. "Did you really create these gardens yourself?"

"Pleased to meet you, too, young lady and, yes, I did create them. Would you like me to show you around?"

"We'd love it" says Dusty.

They spend the afternoon wending their way through the curving paths, in and out of the circular gardens, sniffing fragrant flowers, and marveling at the herb wheel. Autumn had been right about Holly Berry being lucid when gardening. "It's the one time I don't have to worry about her," Chrissy confides.

Autumn asks a multitude of questions, especially about the herb wheel. The wheel, divided into eight quadrants contains rosemary, oregano, thyme, tarragon, sage, basil, and chives. In the hub is catnip. The quadrants shoot out from it like the spokes of a wheel. Autumn grows her herbs in separate containers, but the wheel has her fascinated. Holly gives her detailed instructions so she can plant her own herb wheel next spring.

"Thank you for the garden tour," says Dusty as they sit down to rest at the iron table.

"You're welcome, my dears. My plants are the joy of my life. Always have been, ever since I was a kitten. I still remember toddling after my Mama Cat as she tended her gardens. She taught me to prepare the soil, spread the seeds, water them regularly, and keep out the weeds."

"Did she have a garden like yours?" asks Autumn.

"Oh, no. Hers was like what we have out front. Flower beds, some herbs, and a lovely patch for vegetables. It was my Grandmama Cat who had the truly spectacular gardens. Mine can't begin to rival hers."

"That' hard to imagine," says Dusty.

Holly closes her eyes. Her face takes on a wistful expression as she gently sways in her seat.

"Are you okay, Your Highness?" asks Autumn.

"Oh, yes," says Holly, continuing to sway with her eyes closed. "I'm scampering through Grandmama Cat's gardens." She giggles. "The petals tickle my whiskers."

Dusty nudges Autumn, giving her a questioning look. Autumn shrugs.

"Coming, Grandmama!" Holly calls as if she's just heard the voice of her grandmother beckoning her. "It won't be long, Grandmama. I can't wait to see your gardens." This last is spoken in a normal tone as though her grandmama cat is sitting at the table with them.

Chrissy puts a paw on Holly's arm. "Auntie," she says, her voice gentle.

The Empress opens her eyes. "I'm sorry. I didn't mean to leave my company. I hope Princess Christina entertained you while I was gone."

"Gone?" asks Dusty. "You've been right here the whole time."

Holly pats Dusty's paw as if Dusty is a kitten. "I know you think I was here, dear, but really, I was at the boundary. I go there often these days."

"Boundary?" asks Autumn. She has an inkling of what Holly might mean. "Were you really talking with your Grandmama Cat?"

"Of course, I was. She's on the other side, you know. I can't get all the way there, yet, but it won't be long. I can see her and Mama and Papa Cat. They used to be shadowy, but they've been getting clearer lately. That's how I know I will join them soon."

"Auntie, please don't talk like that," Chrissy begs.

"Don't be upset, sweetie. There's nothing bad about it. They are in the Oneness and that's where I'll be going. We'll all be there someday."

Autumn is more certain than ever that she's right. She doesn't think Holly is deluded at all. Not about this.

"Is the Oneness where we go after this life?" she asks.

"That's right."

"Why is it called the Oneness?" asks Dusty.

"Because, dear, it's where we're all one. All furs, feathers, fins, scales, creepers, plants, water, clouds, mountains, trees — oh, just everything — that's what's so wonderful about it. We are all gathered back to the Great Creator as one, existing in perfect harmony. It's the way we began, though we don't remember it once we get to this life. But it's what we return to. The Oneness should always be honored."

"May I ask you something, Your Highness?" says Autumn.

"Of course, dear."

"Would making a place where all creatures get together to play, eat, and celebrate be a good way to honor the Oneness?"

"It would indeed. I wish such a place existed in this life."

"I think it's about to. My sister is working on designing a park. It was supposed to be a cat park, but it was too close to Rodent Way and the rodents have been protesting. So now it's going to be a park where all can gather, and everyone is invited to help plan it. The problem is that the rodents don't trust the cats so we're not sure if it will happen."

"You must make it happen." Holly's tone takes on a sense of urgency. "It explains everything."

Confused, Autumn asks what she means.

"The dream I had just before I came out here. I dreamed that all the creatures were calling for Oneness to begin on earth. That must be what they meant. Please, tell your sister."

"It's getting close to suppertime," says Chrissy, looking worried as her aunt grows more agitated. "Auntie, why don't we let Autumn and Dusty go home so they can have their meal?"

"Oh, is it time to eat? All right then. Good day to you, ladies. I'm glad you stopped by. Come again."

"What did you make of that?" asks Dusty as they walk back to the cottage. "Do you think she's really in touch with the other side?"

"Smokey would probably say I'm crazy, but yes, I do. And I believe her about her dream too."

"Then I hope they can make this park happen. I wonder what it will take to get the rodents, especially Mr. Ratley to trust us."

"I don't know," says Autumn. "But I have a feeling it will have to be something big."

Chapter Twenty-Two

The Unexpected

"I can't believe it." Stunned, Smokey drops into a kitchen chair.

"I can," says Autumn. "Greyson and Abigail seemed awfully taken with each other when he was here."

Smokey and Autumn have just finished a phone conversation with Greyson who called to say he would be visiting again. This time, however, he was coming at the invitation of Abigail Fluffington and staying at the Faunaburg Hotel.

"So, they're dating?" Smokey asks, still befuddled.

"Sounds that way."

Smokey sighs and shrugs. "It's all too much. First Ratley's harangue and now this."

"Greyson sounds happy. At least this isn't something bad. What do you think Mr. Ratley is going to do?"

"I don't know," says Smokey. "He's purposely keeping us in suspense."

The voice mail Abigail received from Jerome Ratley after the protest was a furious diatribe in which Ratley had accused them of trying to turn his fellow rodents against him. At the end he insisted they meet, saying he wanted to propose something that would end this standoff once and for all.

"When do you meet with him?" Autumn asks.

"Friday night. Abigail, Miguel, Rufus, and I are to meet him in front of City Hall."

"Are you worried about it?"

"Of course, I am. Ratley does not want this park to happen. He's going to do anything he can to stop it."

Ever since hearing the menacing voice mail, Smokey hasn't been able to let go of trying to imagine what scheme Ratley might have up his fur. Thinking about it keeps her awake at night and makes it nearly impossible to concentrate on her work.

"Greyson will be here by Tuesday. Maybe that will take your mind off Mr. Ratley."

Smokey snorts. "And make me think instead of him and Abigail?"

* * *

"Come in," calls Smokey when a knock sounds at her office door.

"How's one of my two favorite cousins?"

"Greyson!" Smokey leaps from her chair to greet him. "It's so good to see you again."

"I'm ready, Greyson," Smokey hears Abigail's voice just outside her office.

"Oh, Smokerina," she says, joining them. "I hope you don't mind me stealing your cousin for a few hours. We're going to lunch.

Just the two of you? I'm not invited. "Um… of course not. Enjoy," she stammers.

Greyson gives her cheek a peck. "We'll visit when I get back.

Smokey returns to her drafting table. Greyson hadn't insisted she come with them. He seemed to want to go alone with Abigail. *Is he really romantically interested in Abigail Fluffington?* Smokey is so lost in thought she nearly jumps out of her fur when her cell phone rings. It's Jasmine.

"What's up Jazz?"

"I just wondered if you know what's going on with Ratley yet. There's a whole team of birds and rodents waiting to brainstorm new survey questions, work on the website, and tabulate responses. It seems Ratley's put out the word that nothing can start until after his big meeting with you on Friday night."

"I wish I knew. He hasn't even dropped a hint. Whatever it is, I'm sure he thinks it's something that will stop the park from happening."

"Drat! The web design team is super excited about this project. We can't wait to get going on it."

"Do you have any sense from the team how others in the rodent community feel about it?"

"Most seem to like the idea, but there's still a lot of suspicion. Siegfried, one of the rats here, told me that they want it to be for real, but most can't shake the feeling it's a trap."

Smokey feels her energy drain way. "So, Ratley could easily turn them against it?"

"I'm afraid so. What a shame that would be. But after all the talks I've been having with the rodents and birds on team, I can understand how they feel. The trust just isn't there yet. I wonder if we're rushing things."

Tears prick Smokey's eyes. "If we abandon this project, what could we do instead to start building trust?"

"Maybe our team could brainstorm some ideas. Maybe that's what the survey could be — how to build trust."

A sigh escapes Smokey.

"I know it's a disappointment, Smokey. I know what this means to you. But if Abigail trusted you enough to give you this project, she'll trust you with another one."

Smokey feels a knot tighten in the pit of her stomach. "Jasmine, it's not that," she says. "Well, mostly not. I mean it was before. But now, it's different. I really believe in this. It's not just about me or my career anymore. I've thought a lot about this. If we can make this happen it could start a monumental shift in the way we all live together. Hey, are you free for lunch? I want to tell you about Autumn's visit with Holly Berry."

"The Empress? Wow, you shifted gears pretty fast, Smokey."

"Actually, I didn't. Lunch?"

"Sure. Meet me at Meowers in about fifteen minutes."

"I'll be there."

* * *

"Maybe the Empress should become the spokescat for the park," Jasmine says as Smokey finishes relating all that Autumn told her about her afternoon with Holly. Their lunches have just been served. Jasmine giggles as she bites into a pickle.

"Oh, sure. She could decree that everyone love each other."

Jasmine laughs. "Yeah. Maybe not. That was a pretty amazing conversation she had with Autumn and Dusty, though. By the way, is Autumn Amelia still on Ms. Fluffington's scratch list?"

"Probably. She hasn't said anything about it. I don't know if she's aware that Dusty spent the day with Autumn."

"Sounds like Dusty's been doing a lot of things her sister doesn't know about."

"Mm-hmm," Smokey agrees, taking a sip of sparkling water. "Doesn't seem to care if Abigail finds out, either."

"Good for her, I say!"

Smokey's cell phone rings. "It's Greyson. Sorry, Jazz. I should take this."

239

"Go ahead." Jasmine digs into her tuna salad while Smokey talks.

"Tonight?" Smokey inquires when Greyson asks if she and Autumn can come to dinner with Abigail and him. "And Autumn, too? Are you sure?"

"Absolutely," Greyson assures her. "Meet us at The Red Dot at seven. I've made reservations."

"I guess that answers your question," Smokey says as she disconnects.

"What does?"

"Greyson just invited Autumn and me to join Abigail, Dusty, and him at The Red Dot for dinner tonight."

Jasmine's eyes grow huge. "The Red Dot? I've been dying to go there. It's nearly impossible to get in. You simply must call me right afterwards and tell me all about it. How did he get reservations?"

"Dropped Ms. Fluffington's name, maybe? Or maybe he didn't need to. Having been CEO of PAWS UNITED gets him into a lot of places."

"You look apprehensive, Smokey. What's wrong?"

"I do?" Abigail has been after Smokey about not letting her feelings show, so as not to give anything away. 'Be a cat of steel,' she counsels her. Smokey's trying hard. She thought she was getting better at it.

"You do. I know you've been trying to put your emotions on ice, but I've known you too long. You can't fool me."

Smokey sighs. "It will be the first time Autumn has been with Abigail since the matatabi incident. And we will be in a restaurant. A very posh restaurant. Can you imagine all that could go wrong?"

"You can't afford to focus on that. Assume you'll all have a wonderful time. If anything happens, think of it as a hilarious story to tell your grandkits someday."

"Oh, please." Smokey rolls her eyes. "I'd better call Autumn. I don't know whether to hope she declines or not. It wouldn't do for her to appear rude.

Abigail doesn't know about her...um...restaurant problem. She'd just think she didn't want to be with her. On the other paw, I'd worry less if Autumn wasn't there. This is no-win."

"Dusty's going. She can keep Autumn out of trouble."

When Smokey gets Autumn on the phone, she finds out that Dusty has already told Autumn about their dinner plans. "I can't wait! The Red Dot is the most upscale restaurant in Faunaburg. My mouth is watering just thinking about it. I'm already picking out my clothes."

"Oh, that's great," says Smokey, her heart sinking.

"Will you have time to come home and change first? I could meet you at your office and bring clothes," Autumn offers.

Smokey had been wondering how she would get home, change, and get back to Faunaburg in time. "Thanks. That would be a big help. My silver dress with the matching heels and purse."

"You got it. See you in a few hours."

"Well?" asks Jasmine as Smokey ends the call.

"Dusty already called her. She's very excited about it."

Jasmine smiles. "I wish I could be a flea on a fur for that one!"

"This could be a disaster."

"Stop it, Smokey. You always expect the worst."

Do I? Smokey wonders.

* * *

Back at her office, Smokey can't stop thinking about Jasmine's comment. *Am I a pessimist?* She asks herself. It always seemed easier to expect the worst. That way if things turn out well, she'll be happy and if not, she's not disappointed. *Is that working? I still feel let down when things don't go the way I want them to.*

Her mind turns these thoughts over all afternoon while she works at her drafting board. A knock at the door makes her jump. She looks at the clock. It's already five. Where did the time go?

"Come in," she calls.

Autumn Amelia enters with Smokey's dress slung over her arm.

"Here you go," she says, laying the clothing and accessories on a nearby chair.

"Autumn, you look gorgeous!"

"I hoped this would do," Autumn says, twirling around to show off her lavender wrap dress with off-the-shoulder sleeves and sweetheart neckline. The ruffles at the hem and ruched sides provide a slimming look.

"Very chic," Smokey says.

"This is so exciting," Autumn gushes as Smokey exchanges her skirt suit for more elegant attire. "I can't wait to get there. I looked at The Red Dot's website. Did you know they offer a nine-course meal from a tasting menu?"

Smokey stops cold while slipping on her heels. "Nine courses?"

"That's right. We'll be eating all night."

"I feel faint," says Smokey, collapsing into a chair.

"That's how I felt when I read it. Wait. Smokey, you're not sick, are you?"

Smokey sighs. "No, I'm fine. Autumn, aren't you worried? I mean, about, you know."

"Oh." Autumn casts her gaze down. "That's what's bothering you. I know. I know. I shouldn't go, but Smokey, The Red Dot! When will I ever get another chance to go there? And with nine courses, I'll be so busy eating, I can't possibly get into trouble, can I?"

Smokey does not want to answer that question. "I guess not," she says.

"I talked about it with Dusty. She's promised not to leave my side for a minute. She won't let me get into anything, so you can enjoy yourself and not worry about it. I promise."

"You and Dusty have really bonded, haven't you?" Smokey asks, thinking it ironic that Dusty should be the one promising not to leave Autumn's side.

"We've become close friends. We both have certain issues to overcome. We've been able to help each other with them." Autumn crouches in front of Smokey's chair. "Oh, but Smokey! She'll never replace you. You're my sister."

Smokey can't help but smile at the look on Autumn's face. "I wasn't worried about that, Autumn. I'm really glad you've found such a good friend. I'm happy, too, that Ms. Fluffington has come to realize it."

"Has she?"

"Well, I suppose. Why else would she agree to you and Dusty coming to dinner with us?"

"Dusty thinks that was Greyson's doing. She thinks he's trying to fix things."

"Oh." Smokey hadn't thought of that, but now that Autumn says it, it does sound like something he would do.

Straightening up, Autumn smooths her dress and adds, "Dusty and I don't care anyway. We're grown cats, after all. We can make our own decisions about who we have for friends. Dusty told Abigail that if she doesn't like it, she can stick it in her litterbox."

"What!" Smokey is aghast. "She said that?"

"She did. I think Ms. Fluffington is slowly coming to realize that her days of running Dusty's life are over."

Chapter Twenty-Three

The Red Dot

Autumn Amelia has never been so excited in her life as Smokey's car pulls into The Red Dot's parking lot. A crisp, white building rises above them. Soft lighting emanates from the enormous front window illuminating the restaurant's interior. In gold above the window are the words The Red Dot with a glowing red circle above and slightly to the side of them as if the words are a laser pointer. In front of the window stands a row of perfectly manicure bushes set into a black wrought iron holder. Slender doors on either side lead into the restaurant.

"Oh, Smokey, just look at it." A light, sultry breeze lifts Autumn's fur.

"There they are," says Smokey.

Autumn looks away from the building to see Greyson opening the passenger door of his rental car for Ms. Fluffington. Then he opens the back door to let Dusty emerge. Greyson looks dashing in a dark charcoal suit, white shirt, and matching charcoal tie. Ms. Fluffington is in a pewter colored dress with a matching cropped jacket, embellished with swirls of sequins. Dusty's dress is a rich forest green with three thin gold bands encircling the waist.

"You look beautiful!" Autumn says as they greet each other. "Did you make your dress?"

"Yes," says Dusty. "And Abby's, too."

"Amazing!"

Neither dress would be out of place in the inventory of the most fashionable designer.

"Are you ladies ready?" asks Greyson. "Shall we?" He offers and elbow to Ms. Fluffington who slips her arm into his.

"Don't forget, Dusty," Autumn whispers. "You have to keep me in line. Smokey will never forgive me if I embarrass her tonight."

Dusty laughs. "I'll make sure you behave," she says linking arms with Autumn.

As Greyson opens the door, delicious scents wash over Autumn. Her eyes roll back as she breathes them in. "This is heaven!"

Autumn doesn't realize she's stopped walking until she feels Dusty tug her arm. She'd become lost in the aromas as if they were a gentle wave carrying her out to sea. She comes back to herself enough to follow as the maître de, a formally attired Irish Setter, leads them to a larger alcove, leaving them in the paws of a gray and white Borzoi.

"My name is Leonid and I will be your waiter for the evening," says the Borzoi.

After taking their drink orders he leaves them to the hors d'oeuvres arranged on a long table against the back wall. From within the three-sided room, they can see the other diners while remaining secluded.

"Greyson, did you request this spot?" Smokey asks. "It's perfect."

"Yes. Abigail told me all about The Red Dot when I was last here. I looked it up online and saw that they have a private alcove for small groups. I thought that would work well for us."

Autumn can't believe her good fortune. She can enjoy the full atmosphere of the restaurant without fearing that she will unwittingly grab something off the tray of a passing waiter. She must remember to thank Greyson for his thoughtfulness. Turning to the spread of delicacies arrayed on the table she wonders where to start.

"Here you go, Miss Autumn," says Greyson, handing her a plate and napkin.

"I don't recognize some of these," Dusty admits. "Autumn, what are those?" she asks, pointing to a set of six white porcelain ladle-like spoons arranged in a circle like spokes in a wheel.

"Hot and cold appetizers," Autumn tells her. "Try this one," she says, placing the contents of one of the spoons on Dusty's plate. Dusty bites into the creamy lump topped with chopped scallions.

"Mm…" she says. "Delicious."

Autumn's stomach growls. She's barely eaten all day in order to save room for this experience. She wants to try some of each, but with eight more courses to come she's afraid she'll be too full. The dilemma of which to choose is overwhelming.

As if reading her mind, Greyson says, "There's too much to have one of everything. Might I suggest we each take a few and share so we can all get a taste of each one?"

"Wonderful idea," says Abigail. "I'm going for the smoked salmon mousse canapes on cucumbers. Those are my favorite. I suppose you'll want the bacon-wrapped shrimp, Greyson?"

"You know me too well already, Abby," he says, chuckling.

Autumn places three hors d'oeuvres on her plate — a sausage and mushroom stuffed cherry tomato, a sweet potato chip topped with goat cheese and caviar, and blue cheese crostini with balsamic roasted grapes. The tastes and textures pop on her tongue like fireworks.

"What sort of drink is that?" asks Smokey, pointing to a glass filled with a frothy green substance.

"That is green pea soup," says Abigail, handing a glass to Smokey. "See," she says, tapping the slice of bacon standing upright in the glass.

Autumn cannot help herself. She takes a glass from the table. The pea soup is delicious, the bacon a perfect complement. Lost in the flavors, her resolve to be selective evaporates. By the time the waiter returns with their drinks, she's had one of each item on the table. If her tummy is full, she doesn't notice. She feels as if she's in a different world, barely hearing the conversation around her. She comes out of her trance only when Dusty tugs her arm, leading her towards the large round table in the center of the alcove.

As they take their seats, lists of ingredients and methods of preparation for each food she's just sampled chase each other through Autumn's mind. It's not long before the waiter reappears.

"May I take your soup orders? He asks them. "Tonight's choices are broccoli almond soup, chilled melon and mint soup, and wild mushroom soup."

The others place their orders. When the waiter turns to Autumn, her brain is reeling. How can she choose?

"I would like…well, all of them." Autumn steals an embarrassed glance at Smokey.

"Very good, Madam," says the waiter, then turns to leave.

"Oh, my. I'm sorry," says Autumn. "I should call him back and pick just one." She starts to rise from the table, but Greyson, seated to her right, puts a paw on her shoulder.

"It's all right, Autumn," he says. "This is a tasting dinner. They are going to serve very small portions of everything so we can try a wide variety of foods without getting stuffed. It's perfectly fine to have ordered all three soups."

"Really?" both Autumn and Smokey ask in unison.

"Really," says Greyson.

Relief floods Autumn, followed immediately by unbridled joy. She can eat everything they offer and it won't be a faux pas! Could anything surpass such a treat?

The waiter sets their soups before them, placing extra spoons before Autumn. The pure taste of the wild mushroom soup is followed by the creamy, nutty broccoli almond soup. Autumn sips some water then spoons up a taste of the chilled melon and mint soup. She's saved this for last because she's been marveling at its beauty. Half the bowl is orange with crushed green mint on top and the other half is green with dollops of orange melon. It's like a work of art.

"How is it, Autumn?" asks Dusty who only ordered the wild mushroom soup.

"Delicious," says Autumn, licking the froth from her lips. "Try some." Autumn spoons some into Dusty's empty bowl.

Conversation between Smokey, Abigail, and Greyson has turned to Ratley and the park.

"So, you've truly no idea what he has planned?" asks Greyson. "Not even an inkling?"

"No," says Abigail. "Other than it's an attempt to derail plans for the park."

"How are you preparing for this meeting?"

"That's a good question. I've spoken with Miguel. He hasn't the foggiest notion what Ratley is up to, either, but he says that whatever it is we should remain positive. He wants to take whatever Ratley throws at us and turn it to our advantage."

"I'm glad you and Miguel think fast on your paws," says Smokey. "I'm not as good at it."

"You did fine at the protest," Abigail assures her.

Autumn listens but doesn't take part in the conversation. She is engrossed in sampling a bit of every appetizer on the table. A variety of freshly baked breads, roasted garlic, cheese and fruit assortments, and a small plate of crab and squid atop celery sticks and covered with sprouts has her attention.

"Who will be at the meeting?" asks Greyson.

"Well," says Abigail, "Originally, I assumed it would just be Miguel, Ratley, Smokerina, and I, but I quickly realized it will be much larger. Not that Ratley has told us, but he's asked us to meet him on the steps of City Hall. He must be bringing a team of rodents with him."

"And Miguel got word that Ratley has contacted the media," Smokey adds. "They'll all be there. He wouldn't have done that for a private meeting."

"It sounds as though he's going to try to paint you into a corner and he wants it all on record," says Greyson.

"Any suggestions?" Abigail asks.

Greyson is about to answer but is interrupted by the waiter carrying a tray with four types of salad mixtures. He tips each plate towards them as he explains the combinations.

"Field salad with snow peas and grapes. Mixed greens with goat cheese and feta. Mixed greens with carrots, pepper, and sun-dried tomatoes. And for dressings we have sesame ginger, raspberry vinaigrette, and lemon garlic."

The others easily make their choices, but again Autumn finds it impossible.

"Could I have one of each if you put them in small bowls?" she asks, hoping she's not embarrassing the others.

"Of course, Madam. And your dressing?"

"Oh dear." Autumn hesitates. How can she ask for one of each salad with one of each dressing?

"Perhaps Madam would like one of each on the side?" the waiter suggests.

"Perfect!" says Autumn.

The conversation returns to the coming meeting as they await their salads.

"If you really think he's going to bring others along," says Greyson, "perhaps you should, too."

"Hmm..." says Abigail. "Rufus should be there."

"Yes," agrees Greyson. "And what about Jasmine? She's part of this now. And didn't you say she has a team of birds and rodents all raring to go? They should come, too."

"Excellent idea," says Abigail.

Once the salads arrive, Autumn no longer hears them. All her concentration is focused on the flavors and sensations dancing on her tongue. She's managed to parcel out each dressing on a different section of each salad so she can try every combination. It's not until she feels the tap of Dusty's paw on her arm that she looks up to see all the faces turned towards her. She looks to Dusty.

"Greyson asked you a question," Dusty whispers.

Autumn turns to Greyson. "I'm sorry. I didn't hear you."

Greyson's face breaks into a huge grin. "Lost in the salads, were you?"

Autumn feels the tips of her ears burn.

"Don't worry, Miss Autumn," he says. "I'm delighted that you are so thoroughly enjoying yourself."

"I am!" says Autumn. "This is amazing, Greyson. I don't know how to ever thank you for inviting me."

"No need. I'm glad you came."

As they talk, the waiter returns, moving silently around their table clearing away their salad plates and forks.

"What I asked," Greyson continues, "is if you have considered Miguel Gato's offer to run a restaurant at the park?"

"Oh, that." Autumn's heart sinks. Having her own restaurant is the dream of her life, but how can she do it if she eats all the inventory? "I'd truly love to, but I don't think it's a wise idea."

"Why not?" asks Greyson. "Autumn Amelia, you are the best chef I've ever known."

"It's true," puts in Abigail. "Anyone who can improve on Gustav's secret sauce to the point where even the great Gustav himself agrees that it's an improvement has a talent most rare."

Autumn is amazed that Abigail praises her so highly. Perhaps she has forgiven her for taking Dusty out and getting her stoned on matatabi. The waiter, reaching for the last empty dish, quickly glances at Autumn, a look of awe shining in his eyes.

Autumn's gaze lowers so that she's staring at her stack of plates awaiting the coming courses. She waits for the Borzoi to leave before speaking.

"I have a problem," she begins, her voice soft. "It's better for me to work from home."

"But Autumn," says Smokey, "it would be your kitchen. You'd be in charge. It wouldn't matter."

Autumn looks up. "I've explained before, Smokey. It wouldn't be my kitchen. Not really. It would be Miguel's."

"It's not like he'd be there."

"It doesn't matter. He'd get rid of me once the stock started disappearing and money was wasted on replenishing it. I don't know if I'd be able to get my old job back. And…well, I think I'd die of embarrassment and a broken heart."

"What is this all about?" asks Abigail. "Why would the stock disappear?"

"You can find a way to manage it, Autumn," says Dusty. "I never thought I'd be able to leave the apartment and now look at me. And that was all because of you."

"That's different, Dusty. You just needed to learn to find your way around and gain some confidence. But I don't even know I'm doing it."

"Doing what?" asks Abigail.

"If you could come up with a creative way to deal with the problem, would you accept the position?" asks Dusty.

"What problem?" asks Abigail. "Greyson, do you know what they're talking about?"

The waiter returns to take their orders for the fish course. Mako shark with citrus, cashew shrimp, grilled sea bass, and steamed mussels with fennel, tomatoes, ouzo, and cream are the choices. The decision is more difficult for each of them than it had been with the previous ones.

"I believe this is where we take a cue from Autumn Amelia and begin to sample a bit of each," Greyson suggests.

"Shall I bring a small portion of each for everyone?" the waiter asks.

All nod in agreement.

"Very good," says the waiter and hurries away.

"Back to what we were talking about," says Abigail. She looks directly at Autumn. "What is the problem with you having your own restaurant?"

Autumn sighs heavily. "While I'm cooking, I eat whatever is near me. I don't know I'm doing it. I'm not sure how to explain it but having something to munch on gives me inspiration. It's how I come up with new recipes. Unfortunately, it means I eat the inventory. It's why I bake from home now. My boss, Tabby Furry, couldn't afford the loss when I was working in the bakery. It's not something I can control since I don't know I'm doing it. I go into a sort of trance when I'm cooking?"

"A trance?" asks Abigail.

"I guess that's what you'd call it. I stop noticing anything but the food. I'm totally focused. It's as if everything else disappears. That includes any food within reach."

Autumn notices Abigail looking at her thoughtfully. *Does she think I'm crazy? Will she try to stop Dusty from associating with me again?*

"It seems to me your munching is not a problem, but an integral part of your creative process," Abigail surprises her by saying. "Tell me, does it matter what you eat?"

"No. Anything within paw's reach will do."

"Then the solution is simple. Bring your own snacks from home and keep them nearby when you cook. That way you'll eat your own food, not the restaurant's."

Autumn is astonished. The faces of the others show that she's not alone.

"I can't believe no one's ever thought of that," says Smokey. "What about it, Autumn? Would it work?"

"I think it might," she says, excitement welling inside her. Could it be possible? Could she really attain her dream?

"I do hope you will give it serious consideration," says Abigail. "If you ran a restaurant at the park, I'm sure it would be a huge draw."

"You'll have to learn what all the different animals like to eat," says Dusty.

"That would be fun," says Autumn. "I love learning new recipes."

The table becomes crowded as the waiter sets several small plates each with a different fish, before them. Again, the presentations are works of art. This time it is the colors that stand out most to Autumn. The shark filet lies in a sunny yellow sauce, sliced lemons atop it. The cashew shrimp soaks in a pool of rich brown sauces and light green scallion slices. The sea bass glistens with a golden texture. It, too, is topped with green, but the darker shade of parsley. The shiny black shells of the steamed mussels contrast strikingly with the peachy colored cream sauce.

As Autumn eats, she imagines creating such delicacies in her own restaurant. The thought delights her almost as much as the lemony, creamy, and oceany tastes of the fish.

"If Miss Autumn is going to seriously consider running a restaurant at the park, then she should attend this meeting too," says Greyson. "What do you say, Autumn?"

Autumn thinks for a moment. Then, inspired, she says, "I'll bring refreshments. Food always puts everyone in a good mood."

"Splendid!" says Abigail.

"What will you make for the rodents?" Dusty asks.

"I know the squirrel brothers love seeds and nuts, but I'm not sure what mice and rats like. Would you mind asking Mr. and Mrs. Mouse for me?"

"Of course. I'll let you know right away what they say."

"Abigail, have you met the Mouse family, yet?" Greyson asks.

"I'm afraid not. I asked Dusty to introduce me, but they were too frightened to meet me."

"Pity," says Greyson. "Their assistance would be helpful. I suppose there's no chance of talking them into attending the meeting, is there?" he asks, turning towards Dusty.

"Not likely, but I will ask them."

"I don't understand," says Smokey. "They get along so well with you, Dusty, and they seem to accept Autumn. Why are they still so afraid?"

"They finally told me that Mrs. Mouse's mother and Mr. Mouse's grandparents were eaten by feral cats. I cried so hard I almost flooded their home when I heard."

Autumn rubs Dusty's back when she sees tears glistening in her eyes.

"It's amazing they trust any cat," says Greyson, looking sober.

Autumn notices that Smokey has stopped eating and is staring at her plate.

"Are you all right, Smokerina?" asks Abigail.

"I don't think I could ever face them." Smokey speaks so softly Autumn barely catches her words.

"No one can undo the past," says Greyson. "But the all-inclusive park you are proposing is a huge step towards creating a better present and future. It would be a crime if it were to be prevented."

"Greyson, you'll still be here on Friday," says Abigail. "Why don't you come to the meeting. I know you're not directly involved in the park, but as the former CEO of PAWS UNITED you are in a unique position. PAWS UNITED has an unblemished worldwide reputation for helping all creatures without exception. In fact, if you'll agree to it, I'll contact Miguel and ask if he can make you our spokescat for the park."

"I'd be delighted. I've been looking for a worthy project since I've retired. This would be perfect."

The waiter returns announcing that the main course is about to be served. The choices are beef bourguignon, kalamata pork tenderloin with rosemary, and coq au vin.

This time Autumn is the first to order. "Yes," she says.

"Pardon?" asks the waiter.

"Yes. I'll have one of each."

"I think we all will," says Abigail as the others nod their agreement.

Autumn's senses sing when the main course arrives. The aromas send her into ecstasy. The flavors frolic on her tongue. All conversation is gone. She is euphorically engaged in mentally deciphering the ingredients of each dish.

"It really is the sauces that make them special," she says, though not meaning to speak aloud. "This one is particularly superb," she mumbles as she lets the beef bourguignon sauce swish around her mouth. She feels as if each tastebud is grabbing hold of her food to make its own assessment.

When they have finished the main course and the waiter has cleared their plates, he returns to offer them a palate cleanser. Abigail and Greyson request prosecco. Smokey and Dusty opt for water with lemon and Autumn orders a lime sorbet. These are followed by desserts of flourless chocolate cake sprinkled with confectioner sugar and topped with raspberries, and lemon crème Brule topped with two strips of lemon peel and a sprig of white rosebud. True to form, Autumn has one of each.

There is only one course left, the mignardise. The waiter arrives with colorful French macarons, French Madeleine biscuits, and an assortment of small chocolates. Though Autumn is stuffed, she can't dream of missing a bite of this magnificent dinner and consumes one of each. When finished, she wonders if she'll ever be able to move.

The waiter returns, presumably to present Greyson with the check. However, it is Autumn's chair at which he stops.

"Madame, the chef has a request," he says.

"Oh?" asks Autumn. She looks at Dusty and whispers, "Did I do anything wrong?"

Dusty shakes her head.

"Yes, Madam. The chef would like to know if you are indeed the same Autumn Amelia who improved Chef Gustav's bourbon sauce?"

"How does your chef know about that?" she asks.

"Madam, the entire restaurant community knows about it. When I heard your name and Madam Fluffington mention the occasion of your improvement of the sauce I was compelled to tell Chef Luna. She asked me to inquire as to whether you are indeed the same Autumn Amelia."

"Yes, it was me," Autumn admits, perplexed.

"Splendid!" the waiter exclaims. "In that case, Chef Luna would be most honored to meet you."

"Really?"

"Oh, Autumn, how wonderful," says Greyson.

"Yes, Madam. She would like to give you a tour of the kitchen."

Autumn can hardly believe her ears. Just when she thought this night couldn't get any better.

"Autumn, please be careful," says Smokey.

Seeing the worried look on her face, she knows Smokey is imagining all the trouble Autumn could cause in the kitchen. Torn between wanting to meet the chef and see the kitchen and fearing what might happen, she finally asks, "Could Dusty come with me, please?" hoping she's not being rude.

"Of course, Madam."

Overjoyed, Autumn bounces out of her chair forgetting how full she is. She grabs Dusty's paw. As they follow the Borzoi, Autumn whispers, "Don't let me do anything bad."

The large, immaculate kitchen bustles with activity. Chefs and their assistants work busily at a variety of stations while waiters constantly come and go. It is the biggest, most fascinating kitchen Autumn has ever seen. She takes it all in, imagining herself in charge.

"You must be Autumn Amelia." A beautiful Alaskan Malamute says as she approaches Dusty and Autumn.

"Yes," says Autumn. "This is my friend, Dusty."

"I am Luna, the executive chef. I am so very happy to meet you." Luna shakes paws with both cats.

"Your kitchen is amazing. I wish I could cook in a kitchen like this."

"From what I've heard, you should be running one," says Luna.

Autumn is still baffled as to how word of her improving Gustav's sauce got to Luna's ears. "If you don't mind my asking, how did you find out about my little adventure in Mr. Gustav's kitchen?"

Luna barks out a laugh. "Everyone knows about it. It's the talk of the Faunaburg culinary community. But I heard it from my pastry chef. She heard it from the sous chef at Top Cat."

"Oh my. I hope Mr. Gustav doesn't think I talked about it. I didn't tell anyone."

"I daresay you and Gustav weren't alone in that kitchen at the time."

"That's true." Autumn realizes that Sukey and Sally must have been spreading the tale to all of their restaurant colleagues. "Poor Mr. Gustav. I hope he's not terribly embarrassed. I could tell he's sensitive about his cooking."

Luna's barking laugh resounds again. "Gustav needed humbling. He's too big for his whiskers. It probably did him good. Now, I must ask you, Miss Autumn, did you enjoy your dinner here tonight?"

Autumn is suddenly aware that all the noise in the kitchen has stopped. Every employee has turned to look at her, anxious expressions on their faces.

"Everything was superb," she says.

The entire kitchen seems to breathe a sigh of relief.

"I am delighted. And you, Miss Dusty? Did you enjoy your dinner as well?"

"Very much, thank you."

"I'm so glad. Would you ladies like a tour of the kitchen?"

"We'd love it," says Autumn.

Luna takes them from one cooking station to the next, introducing her to each chef. Besides Luna, The Red Dot has seven chefs, and each has an assistant. Each chef gives Autumn a brief overview of their work. The saucier makes all the sauces, the poissnnier makes all of the fish dishes, the rotisseur makes all the meat dishes, the entremetier is in charge of all vegetables and oversees the legumier — the vegetable chef and potager who prepare the soups — and the pâtissier creates the desserts. Autumn marvels at the variety of equipment at each station and the skill with which the chefs handle them.

"This is amazing," she says, as Luna leads them from the last station. "Mama Cat certainly didn't have so many gadgets. Imagine what she could have done with them."

"What is amazing is that you have such talent without ever having attended a school of culinary arts."

"Would I have to have gone to a cooking school to run a restaurant?" Autumn asks.

"Not necessarily," says Luna. "To run a restaurant like The Red Dot, yes, but anyone who knows how to cook can open a family restaurant. Are you thinking of doing that?"

"An offer has been made. I would love to do it."

"Autumn, would you like to go to culinary school?" asks Dusty.

"I'd love to, but I haven't the money for it. Besides, I don't think the restaurant at the park would be the type that would require it."

They are standing at the back of the kitchen. A door swings open to their left as a furry creature carrying a tray of clean dishes emerges. The stack of dishes is so high she can't see his face.

"Careful, ladies," says Luna, ushering them out of the way.

Autumn looks towards the door. "Is there more to the kitchen?" She can hardly believe it.

"That's where the dishes are washed, but you can see it if you like," Luna explains, pushing the door open.

The room is warm and humid. Several dishwashers rumble. At one end of the room a pair of French Bulldogs scrape and rinse dishes and serving plates. Then they are passed to the Labrador Retrievers who load them into the dishwashers. The door swings open again, and an animal Autumn does not recognize enters. It is the same one who, moments ago, carried out the huge stack of plates. She looks at him curiously. He appears to be a dog, but he's not a breed with which she is familiar. His coat is like a German Shepherd's but not as thick. He's slightly smaller than a Shepherd, but with very long legs and a bushy tail.

"Is everything okay?" asks Luna.

Autumn realizes she's been staring. "I'm sorry," she says. "I didn't mean to be rude. It's just that I've never seen one of those dogs before. What breed is he?"

"Oh, you mean Irving? He's a coyote."

Autumn gasps. Irving turns to look at her.

"Don't worry," says Luna. "He won't harm you. Irving is very nice."

Irving casts his gaze down.

Afraid she has hurt his feelings Autumn approaches the coyote. "Hello, Irving. I'm Autumn Amelia. It's nice to meet you," she says, holding out her paw.

Irving looks up. He shakes her paw. "Nice to meet you too," he says. Suddenly his eyes widen. "You're not *that* Autumn Amelia, are you?"

"Yes, she is," says Luna. "See, Autumn. I told you. The *whole* culinary community is talking about you."

As they ride back to the Faunaburg Office Towers so Autumn can pick up her car, she tells Smokey everything about her visit to the kitchen.

"I've made up my mind, Smokey. I will take the job as head chef of the park's restaurant. After seeing The Red Dot's kitchen, I know I'd be in heaven running one even half as nice. And I think Ms. Fluffington's idea about bringing my own snacks will work. Oh, I do hope Mr. Ratley doesn't manage to stop it. I'm going to get started right away on planning the refreshments for the meeting. I wish I knew his favorite food."

Smokey has been silent all the way home, mostly because Autumn has talked non-stop. She turns into the parking lot and pulls up next to Autumn's car.

"See you at home," says Autumn, reaching for the door handle.

A paw grips her arm tightly. Startled, Autumn turns to Smokey. The dashboard gives enough light for her to clearly see that Smokey looks terrified.

"What's wrong?" Autumn asks.

"Never, ever go anywhere near a coyote again!"

Chapter Twenty-Four

The Challenge

Smokey's heart pounds as she approaches the steps of City Hall. It's close to dusk on Friday. Already a crowd is gathering, though she is early. Autumn and Dusty arrived at least a half hour ago to set up food tables on the common. She spies them bustling about, setting out stacks of plates, warming pans, cups, and utensils. Autumn Amelia is fussing with the layout of the table.

Smokey watches the TV crews setting up their equipment. Jerome J. Ratley's sedan is parked near the steps. An influx of rodents slowly descends upon the cement steps and mills about the common. More arrive each minute. As she gets closer, she sees that many appear apprehensive, though a small number of brave souls head towards the tables, drawn, no doubt, by Autumn's cooking. When Smokey reaches the tables she recognizes the Squirrel brothers, Simon and Sam. They are racing between the tables and the coolers helping Autumn Amelia and Dusty set out the food.

"Where is Ms. Fluffington?" Smokey asks. "She told me to get here early, but I don't see her anywhere."

"She's just arriving," says Dusty, pointing as her sister pulls up behind Ratley's vehicle.

Smokey watches as Abigail Fluffington steps from her cream-colored luxury car. Poised as always, if

Abigail Fluffington feels any dismay about the gathering crowd, she hides it well. Abigail catches sight of them and heads towards the table.

"Can you believe how many are here?" Smokey asks as Abigail joins them.

"It's just as Miguel predicted."

"It is?" Smokey asks. She knew the media would be here, but she hadn't expected so many rodents. Now all manner of birds were flying in, as well.

"He's had enough contact with Ratley to know what to expect. By the way, where is Miguel? He was going to pick up Greyson on his way. I thought they'd be here by now."

"Over there," says Autumn, indicating a small crowd huddled on the common.

Smokey sees rodents, birds, cats, and dogs, but she does not see Miguel or Greyson.

"He's in that mix, somewhere," Autumn explains. "Word got out quickly that Greyson is the retired CEO of PAWS UNITED and suddenly everyone wanted to meet him."

Abigail chuckles. "That must be Miguel's doing. He knows how well-loved PAWS UNITED is."

Smokey hears a soft squeak. It seems to be coming from Dusty.

"Of course, I'll introduce you," says Dusty, looking into her apron pocket.

Dusty holds her pocket open. Smokey peers in to see two mice, one wearing a suit and tie, the other in a floral dress. The lady mouse is checking her whiskers in a tiny mirror.

"Abby, Smokey," says Dusty. "This is Mr. and Mrs. Mouse. They live in the wall in my bedroom. Mr. and Mrs. Mouse, this is my sister, Abigail, and Autumn's sister, Smokey."

"I'm pleased to finally meet you," says Abigail. "But whatever are you doing in Dusty's pocket?"

"They feel safer in here," Dusty explains.

Abigail bends, speaking into the pocket. "I want you to know that we are delighted you've made a home with us, and you are always welcome in our apartment."

"Thank you," say the mice.

"It's nice to meet you," says Smokey. I've heard a lot about you from Autumn Amelia. She thinks your babies are adorable."

Mrs. Mouse beams.

Smokey feels a tap on her shoulder and turns to see Jasmine, two rats, a woodpecker, a blue heron, a chinchilla, and a groundhog. The web design team, apparently.

"Hi Smokey," says Jasmine. Turning to the others she says, "Hey, everyone, this is my best friend, Smokey. She's the lead architect on the park."

"Only for now," says Smokey. "If we are able to go through with this park there will be co-leads."

Jasmine introduces everyone. Siegfried and Poppy are the two rats. They're holding paws and only stop gazing starry-eyed at each other long enough to say hello. Chipper, the woodpecker, nods at everyone. The great blue heron named Louisa extends the leg she's been holding up since they arrived towards Smokey who shakes it in greeting. Scooter, the chinchilla could almost rival Autumn for fluffiness. And Shadow, the groundhog stands on his hind legs appraising everyone with a knowing look.

"Good thing Autumn brought a lot of food," Jasmine says, looking at the heavily laden tables. "This is quite a crowd."

"She's been preparing all day," says Smokey. "Her friend, Sukey, came over and helped her cook and Dusty is assisting with the set up."

"After they taste her food, all the furs and feathers will probably beg for the park just so they can go to her restaurant," says Jasmine.

"Hello, ladies."

Smokey looks up to see that Greyson and Miguel have joined them.

"Hi, Greyson. Nice to see you again," says Jasmine who then proceeds with another round of introductions.

"Have you spoken with Ratley, yet?" Abigail asks.

"Briefly," says Miguel.

"Any clue what he's up to?"

"All he'd say was that he has a proposal to make."

"Does that mean he might be willing to negotiate something?" asks Smokey, feeling hopeful for the first time.

"Possibly," says Miguel. "He was amazed to find the former CEO of PAWS UNITED here. It seems he has an uncle who was rescued by them a few years ago when the island he lives on was hit by a hurricane."

"Oh!" exclaims Abigail. "Now I have yet another reason to be glad you're here, Greyson."

Smokey notices the way Ms. Fluffington playfully twitches her whiskers at Greyson and the grin he gives her in return. She is still not sure how she feels about this relationship. She does not have to time ruminate on it, however, as Mr. Ratley has taken his place on the top step of City Hall and is calling the crowd to attention through a microphone.

"We'd better get up there," Miguel says and he, Smokey, Abigail, and Greyson head for the steps where they meet Rufus Tailwagger.

"Welcome, every fur and feather," Ratley says. "I am delighted that so many of you could make it. As you all know, we have a matter of great urgency to resolve. Recently, the City of Faunaburg sold a large piece of land adjacent to Rodent Way to Miguel Gato who in turn hired Fluffington ArCATecture to build a cat park. But you, my friends, did not allow it. Thanks to your willingness to protest such an abomination, those plans have been rightly scraped. Now, however, these cats have changed their tactics.

They'd like us to believe that they now want to build a park for all furs and feathers. They claim they want an end to all animosity between cats and rodents and to build new friendships and a better future for all. Well, my friends, I say that we'd all like such an occurrence. We'd all like to feel safe and secure in the knowledge that no fur or feather need live in fear of any other. That is, after all, the way it should be. And if…IF…they are truly sincere, then I am willing to lend my support in any way possible. However, they must prove their sincerity. I have labored far too many years for the rights of rodents to allow any underpawed schemes to bring harm to the rodent community. So, without further ado, I would like to announce my proposal to the team of Miguel Gato and Fluffington ArCATecture."

By now Smokey, Abigail, Miguel, Rufus, and Greyson are lined up on the top step a few feet from Ratley. Smokey watches intently as Ratley turns towards them. There is a gleam in his eye she can only term dangerous. Her anxiety grows as Miguel walks towards Ratley.

"Mr. Ratley," he says, taking the microphone handed to him by Rufus. "We are extremely grateful for your offer of cooperation. Whatever we can do to show our sincerity we will welcome."

Ratley's whiskers twitch as a wry smile inches across his face.

"I'm so glad to hear that, Señor Gato."

Ratley looks towards the group standing on the steps. Miguel follows his gaze, then motions for them to move closer. Once they are assembled, Ratley turns back towards the silent crowd staring in their direction.

"Well, then, Mr. Ratley," Miguel begins. "What is your proposal?"

"It's simple, really. All you have to do to show that you are truly sincere is to host a small dinner party at the site of the proposed park."

The look on Ratley's face and the tone of his voice tell Smokey that whatever he's suggesting is going to be far from simple.

"For the rodents?" asks Miguel.

"Oh, no, Señor. For another group of guests. A group that I will have my friend, Jay, fly this invitation to. Should you accept that is."

Ratley takes a piece of cardstock from his breast pocket and hands it to Miguel. Smokey wishes she could see Miguel's face as he reads it, but his back is to her. She does note a slight stiffening in his posture. The smile on Ratley's face has grown wider.

"Well?" asks Mr. Ratley. "Do you agree?"

"I can't speak for everyone. I must ask the rest of the team."

"By all means. In fact, why don't you read the invitation aloud. I'm sure everyone here is curious as to its contents and would love to know your team's reaction to it." Ratley bobs on his feet with excitement.

"I'm sure they would," agrees Miguel, his tone measured.

Miguel glances towards them and Smokey notes with some trepidation that his glance rests longest on her. There is a look on his face that seems to convey an apology. Smokey feels her claws dig into her pads and realizes she's been holding her paws in tight fists.

Miguel clears his throat, then reads the invitation aloud.

"Miguel Gato and Fluffington ArCATecture cordially invite the coyote colony of East Faunaburg to a dinner party in their honor on August 18th. A cocktail hour will begin at five o'clock p.m. followed by dinner at six. Please RSVP via Blue Jay post."

Smokey is certain her heart has stopped beating. Host a dinner party for a pack of coyotes? That is beyond her endurance.

"Of course, Señor Gato," says Ratley, "There will be witnesses to this dinner party should you actually go through with it. Myself, and a few others, will be posted within sight but safely out of reach. If, indeed, you are sincere about wanting all furs and feathers to live peacefully together I can only assume you mean *all* furs and feathers. That would include your own predators, would it not?"

Smokey's body feels frozen. She does not think she could move were the steps to suddenly burst into flame.

"And that does mean," continues Ratley, "that all of you must partake in this dinner party."

Ratley turns his gaze upon Smokey, the gleam in his eye practically glowing.

He knows I can't do it. It's what he's counting on. He'll say we were never sincere. We'll be disgraced. Miguel will have to accept to save face, but, no, I can't. I just can't!

"Smokey, are you okay?" Greyson's voice breaks through her racing thoughts.

"No," she mewls like a kitten.

Miguel turns to them. "What's it to be?" he asks, his voice low, his microphone turned off.

They all look at Smokey.

"Is there a way we could do it without Smokey being involved?" Greyson asks, though his tone says he already knows the answer.

"Not likely," says Miguel who turns to Smokey. "Smokerina, I'm going to let you make the decision. You're the one who will be most affected by this. And please be assured that if you say no, it will never be held against you."

"I...I c-can't." Smokey can barely get the words out.

There is a collective sigh among the group. Tears well up in Smokey's eyes. She hates being the weak link, letting them all down.

"All right," says Miguel. He turns back towards Ratley, but before he can say a word, he is nearly run over by Autumn Amelia who has just bounded up the steps of City Hall.

"We accept!" she cries. "Send the invitation, Mr. Ratley. We'll do it!"

Ratley suddenly appears as though a thunder cloud has settled upon his face.

"Who exactly are you?" he bellows.

"Mr. Ratley," says Miguel. "This is Smokerina's sister, Autumn Amelia. She's responsible for all the food here this evening. She's also to run a restaurant at the park."

"So, she's part of your team?"

"In a manner of speaking, yes but —"

"Don't worry, Mr. Gato," says Autumn. "I can make a dinner that will have the coyotes swooning. And Mr. Ratley," she says turning towards him. "I understand your point completely. We cats are asking rodents to trust us when since from time immemorial we've given you no reason to do so. It's only fair that we should show ourselves willing to be put to the same test."

Though Miguel's microphone is off, Ratley's is still on. Autumn's words ring out for all to hear causing a mighty cheer to erupt from the crowd.

Smokey can scarcely breathe. How could Autumn do this to her? Suddenly very fluffy arms wrap around her, and she is enfolded in Autumn's luxurious fur.

"Smokey, don't worry," Autumn whispers. "I know you're frightened, but we can do this. I'll handle everything. All you have to do is show up long enough for Mr. Ratley to see you. We can't lose this opportunity. It's what we've been waiting for."

Smokey steps back, holds Autumn at arm's length.

"What we've been waiting for? To be eaten by coyotes?"

Autumn has maneuvered them far enough away for their voices not to be picked up by the microphone.

"That won't happen. I'll make such a magnificent meal it will be all they'll want. And just think, this could be the start of good relations between cats and coyotes. Remember the Oneness the Empress talked about? This is it. This is how it will happen."

"Autumn, I wish I could believe that. But I'm terrified we'll be eaten."

"That's what the rodents are terrified of about us too. Yet we expect them to accept us at our word that we won't do it."

"The coyotes haven't made any such promise."

"True. But I'll talk to the coyote at The Red Dot. He was nice. I'm sure he'll help. Please, Smokey. We have to do this. It's not just about us. It's about what the Great Creator wants for us. Let's not stand in the way."

Smokey's mind reels. She wants desperately for Autumn to be right. She wants to honor the Great Creator. But she's still afraid.

"Have faith, Smokey," says Autumn. "We'll pray to the Great Creator every night between now and the eighteenth. If we're working in the Creator's service everything will be fine. I feel it. This is the right thing to do."

"Well, what's your answer?" asks Ratley, a note of impatience in his voice.

"Smokerina?" asks Miguel.

"We'll all be there," says Greyson. "And for what it's worth, I've worked with coyotes and wolves at PAWS UNITED. I've lots of contacts. I'll get in touch with them. We'll make sure everything is safe.

Greyson's words give Smokey a measure of reassurance. She glances at Abigail who nods.

"Well. I guess…okay," she says, feeling as though she's just sealed their doom.

"Send the invitation, Mr. Ratley," Miguel announces into the now live microphone.

Another cheer goes up from the crowd, louder than before as a blue jay swoops down, grabs the invitation in his beak and flies off. Once the ovation dies down and he can be heard again, Miguel says into his microphone, "Mr. Ratley, do we have your word that once this dinner party has concluded you will honor your promise to cooperate with the forming of a park for all furs and feathers?

"Sir, I am nothing if not a rat of my word. It is agreed."

The two shake paws as flashbulbs from the many TV and news camera crews capture the momentous event.

"May I?" asks Autumn, holding out her paw.

"Of course," says Miguel, handing her the microphone.

"May I have your attention, please?" says Autumn addressing the crowd. "There is plenty of food on the tables. Please see my friends, Dust, and Simon and Sam Squirrel. They'll help you find whatever you need."

Smokey spends the rest of the evening in a daze. Though she helps at the table, her mind isn't on what she's doing. In fact, she can't focus at all. She feels shaky, sure her legs will give out.

"Smokey, that's the wrong one," she hears Dusty say. "He wants the one with blueberries."

Looking down she sees she's picked up a peanut butter suet cake.

"Oh, sorry," she says, replacing it on the plate and serving the correct one to the waiting house wren.

"Are there any more seed and berry pies?" asks a racoon.

Smokey looks around. Not seeing any, she says, "Um…I guess not. Sorry."

"There are more in the food chest," says Simon Squirrel. "We'll get them."

Simon and Sam scamper off.

"You are all very brave to have agreed to Mr. Ratley's proposal," says the racoon.

"Thank you," says Smokey, feeling anything but brave.

"Will the park be open at night?"

"Yes. Many of the furs and feathers are nocturnal or semi-nocturnal so it will be open day and night."

"Wonderful! And your sister's restaurant? Will that be open at night, too?"

"I don't know. She has to sleep sometime, but we'll discuss it."

"This food is fabulous. I certainly hope we nocturnals will get to have our share."

"I'm sure Autumn will figure out something. She's very accommodating."

Smokey nearly jumps out of her fur as Simon lands with a thump on the table in front of her.

"More pies!" he calls, dropping a few warm pie plates in front of him.

"Coming through!" yells Sam, who runs up Simon's back and springboards off his head with even more pies.

"Hey!" yells Simon.

"I said, 'coming through.' You didn't move."

"You didn't give me time."

"Boys!" says Autumn, just returning to the table after seeing to the fish she's been frying over a portable charcoal grill. "No running over each other."

"Sorry, Miss Autumn," they say in unison.

"That's better. The fish is ready, and a line of wading birds is forming. Please see to them."

"Right away, Miss Autumn," they say, scurrying off the table.

Smokey watches, transfixed, as the Squirrel brothers scamper towards the grill.

Autumn sighs. "I suppose no one has ever informed them that the fastest way between two points is a straight line."

Smokey can't help but smile as Simon and Sam zigzag across the common, running halfway up the flagpole, leaping over each other, scooting in and out of the openings in the gazebo. Still, they move so fast they reach the grill in no time and begin plating and handing out fried fish to the herons, loons, and kingfishers lined up before them.

Greyson is still chuckling over them when he reaches Smokey and Autumn.

"If this dinner is any indication, all the furs and feathers will be begging for the park to be built," he says as he reaches them. "Everyone is raving about your food. And just look," he says, gesturing to all the diners scattered about the common. "Cats, dogs, rodents, birds, all eating together. Why even Mr. and Mrs. Mouse ventured out of Dusty's pocket. They're sitting over there with Jasmine and the website team, chatting away like old friends. What a blessing this park will be."

"If we live to see it," Smokey mumbles.

"Greyson, will you take over here for a minute?" Autumn asks as she guides Smokey to an undisturbed section of the common.

"Are you angry with me?"

"No," says Smokey. "I'm scared."

"It will be all right. Tonight's festivities will be all over the news by morning. Everyone is going to want this park built."

"I want the park to be built, too. I just don't want to get eaten."

"Smokey, look around. Look at what's already been accomplished. It's happening because all the furs and feathers want it to. We all really want to live in peace with each other. Don't you think the coyotes might want that too?"

This was something Smokey had never thought about. Could it be?

"They'll see the news too," Autumn continues. "It's very possible they will be just as eager for peace as any of the rest of us. After all, the last time they raided they only ate the confections at Tabby's. That must say something."

"Well," says Smokey. "Maybe." She wants it to be true, but barely dares to hope.

"We'll start praying to the Great Creator as soon as we get home tonight. And tomorrow I'm going to start planning the dinner party. Will you help?"

Despite the jitterbugs dancing in her stomach, Smokey agrees. The sight of all these furs and feathers enjoying each other's company is heartening. She even spies Mr. Ratley talking to a cat, a dog, and an owl while obviously delighting in Autumn's cheese puffs.

Smokey draws a deep breath. She's not sure how the dinner party for the coyotes will play out, but she knows that the way things are at this moment is the way they should always be. If she has to die trying to bring it about, so be it.

Chapter Twenty-Five

The Dinner Party

Autumn looks over the long tables set up on the site of the proposed park while Dusty arranges white linen napkins on the tablecloths. She's made them specially for the occasion, midnight blue with images of the moon in various phases.

"What do you think?" asks Dusty as she folds the last napkin into the shape of a star and sets it atop a gold-rimmed plate.

"Beautiful," says Autumn.

"It will be dusk soon, Dusty says. "Where is everyone?"

"They should be back anytime."

Sukey and Sally have been working all day in the kitchen at Miguel's. With Autumn in charge, they've prepared a spectacular meal. Once Autumn knew everything was under control, she'd left for the site where she met up with Dusty. Earlier, Greyson, Miguel, and Rufus had set up the tables and prepared a fire pit while Smokey, Jasmine, and Abigail hung lanterns from trees and a banner proclaiming, WELCOME FRIENDS above the table.

"Look," says Dusty, pointing to a car pulling up to the edge of the site.

"That's Sukey," says Autumn. "She's brining the appetizers."

Autumn and Dusty hurry to the car to help Sukey carry trays of cold smoked salmon, cheese and crackers, pastry cheese puffs, fruit, and yogurt dip to the food table.

"Everything looks great," says Sukey.

"Thanks," says Autumn. "I'm anxious for it to be perfect."

"Speaking of anxious, how is Smokey?"

"Nervous. I've been working on her since the meeting at City Hall. I've had to talk her out of calling it off more times than I can count."

"Wasn't Greyson going to have one of the coyotes from PAWS UNITED talk to them?" asks Sukey.

"He was, but Mr. Ratley knows how well connected he is. Before Greyson could do anything, he added the stipulation that no outside influence could be exerted and that includes PAWS UNITED."

"Oh dear," says Sukey.

"Are you worried too?" asks Dusty.

"I'm not afraid they'll do anything bad." Sukey hesitates, then adds. "I think. I just want everything to go well."

A van pulls up beside Sukey's car. "That's Sally," she says. "She's got all the food and warmers."

As they walk towards the van, several more vehicles pull into the parking area. Greyson and Abigail emerge from one car, Miguel and Rufus from another, and Smokey and Jasmine from a third. Autumn is surprised to note that it's Jasmine's car. She thought Smokey was taking her own.

"I had to drive," Jasmine explains. "Smokey's a nervous wreck. I was afraid she'd total her car. All the way here she kept muttering about how we'll all end up on the coyote's dessert plates."

"Dessert is key lime pie and lemon tarts," says Autumn, loud enough for Smokey to hear and look up.

Just as they finish setting up the chaffing dishes and arranging the food, they hear a rustling in the fields just beyond the tables.

"Are they here?" asks Autumn, looking towards the fields, but seeing no one.

"Hi, Miss Autumn," calls a familiar voice.

"Simon!" Autumn runs towards the field.

"What are you doing here?" she asks as Simon Squirrel leaps from the tall grass to land in her arms and just as quickly jump down.

Sam Squirrel pops up next to him. "We're both here," he says.

"I can see that. Did you come to help?"

"In a way," says Simon. "Mr. Ratley and his crew are here to keep an eye on you, so we came to keep an eye on him."

"Don't you trust him?" asks Autumn.

"It's not that," Sam explains. "He doesn't know you like we do. We just want to make sure everything is on the up and up."

"Aren't you boys sweet!" Autumn gives each squirrel a kiss on the top of his head sending them into rapturous scurrying up the nearest tree. The lanterns sway wildly as they leap from one branch to the next.

"Okay, boys. That's enough," calls Autumn, but either they don't hear or are too excited to pay attention.

Autumn moves directly under a lantern strung from a low branch and looks up. Her face is inches from Simon's who is hanging upside down from the bottom of the lantern.

"Get down right now. The ladies spent a long time putting those up. You'll be in big trouble if you break them."

"Sorry, Miss Autumn," says Simon. He pushes off the lantern, executes a back flip and lands next to his brother at Autumn's feet.

"That's better. Now, is Mr. Ratley here yet?"

"Yup," says Sam. "Over there."

Autumn looks to where Sam is pointing. The tall grass waves jerkily in a way obviously not caused by a breeze.

"What's going on over there?" she asks.

The others have joined her. They all stare in the direction of the commotion.

"It's Mr. Ratley," says Simon. "He's brought his recording equipment. He's going to film everything. He says he wants to document this dinner party so there can be no way anyone can dispute whatever happens."

"But he wants the cameras hidden," says Sam. "He doesn't want the coyotes to know they're being filmed. I don't think he wanted you to know either."

"Hmph!" says Autumn. "He certainly is cynical, isn't he?"

"Is that even legal?" asks Jasmine.

"I don't know," Miguel answers, "but I refuse to make an issue of it. This dinner party will be a success and a recording will mean he can't dispute it either."

The tall grass parts allowing Ratley to step into the clearing and head towards them.

"Good evening," he says upon reaching the group. "I see you're all set up." He smiles, but his darting glances betray his apprehension.

"We are all ready, Mr. Ratley," says Autumn Amelia.

"We expect a delightful evening," says Greyson.

"We're fortunate to have such splendid weather," Abigail puts in.

"Indeed," says Ratley.

"Look!" says Dusty. "They're coming."

Autumn turns to see a band of seven coyotes striding towards them, the setting sun's rays blazing like golden shards between them.

"Ah, well…" says Ratley. "Good luck to you." With that, he scurries back to the tall grass out of sight.

Autumn smooths the yellow wrap dress she donned before leaving Miguel's kitchen and starts forwards to meet their guests. She feels a tug on the back of the cloth belt holding her back. Turning, she sees Smokey staring wide-eyed at the approaching coyotes. Her mouth is open as if to scream, but nothing comes out.

"Smokey? Are you alright?"

Frozen with terror, Smokey doesn't answer, but her whiskers tremble.

"Come with me, Smokey," Jasmine says, putting an arm around Smokey's shoulders. Guiding her towards the food table, she turns back to Autumn. "We'll start uncovering the appetizers," she says as she moves Smokey along.

Autumn stares after her sister in dismay, wondering how Smokey will make it through the evening. She offers a silent prayer to the Great Creator that all goes well, then turns her attention to the approaching guests.

Miguel, Abigail, and Rufus are the first to greet the coyotes. Autumn and the others stand just behind while introductions are made. Four of the coyotes are adults and three are pups. Autumn wants to cuddle the pups, especially the shy one hiding behind his mother's skirt.

"May I present to you the chef for tonight's feast, Autumn Amelia," says Miguel.

Autumn tears her gaze away from the adorable pups to shake paws with their parents. Mr. and Mrs. Alistair and Celia Wooders and their pre-teen twins Tobias and Myra and Mr. and Mrs. Leo and Ivy Birch and their little pup, Rusty, are presented as the honored guests.

Autumn crouches near Rusty who peeks out from behind his mother.

"Welcome, Rusty," she says. "Do you like fruit?"

He nods.

"Well, I've got a big plate full of fruit and some delicious yogurt to dip it in."

Rusty's eyes grow big.

Ivy gently presses him forward. "Say hello to Miss Autumn Amelia," she tells him.

"Hello," he says, his voice a tinny squeak, then darts back behind his mother.

Autumn stands up. "He is adorable," she says to Ivy.

"And just look at you, two," she continues, turning to the twins. "You look very grown up in those nice outfits."

Tobias and Myra break into huge grins.

"Please, come to the tables," says Miguel.

The group moves forward, the cats and dogs falling into step with the coyotes. When they reach the table with the appetizers, Jasmine is alone behind it. Autumn looks around but doesn't see Smokey. Where could she have gone? There are no buildings on the site and she would have had to pass them to get back to the vehicles. Autumn steps closer to the table, her foot compressing something soft and cylindrical. A high-pitched screech rends the air as the table jolts upward. Jasmine, Greyson, and Sukey grab for the dishes near the table's edge. Smokey pops up from underneath holding her tail.

"Smokey, what were you doing under the table?" Abigail asks as Dusty rearranges the disheveled table skirts.

"I…um…I dropped something. I was looking for it," she stammers, unable to lift her gaze.

Jasmine gives her such a pitiable look that Autumn knows she was hiding. She hopes the coyotes mistake her behavior for embarrassment over disrupting the contents of the table.

"No harm done," says Rufus. "Everything's set to rights."

"Yes, and I'd like to present to you the lead architect on the park project," says Miguel to the coyotes. "This is Miss Smokerina. She and her co-leads will be responsible for creating the design that will turn this parcel of land into a beautiful park for all furs and feathers."

As Miguel introduces the coyotes one by one, Autumn wills Smokey to look at them and speak politely.

"It's a pleasure to meet you," says Celia. "We've been following the story of the future park in the newspapers. I'd love to hear what you're planning."

"Nice to meet you, too," says Smokey in a voice so timid Autumn almost doesn't recognize it.

"Is your tail hurt?" asks Ivy. "You're still holding it. I'm a nurse. Would you like me to look at it?" She puts a solicitous paw on the tip of Smokey's tail causing Smokey to jump back.

"Wow! It must really hurt," says Autumn, hoping the coyotes believe that's the reason Smokey recoiled. "I'm sorry. I didn't see it sticking out under the table."

"It's all right," says Smokey. "It will stop hurting in a minute."

"Well," says Abigail, shooting Smokey a look of disdain. "Please everyone, help yourselves to appetizers."

A little nose pokes up over the table's edge. "Is this where the fruit and yogurt dip are?" asks Rusty.

Autumn can't resist a delighted smile. "Yes, it is. Let's get you a bowl."

As the rest mingle, Autumn, Sukey, and Sally check the contents of the chafing dishes.

"Is your sister alright?" Sally asks.

"She's terrified of coyotes," says Autumn. "She thinks they're going to eat us."

"Why would they do that when they've got such a splendid meal?" asks Sally, shaking her head.

"That's what I said, but Smokey is convinced. I just hope we get through this evening without her creating an inter-species incident," says Autumn. She tests a spoonful of the wine sauce covering the filet mignon. "Perfect! How's that polenta?"

"Exactly the right amount of creaminess," Sally says.

"Excellent."

Autumn looks over at the group seated around the fire pit, their forms silhouetted against the deep blue, almost black, sky. Talk and laughter waft over the open expanse. Movement to her left catches Autumn's attention. Smokey is seated behind the appetizer table.

"Oh dear," Autumn mutters and heads over.

As she nears the table, she hears Smokey's voice softly repeating, "They aren't the same coyotes. They won't hurt us."

Autumn crouches next to Smokey's chair. "What are you doing Smokey?

"Trying to make myself join them. I saw how Abigail looked at me. She's disgusted. She'll probably take me off the account. Maybe she'll fire me. If I want to salvage my job, I have to at least make an effort, but I'm just so scared." Tears streak the fur on her face and drip from her whiskers.

"They seem awfully friendly to me. Look at everyone." She gestures towards the group at the fire pit. "They all seem to be enjoying themselves. And the pups are just the cutest things. That Rusty is a darling. Why don't you try playing with the pups? That shouldn't scare you."

"I'm not good with kits and pups like you are. I never know what to do around them."

"Okay, then talk to Ivy. She was quite concerned about your tail. Thank her for offering to look at it. Ask her where she works. Get a conversation going. Sukey and Sally have everything under control here. Let's join them."

Autumn grabs a bottle of wine from under the table, pours a glass for Smokey, then taking Smokey's paw, leads her towards the fire pit. Ivy is easy to spot since Rusty is climbing all over her.

"May we join you?" she asks.

"By all means," says Greyson. "Smokey are you feeling better? Has your tail stopped hurting?"

"Yes, thank you. It's fine now."

"He is a rambunctious little fellow, isn't he?" says Autumn to Ivy.

"Yes, and if he's not careful, he's going to spill his Papa's beer."

"Hey, Rusty," says Autumn, "why don't we play a game together so your mom can talk to Smokey?"

"Okay."

"Can we play, too?" asks Myra.

"You sure can."

Rusty jumps into Autumn's arms and she carries him off with Myra and Tobias trailing after them. When they're far enough away not to bother the adults, Autumn kicks off her shoes and suggest a game of tag. She is having so much fun with the pups, she forgets the time until Miguel steps into the fray to ask when dinner will be served.

"It's all prepared. We've been keeping it warm until everyone is ready. Please have everyone take a seat at the table and we'll serve."

Autumn shoos the pups back to their parents and returns to help Sukey and Sally place the filet mignon atop a large scoop of creamy polenta on each plate along with a side of haricot vert with slivered almonds.

Once all the plates are filled, Alistair stands. "May I offer the blessing?" he asks.

"We'd be honored," says Abigail.

He lifts his paws and looks to the sky. "Great Creator, we thank you for this food and ask your blessings upon it. We thank you, also, for bringing us together this evening and we ask that you bless everyfur here with good health and peace and allow the park that will be built here to become a major step towards the Oneness of all creatures. Amen."

Oneness thinks Autumn. *The same word the Empress used. That must be a good omen.*

"This is delicious," says Leo Birch. "The rumors are true."

"What rumors?" asks Autumn.

"Everyone's heard about your cooking, Miss Autumn Amelia," Tobias says. "That's why the coyote band from Nestle Nook broke into Furry Confections. They wanted to see if what every fur and feather says about your cooking and baking was true."

"Tobias!" Celia exclaims.

"But it's true, Mom," Myra adds.

"They made an awful mess," says Celia Wooders. "That poor cat who owns the bakery must have been terribly upset."

"But they did say the food was awesome," Tobias claims.

"How would you know what they said, young pup?" asks Tobias' father, sternly.

"I heard it around." Tobias suddenly becomes enormously interested in the food on his plate.

"I'm glad to know they liked it," says Autumn. "But they could have just gone to the bakery and purchased whatever they wanted."

"Oh, those coyotes don't have any money," says Myra. "They're poor."

"That doesn't make stealing and destroying property excusable," says Celia.

"You work for Furry's, Miss Autumn," says Myra. "Did you see them?"

"No. It happened at night, but I did see the mess the next morning."

"Was it awful?"

"Lots of broken glass. Tabitha Furry was beside herself. The police dogs were there. I never heard what happened afterwards."

"They were arrested," says Leo. "A band of rogue coyotes. Just a few troublemakers."

"Are they in jail?" asks Rusty.

"Yes," says Celia. "I think we should talk about something more positive now."

"Good idea," says Ivy. "Smokey and I were talking earlier about plans for the park. It sounds wonderful."

"Please tell us about it, Smokey," says Alistair.

Autumn glances at Smokey. At least she did have a conversation with Ivy. But talk of the break-in at Tabby's has surely reminded Smokey of how terrified she was that night. Afraid Smokey won't be able to respond, Autumn says, "I'm looking forward to the slide."

"There's going to be a slide?" asks Rufus. "Can I slide down it?"

"Of course. I made Smokey promise that it won't be made of plastic. I hate when my fur gets full of static," says Autumn making the pups laugh.

"The slide will be in the tower."

Autumn looks up. It's Smokey who's spoken.

"Tell them how you came up with the idea for the tower," Greyson encourages. "And about the lighthouse and how you want to adapt it."

As Smokey begins, her words are choppy, staccato. Then Greyson interjects here and there and before long Smokey is blithely telling the story of their trip to Niptucket Island while being peppered with questions and comments from everyfur at the table.

"So, what would you like to see in the park?" Jasmine asks the coyotes when the story finishes.

As the conversation continues, Autumn, briming over with pride in her sister, gives Smokey a wide smile.

Once dessert is finished, Sukey and Sally clean up the dishes while the others return to the fire pit.

"Mommy, I'm tired," says Rusty, settling into Ivy's lap with a yawn. "Will you sing me to sleep?"

"I think we should wait until we get home, sweetie," she says.

"Oh, but Ivy, you have such a beautiful voice," says Celia. "You should sing."

"I love lullabies," says Dusty.

"Please do sing for us," says Miguel. "If you don't mind, that is."

"Well, all right," says Ivy. She clears her throat, looks down at Rusty curled in her lap and stroking his fur, begins to sing: "Little coyote pup looks at the moon. Can I climb up to it, Mama, he asks. You have to sing for the moon, my son. Sing your love to the moonbeams."

Entranced by Ivy's pure, soft voice Autumn feels all the tension she hadn't known she was carrying drain away. Each verse ends with "Sing your love to the moonbeams" and by the third verse all quietly add their voices.

When the song ends, there is silence. Rusty is sound asleep as are Myra and Tobias.

"That was lovely," Greyson whispers.

"You know," says Celia in quiet tones, "I'm glad we're here. At first, I didn't want to come to this dinner party."

"Why is that?" asks Rufus.

"Everything that's gone on with this park has been in all the papers and on TV. It felt as though we were being used as pawns in the power struggle between you and Jerome Ratley. We didn't like that."

"We also weren't sure if it was some sort of trick," adds Ivy. "Cats and coyotes haven't always been on the best of terms. I think Smokey can vouch for that."

"What?" asks Smokey, her startled tone causing Myra to stir in her sleep.

"It's all right, Smokey," says Leo. "We could tell you were terrified when we first got here."

"We know you were really hiding under the table," says Ivy, her voice conveying sympathy rather than accusation.

"Oh…well…I…um," Smokey stammers.

"Something very bad happened to you involving coyotes, didn't it?" asks Alistair.

Smokey goes silent.

"Not to her, to her father," says Greyson. "It was a long time ago, but he was…" Greyson's voice trails off.

"You don't have to say it. We can guess," says Celia who moves to sit next to Smokey.

"I lost my father when I was very young, too," she says. "It's a heartbreaking experience. I'm so very sorry, Smokey."

As Smokey dissolves in tears, Celia wraps her arms around her, rocking her gently.

"This is why we decided to come tonight," says Leo. "If this will help end the fears and antagonism between coyotes and cats, and every other species, we want to be a part of it. It's time all furs and feathers live together in peace. We think this park will be a great start."

"We also think it was very courageous of you to go through with this," says Ivy. "Especially you, Smokey. You're a very brave cat indeed."

Smokey lifts her head. Through tears coursing down her face, she says, "I want us all to live in peace, too, but how can I ever forget?"

"I don't think you can," says Alistair. "I don't think you should. None of us can pretend as though nothing's happened. That would make things worse."

"It's my belief," says Greyson, "that we must all own up to our faults, mistakes, and bad behavior. We must forgive each other and forgive ourselves. Many of our hurtful deeds were done out of desperation or ignorance. Some of us have a hard time forgiving ourselves for them."

"Yes," agrees Leo. "And some of us try to rationalize everything so we don't have to feel guilty. Instead, we should seek forgiveness and be willing to forgive."

"Every fur and feather have much to offer," says Abigail. "We should celebrate one another. My sister, Dusty, has taught me that."

"I have?" asks Dusty.

"You always assume the best of everyfur. I used to think you were being naïve and, sometimes, you were. Still, assuming the worst does too much damage. Autumn Amelia's the same way. I suspect that's why you two get along so well. The attitudes you both have bring out the best in others. Maybe they even bring out the good we didn't know we had in ourselves."

Autumn watches in delight as Greyson leans over to rub noses with Abigail.

The still night air is broken by a rustling noise coming from the fields, pulling Autumn's attention from Greyson and Abigail. The grass on the edge of the clearing bends to admit a stream of rodents led by Jerome J. Ratley pouring forth towards the fire pit.

"Mr. Ratley, have you come to join us?" asks Miguel, his eyebrow whiskers shooting up in surprise.

"Have you been here the whole time?" asks Alistair.

"Yes. Yes, we have. I couldn't take it any longer," says Ratley.

"What exactly are you talking about, Mr. Ratley?" asks Autumn, using the same tone as she assumes when the Squirrel brothers get out of line.

Ratley straightens his tie and smooths his whiskers. "It's simply that we've been in the field watching and listening."

"And recording," says Simon as he scurries over to plop himself in Autumn's lap.

"Hush," she says. "You'll wake the pups."

"As I was saying," Ratley continues. "We've seen and heard all that's gone on here, tonight. Frankly, things did not go as I expected."

"What did you expect, Mr. Ratley," asks Ivy. "A melee? A feud. Recriminations and insults?"

"At the very least," he admits.

"Sorry to disappoint you, Ratley," says Miguel.

Ratley straightens up to his full height. "You may be sorry, but I'm not."

"You're not?" asks Dusty.

"All I've ever wanted," says Ratley, "is peace and safety for rodents. I've worked for it for years. But to tell the truth, I never honestly believed it was possible. I did not believe the cats were sincere. I was shocked that they were willing to go through with this dinner party, but I assumed it just showed how desperate they were to get to us. After tonight, though…well, I now think that maybe there is hope. I said to myself moments ago, 'Ratley, you are watching the beginning of all you've dreamed of. Get over there and be a part of it.' That's why I brought us out of hiding. I want to apologize. You were right, Mrs. Wooders. I did use you as pawns. It was wrong and I'm sorry. And to the rest of you, I apologize for not believing you."

"Mr. Ratley, it is perfectly understandable why you didn't trust us," says Smokey. She has stopped crying and is looking at Ratley with a sympathy Autumn has never seen in her before. "My family, well not Autumn, but the rest of us hunted and ate rodents. We did it to keep from starving, that's all. But knowing that doesn't make it any less painful for you in the loss of your sister nor for any other rodents who have lost loved ones to cats. I want to be forgiven and have rodents trust and like me." Smokey shifts her gaze from Ratley to Celia. "So, I will work hard on forgiving the coyotes who killed my Papa Cat."

"I hope we can be part of your healing process," says Celia.

"The Great Creator works in mysterious ways," says Alistair. "Perhaps you're coming up with the idea of this dinner party, Mr. Ratley, was actually an inspiration from the Great Creator. It has certainly turned out to be a blessing."

"Mr. Ratley, does this mean you are going to back the creation of the park?" asks Jasmine.

"Indeed, it does. Let's start planning!"

Cheering erupts from every fur. It wakes the pups, but no one minds.

"Join us, then," says Miguel.

"There's still lots of food left," says Autumn "Hey, Sukey, Sally," she calls across the land parcel.

"Unpack those appetizers, bring them over, and join us!"

"Mr. Ratley, did you say you recorded this?" asks Ivy.

"Uh, yes." Ratley clears his throat. "I have the whole thing on video. I must apologize for that, too. I will destroy it, of course."

"No, don't. If everyfur agrees, I think it will be a wonderful documentary of what happened here tonight," says Ivy.

The others voice their assent. Tobias rubs his sleepy eyes and says, "We get to be in a video too? Wow! This is the best night ever!"

I couldn't agree more, thinks Autumn.

Chapter Twenty-Six

One Year Later

"No, Herbie, you may not go up there," Mrs. Mouse says to one of her brood. She stands, paws on hips watching Herbie gaze longingly at the tree tops.

"But Mom! The squirrels are having so much fun."

"What's going on?" asks Autumn Amelia, stopping to chat on her way back to Mama Cat's Kitchen, her new restaurant in Oneness Park.

"I want to climb the trees like the squirrels, but Mom won't let me."

"They are awfully high," says Autumn looking up at the canopy of green.

"Mice can climb trees," Herbie insists

"You're too little," says Mrs. Mouse. "Besides, I know you. You'll try to do everything the squirrels do. Jump from branch to branch, hang upside down from a limb. You'll fall and get hurt or worse. You stay down here where you're safe."

Herbie stamps his foot, curls his paws into tiny fists, and scowls."

"Have you tried the slide yet?" asks Autumn.

"No," says Herbie, kicking the dirt at his feet.

"You should. It's loads of fun. It's tall and it's got curves and bumps. Best of all, it's made of wood. No static." Autumn looks at the tower in the center of the park. Except for Mama Cat's Kitchen it's her favorite place in Oneness Park.

"That sound fun, Herbie. Why don't you try it?" coaxes Mrs. Mouse.

"Okay," he says, sounding less than enthusiastic. With a longing look at the squirrels zipping through the boughs above, he strolls off in the direction of the tower.

"I don't know what to do with him," Mrs. Mouse confides to Autumn Amelia. "He always wants to do things he's not ready for and some things he never will be. I don't want to stifle his enthusiasm, but I'm afraid he's going to get injured one of these days."

"Sounds like he's a real pawful," says Autumn Amelia, chuckling. "Cute, though."

"Autumn Amelia!" A voice calls. Autumn shades her eyes, looking in the direction of the voice. She sees Sukey beckoning from just outside the restaurant.

"I'd better go," says Autumn to Mrs. Mouse. "Enjoy opening day!"

Autumn heads towards Mama Cat's Kitchen. Ever since the finishing touches were put on it a month ago, Autumn has been in love with it. *I have my very own restaurant!* She bubbles over with joy every time she thinks of it. She only wishes Mama Cat was here to see it.

Autumn and Smokey had loads of conversations about the design. It turned out just as Autumn had hoped. Outside it looks like a little cottage with a welcoming front porch. Inside, it has two dining areas. An informal room called Beaks and Whiskers is destined to become a favorite of the youngsters if today is any indication. It's filled with thick wooden tables and benches stained a cheery yellow set on a gleaming hardwood floor. Sunshine streams through the windows, splashing across the red and white gingham curtains, making the room appear to glow.

On the other side of the kitchen is The Meadows, a formal dining room. This room has hardwood floors, too, but of a darker wood. A great fireplace with a stone surround and mantel stands at one end. Wagon wheel chandeliers hang from the ceiling and rustic sconces protrude from the walls. The tables are covered with gold edged champagne-colored linens all made by Dusty. Elegant settings top the tables for two and four. Larger tables await settings depending upon the number who will use them.

Down a short hallway towards the end of the cottage is a conference room and upstairs the employees only section houses the offices.

The kitchen is a grand affair with state-of-the-art equipment. Autumn Amelia feels as though she's dreaming whenever she enters it. Sukey and Sally have left Miguel's and now work at Mama Cat's Kitchen. Autumn felt bad at first thinking they were deserting Miguel and Gustav, but Sukey set her straight. They were sick of being yelled at and there were loads of young chefs waiting for the chance to work with the world-renowned Chef Gustav. "We did learn a lot from him," Sukey explained. "It's time to give others a chance."

A curlew named Arthur, a rat named Luke, a chinchilla named Harriet, and a rabbit named Midge are also on Autumn's kitchen staff for the day shifts. Since the park and the restaurant are open around the clock, two raccoons, Buddy and Sampson, an opossum named Odette, a fox named Marilu, and a bat named Henry work the night shifts.

In a smaller section at the back is a take-out area called On The Side where sandwiches, ice cream, and assorted snacks are served through screened windows. This area is run by two coyotes named Fergus and Cooper and a goat named Gretchen.

In the basement is the wine cellar.

As Autumn nears Mama Cat's Kitchen she sucks in her breath. She still can't believe it's real.

"Autumn, we need help," says Sukey from the porch. "The restaurant is packed. Both rooms. And there's a line waiting to get in and two long lines at the take-out windows."

"Oh, my," says Autumn, hurrying up the steps. "I didn't mean to leave you hanging. There wasn't much of a crowd when I went to see how Smokey is doing."

"It's lunchtime now and we've suddenly got a throng."

Autumn and Sukey go in through the employee's entrance to the kitchen. Autumn peeks out at the dining rooms. Servers are bustling from table to table carrying menus, trays, and table settings. In Beaks and Whiskers, a group of kittens, puppies, starling chicks, and baby field mice share one of the long tables. They are trying out each other's lunches and giggling.

In the formal dining room adult dogs, cats, foxes, coyotes, rabbits, rats, mice, chipmunks, squirrels, and a foursome of brown bears relax at tables either enjoying a hearty lunch or awaiting their orders. A couple seated at a table for two near a window catch Autumn's eye. They look like cats only bigger, more muscular.

"Are those cats?" Autumn asks, as Mark, a beaver carrying a large tray of dirty dishes, passes her on the way to the kitchen.

"Bobcats," he says, backing through the swinging door.

"My goodness, opening day really has brought out everyfur!" she says, turning back to the kitchen. "I'd better get cracking."

* * *

From the top of the lookout tower, Smokey surveys all of Oneness Park. She draws in a breath as her gaze travels over the milling crowd below. The day has the feel of a carnival. Crowds traverse the crushed gravel as they move from one site to the next. To the right is a grassy area with an obstacle course for leaping through hoops, running up and over wooden ramps, and jumping from one stepping paw to the next. Once the sun sets foxes and wolves will take the place of the dogs and coyotes who are now testing their skills. To the left is a field with so many scratching posts of various sizes it appears as though they've grown wild there. Between these two fields is a copse of trees that just now is filled with squirrels and chipmunks racing up and down, leaping from tree to tree. Birds swing gently on some of the trapeze-like bars suspended from branches while in another section squirrels hurl themselves from one bar to the next executing flips in mid-air.

Smokey continues to look over the large park grounds as she makes her way around the track on the outside of the tower's top. Below she spies the giant box filled with shredded paper and wood shavings. The crowd of rodents diving in and out makes it appear as though the box's contents are undulating. Next, she sees the brusselball court with a field of newly planted Brussels sprouts beside it. Jasmine is busy giving tours of the court and spa and signing up members for the brusselball teams.

Jasmine and Louisa, the Great Blue Heron, have done all the decorating in the spa, giving it a relaxing atmosphere. Massage therapists — a Great Dane named Mandy, a Boxer named Ralph, and gerbil named Gilly for the smaller animals — have taken over one wing of the spa and set up rooms with their tables, lightly scented candles, soft lighting, and gentle music.

From the front of the tower, Smokey is directly lined up with Mama Cat's Kitchen. Autumn stopped by earlier to tell her for the thousandth time how much she loves it. Judging by the line waiting to get in and the continually growing lines at the take-out windows, she's not the only one.

All day Smokey has felt as though she's moving through a dream. A powerful sense of serenity enfolds her and she hasn't even been in the spa. It's simply the realization of her dream. In the months and weeks leading up to this moment she's ping-ponged between nervousness and excitement. She's gotten little sleep since the night of the coyotes' dinner party. Her mind has been constantly reeling with ideas especially after requests began pouring into the new website. Her co-design leads, a rat named Helen and a swallow named Earl, have become esteemed colleagues. Here it is one year later and while not everything has been implemented, enough has that they could open. She's been waiting for this day for a long time.

When she'd set off for the park this morning she'd been in a state of high excitement. Standing at the entrance with Autumn Amelia, Miguel, Abigail, Helen, Earl, Greyson, Rufus, and Jerome J. Ratley, she'd eagerly welcomed the first visitors to Oneness Park. Once the park began to fill up, the welcoming committee decided it was time to disperse so they could mingle and see how everything was going. As Smokey walked among the park-goers she saw smiles and laughing faces. She heard exclamations of wonder and delight.

After a while, Smokey wandered into the tower, her masterpiece. Based on the lighthouse on Niptucket Island, it is a tall, cylindrical structure. The foot of the massive spiral staircase greets guests as they step through the door. The walls of the first floor are hung with pictures of Oneness Park in various stages of development to tell the story of the park's creation. On the far end behind the staircase is a small, softly lit chamber. Against the back wall stands a marble altar. On the wall behind it these words are inscribed:

This chapel is dedicated to the Great Creator, our sole and mutual creator, who loves each of us equally and wants us to love one another. Let us honor the Great Creator.

Amen.

Atop the altar is a basket containing hundreds of folded pieces of paper. Each fur and feather are welcome to write their prayers to the Great Creator and place them in the basket, offer a silent or quietly spoken prayer, or simply spend time in reflection. When Smokey entered the chapel after mingling with the crowd, a powerful feeling of serenity came over her. She'd closed her eyes, her heart too full for words and offered up all the gratitude in her heart.

Now, walking along the top of the tower, the feeling lingers. She knows she will sleep well tonight.

"Woo-hoo!" The call comes from a deer zipping down the spiral wooden slide encircling the outside of the tower. Smokey grins as she leans over to see the deer, hooves in the air, whooshing rapidly down the slide. "Hee-hee!" he calls as he skims over a bump halfway down.

Smokey opens a door and slips inside. In a real lighthouse this room is where the giant lantern is kept. Here, in its place is an enormous fire pit. It will be lit once the sun sets. Long sticks and huge boxes of marshmallows wait in a corner. There will be fireworks to celebrate opening night. Chairs placed along the outside track will offer prime seating for the spectacle. Smokey checks that everything is ready for the evening. Satisfied, she takes her leave of the tower by opening the gate on the track and sitting down. With only the slightest push, she propels herself down the slide. At the bottom she flies off to land, giggling, in a giant foam pit.

Crawling out of the pit, she sees a group gathered beneath the copse of trees all staring upwards. Curious, she approaches, assuming the squirrels are putting on a show.

"How did he get up there?" squeaks a little mouse, one of the Mouse family's children.

"Disobedience," answers Mrs. Mouse. "He climbed onto a squirrel's back without the squirrel's permission or knowledge, I might add, and off he went." Mrs. Mouse sounds more frightened than angry."

"Herbie, come down!" she calls.

"I…I…can't," a frightened voice answers.

"Oh my," says Smokey catching sight of the little mouse hanging on for dear life to the fur of a furiously fast squirrel leaping from branch to branch near the very tops of the trees. The squirrel's back twitches violently. It's apparent he feels the mouse but has no notion of what's on his back. Other squirrels call to him, a few try to chase him down, but he's by far the fastest in the trees and so consumed by trying to rid himself of whatever is on his back he pays them no mind.

Mrs. Mouse covers her mouth with her paws, whiskers twitching. "He's going to fall," she cries.

Mr. Mouse, who had been in another section of the park with some of the Mouse children, races to join her. Suddenly a gray streak shoots up the tree and Smokey realizes Jasmine is racing to the top. She's nearly reached them when a small gray ball is flung from the squirrel's back, hurtling towards the ground. Mrs. Mouse screams.

"Look out!" comes a shout Smokey recognizes as Autumn's voice.

The crowd under the tree quickly parts. A flash of gray, white, and orange fluff slides in under the tree.

Herbie lands with a soft *thwop* and disappears into the long, lush fur of Autumn Amelia's tummy.

"My baby!" cries Mrs. Mouse, jumping atop Autumn and diving into her fur to find Herbie.

"Oh! That tickles!" Autumn convulses with laughter which tosses Mrs. Mouse, clutching Herbie tight in her arms, onto the ground, unharmed.

"Thank you, thank you, Autumn Amelia," says Mrs. Mouse. "You saved Herbie's life."

Smokey looks back towards the treetops. Jasmine, who had almost reached them when Herbie fell, is making her way down the nearest ramp. Autumn is sitting with the entire Mouse family in her lap, all of them kissing and hugging her. Once they've calmed down and made their way out of Autumn's fur, Smokey leans down to help her sister up. Greyson, standing behind Autumn, lends a paw. Smokey hears him whisper into Autumn's ear, "Congratulations, Miss Autumn. You've finally caught a mouse."

The End

Also published by BWL Publishing Inc.

Kelegeen

Erin's Children (Sequel to Kelegeen)

Eileen O'Finlan lives in central Massachusetts with her Maine Coon cat Autumn Amelia. Sadly, her Russian Blue, Smokey has gone to the Rainbow Bridge. They were the inspiration for *All the Furs and Feathers*. To visit her website and sign up for her free monthly newsletter, which includes a column called The Cat's Corner, written by Autumn Amelia, go to *www.eileenofinlan.com*.